STICKMEN'S GUIDE TO YOUR BODY

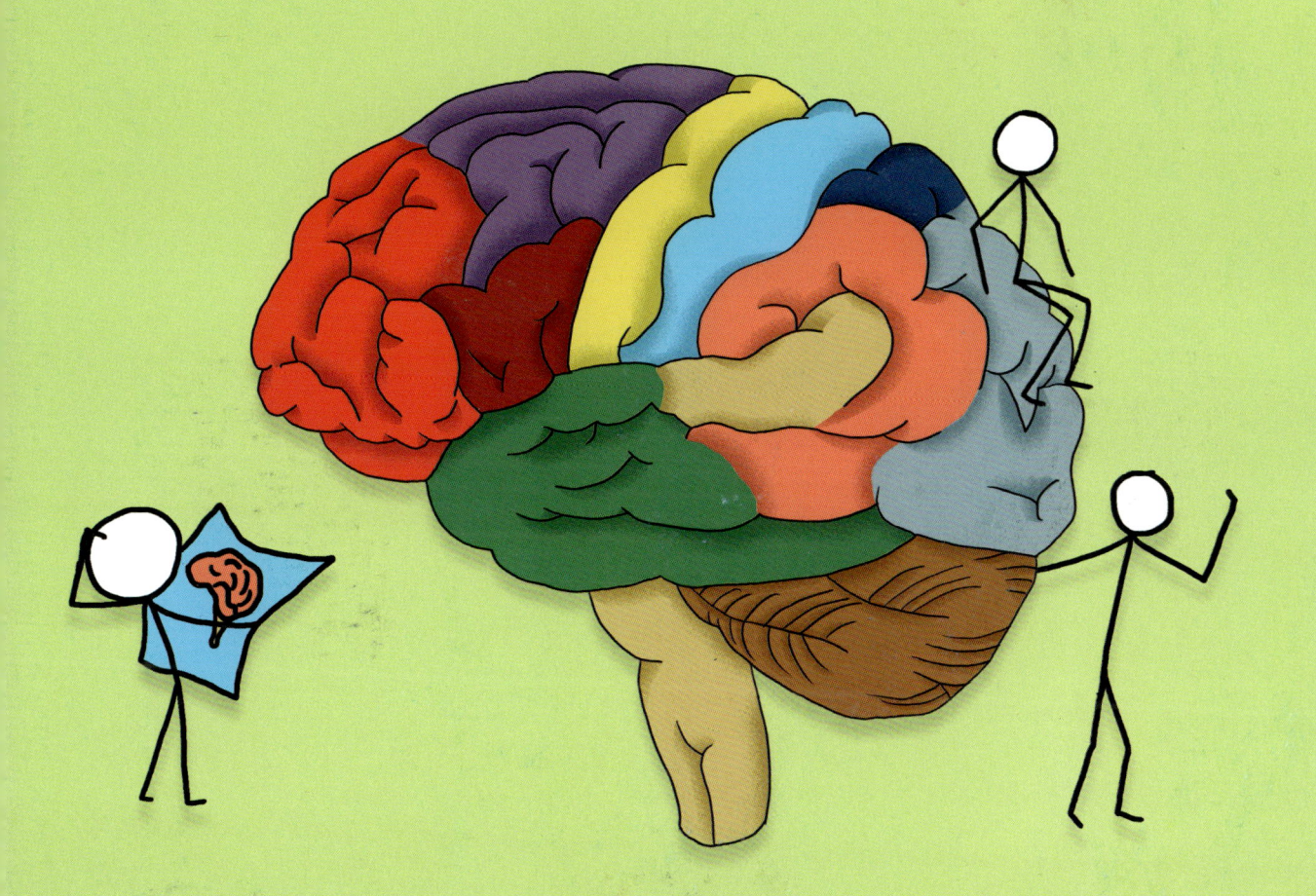

by John Farndon
Illustrated by Venitia Dean

Contents

Stickmen's Guide to your Body — 5

Muscles and Bones — 6
Holding You Together — 8
Your Muscly Body — 10
Pulling Together — 12
Inside a Muscle — 14
How to Get Strong — 16
Your Framework of Bones — 18
Strong Bones — 20
Moving Parts — 22
Binders — 24
Bonehead — 26

Your Brilliant Brain — 28
Central Control — 30
You've Got a Nerve — 32
Brainy — 34
Inside Your Brain — 36
Brain Map — 38
Moving and Feeling — 40
Seeing Things — 42
Hear, Hear — 44
Smell That, Taste That — 46
Remember, Remember — 48

Your Beating Heart — 50
Breathing — 52
Blood Circulation — 54
Heartbeat — 56
Arteries and Veins — 58
How Cells Breathe — 60
What Is Blood? — 62
Blood in Action — 64
Mending Hearts — 66
Staying Fit — 68

Your Gurgling Guts — 70
Body Fuel — 72
Eating — 74
The Food Masher — 76
Guts — 78
The Chemical Refinery — 80
Chemical Powerhouse — 82
Warm Body — 84
Staying Pure — 86
Body of Water — 88
Waste Disposal — 90
Index — 92

Beetle Books is a Hungry Tomato imprint
First published 2020 by Hungry Tomato Ltd
F1, Old Bakery Studios, Blewetts Wharf, Malpas Road, Truro, Cornwall, TR1 1QH, UK

Copyright © 2020 Hungry Tomato Ltd

No part of this publication may be reproduced, stored in a retrieval system, or transmitted in any form or by any means, electronic, mechanical, photocopying, recording, or otherwise, without the prior written permission of the copyright owner.

A CIP catalog record for this book is available from the British Library.

ISBN 978-1-913077-174

Printed and bound in China

Discover more at
www.mybeetlebooks.com

Stickmen's Guide to Your Body

The body is an amazing machine. A living supercomputer sits in our head, housed in a protective shell of bones, made from tough minerals that form part of the skeleton, that holds everything together. A digestive system that breaks big lumps of food into fuel and materials. This is then driven through the body absorbing the good bits to bring energy to all the cells, by a giant beating muscle that never stops. Every single part working together to make the body a briliant machine that keeps us alive and working. Let the stickmen take you on a tour—inside and out!

Your Muscles and Bones

Although your body seems very complicated, it all begins to make sense if you think of it in terms of systems, each with its own task to do. Some systems such as the nervous system (the body's communication system) extend throughout the body. It is the task of the skeleton—the body's framework of bones—to protect you and keep you upright. The skeleton works in conjunction with muscles, which give your body the power to move.

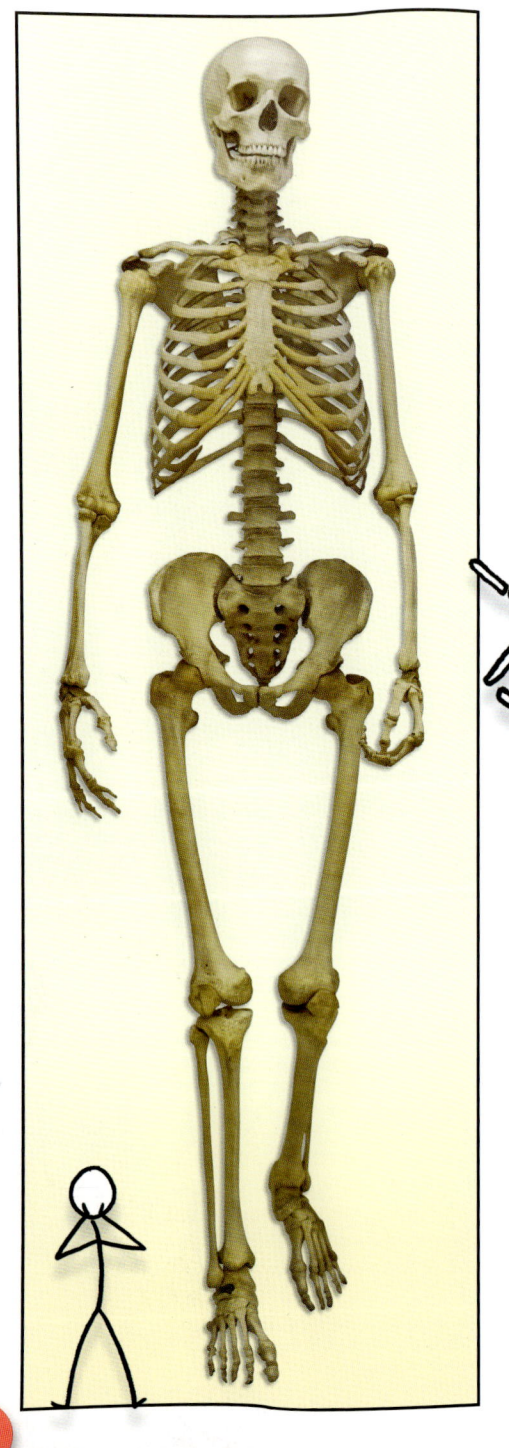

Skeleton

The skeleton is the one part of the body that may last the longest after people die. That's because the bones are made from tough minerals that don't rot away. Altogether, over 100 billion people have lived on Earth so far. That means there could be 100 billion skeletons lying around. Fortunately, most do crumble into dust eventually!

Lucy

The world's most famous skeleton is about 3.2 million years old! It's called Lucy and is the skeleton of a small ancestor of humans called an australopithecine. It was found in Ethiopia in 1974. Its shape shows that even this long ago, our ancestors walked upright on two feet.

Muscles

You have over 600 muscles on the outside of your skeleton. If they could all pull together, they could lift a bus! Of course, that could never happen because they all pull in different directions. The average adult man can just about lift another adult off the ground.

The strongest man

The world's strongest man ever was Canadian Louis Cyr, who lived between 1863 and 1912. He could push a railroad truck uphill, beat two horses in a tug of war, and lift the weight of five adults with his little finger. His most famous feat was the backlift, in which he lifted a bench with 18 men on it on his back.

Meaty muscle

If you want to know what your muscles look like on the inside, go to the butcher. When you eat meat, you're eating mostly the muscle of animals. Only fat, gristle, and bone are not muscle. If you ever eat steak, the chances are you'll be eating the big rump, or bottom muscles, of a cow. Your own bottom muscles look similar!

Holding You Together

If you looked through a powerful microscope, you would see that your body is made of tiny living packets called cells—about 37 trillion altogether! And just as lots of bricks make a wall, so lots of cells joined together make different kinds of tissue. Tissues are the basic building materials of your body.

Four Tissues

There are four kinds of tissue. Most of you is either muscle tissue—the tissue that makes muscle—or 'connective' tissue, which fills the space between muscle and other tissues. But there are also small amounts of 'epithelial' tissue that line and wrap things, and nervous tissue that makes the nervous system, your body's internet.

nervous tissue makes up your nerves and brain

epithelial tissue lines your airways and blood vessels and wraps your heart

connective tissue comes in various kinds, including bone, tendon, cartilage, fat, and blood

muscle tissue is the special fibers that make things move

Connective Tissue

Connective tissue is made of three things: cells, thin fibers, and a matrix. The matrix is basically just a setting for the other materials, like the bread in a currant loaf. It can be anything from a runny syrup to a thick gel.

Smooth Muscle

There are different kinds of muscle. Smooth muscles are the ones deep inside your body. They form tubes or bags and move things around by squeezing. For example, rings of smooth muscle squeeze food through your gut.

Skeletal Muscle

Skeletal muscles are all the muscles you see under your skin covering your skeleton. They are sometimes called striated muscles. Striated means "stripy," and these muscles get get their name because under a microscope, you can see dark bands around them.

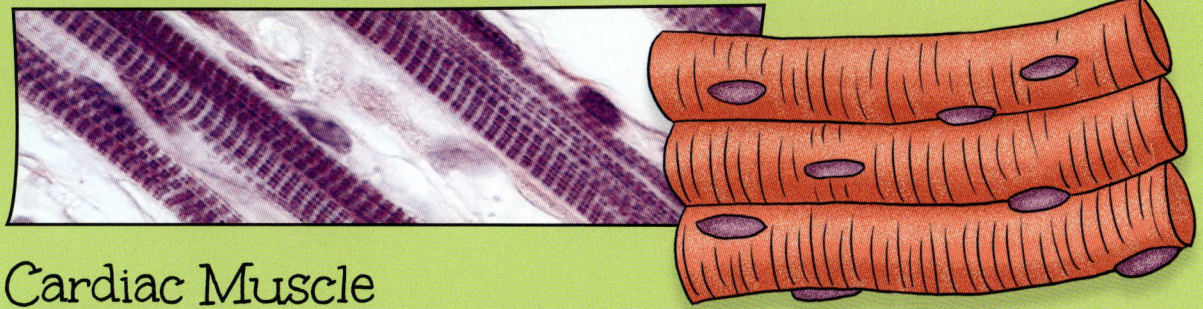

Cardiac Muscle

Cardiac muscle makes the strong walls of your heart. It squeezes automatically 100 or so times a minute to pump blood around your body. It is made from a mix of smooth and striated muscle.

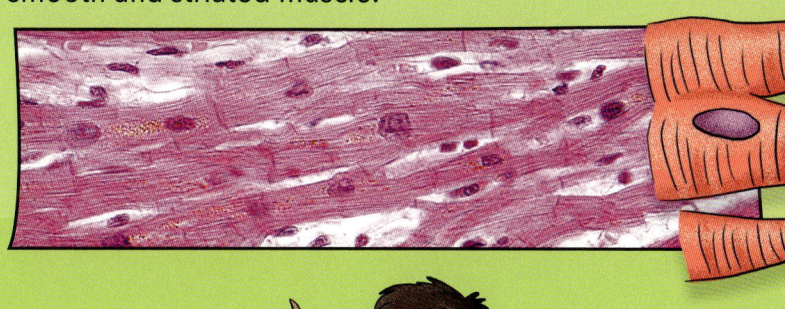

Do it Yourself

When you decide to jump and kick, your skeletal muscles make it happen. YOU can move these muscles if you want to, so they are called voluntary muscles. But you have little control over the heart and other muscles inside your body, so they are called involuntary muscles.

Your Muscly Body

Your body is covered with skeletal muscles. They are all bundles of fibers that tense and relax to move parts of your body. They range from big muscles, such as those in your bottom and legs, to tiny muscles, such as those in your ear.

The Skeletal Muscles

You have 640 skeletal muscles altogether, and they make up two-fifths of your weight. In these diagrams, you only see the muscles on the surface, but there are several layers underneath too. Some are long with a bulge in the middle, some are triangular, and some are sheetlike.

a major neck muscle, the sternocleidomastoid, tilts your head on either side

the pectoral turns your arm

the biceps raises your arm

the triceps lowers your arm

the external oblique holds your side in

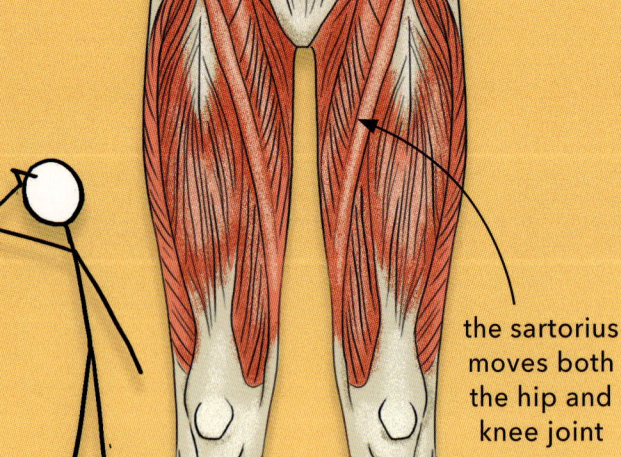

the sartorius moves both the hip and knee joint

the sartorius is the longest muscle in the body

the quadriceps bends your knee

the shin muscle lowers your foot

Long Muscle

The sartorius runs over the hip and down over the knee and turns the thigh. It gets its name from the Latin word *sartor*, meaning tailor. That's because tailors used to stretch this muscle when sitting cross-legged to work.

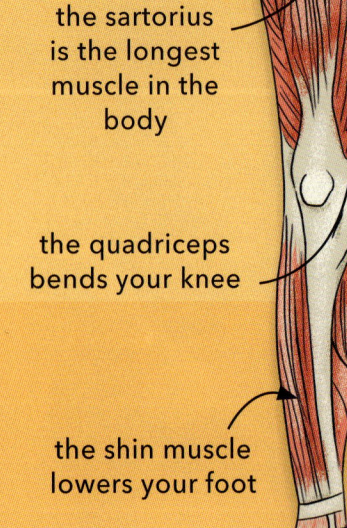

Strong Jaw

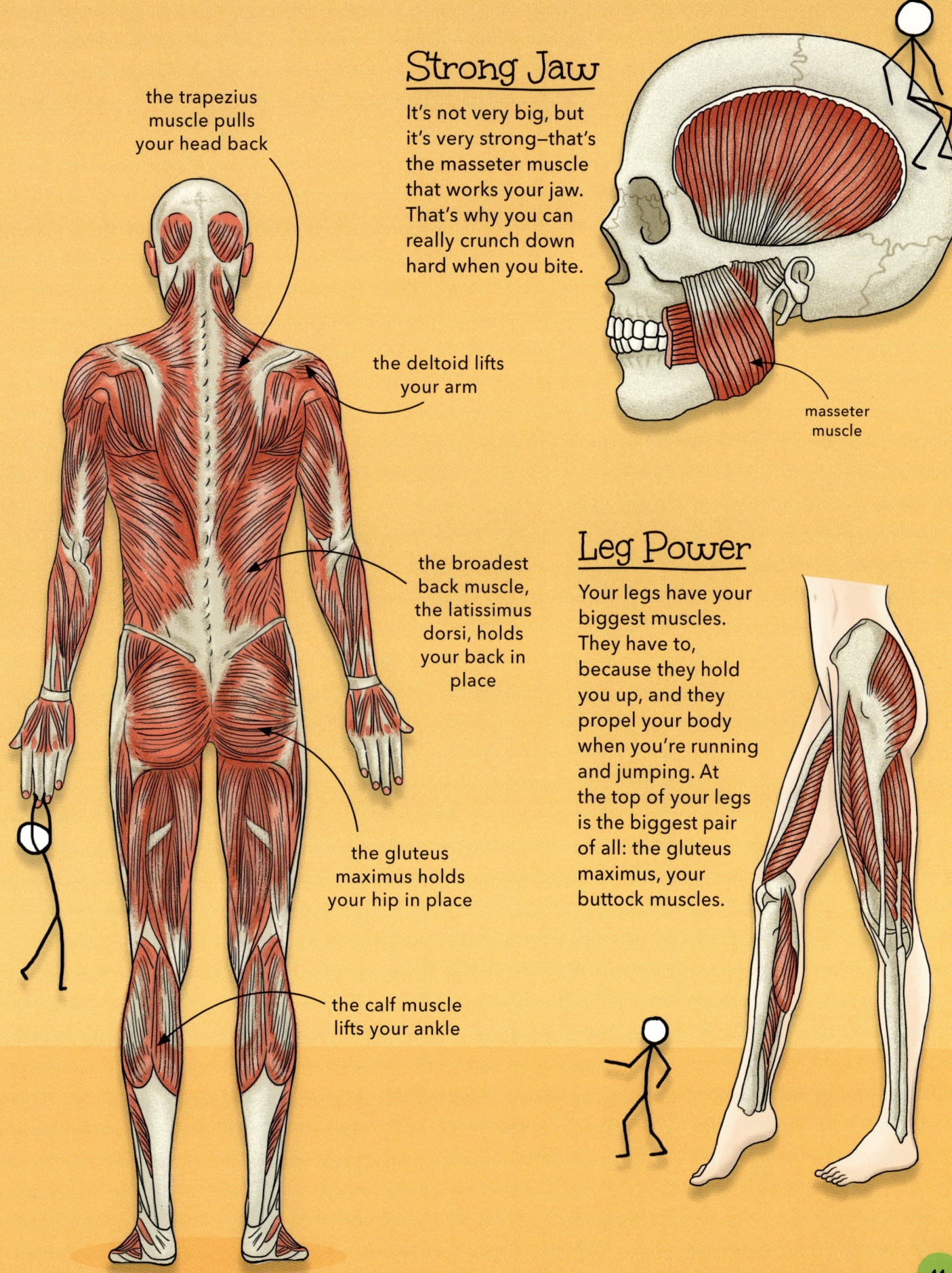

It's not very big, but it's very strong—that's the masseter muscle that works your jaw. That's why you can really crunch down hard when you bite.

masseter muscle

- the trapezius muscle pulls your head back
- the deltoid lifts your arm
- the broadest back muscle, the latissimus dorsi, holds your back in place
- the gluteus maximus holds your hip in place
- the calf muscle lifts your ankle

Leg Power

Your legs have your biggest muscles. They have to, because they hold you up, and they propel your body when you're running and jumping. At the top of your legs is the biggest pair of all: the gluteus maximus, your buttock muscles.

Pulling Together

Your muscles make your body move in all kinds of ways. But they do it all just by pulling themselves shorter (contracting) or relaxing. Each muscle works simply by pulling two bones together, so they must be anchored to bones at both ends.

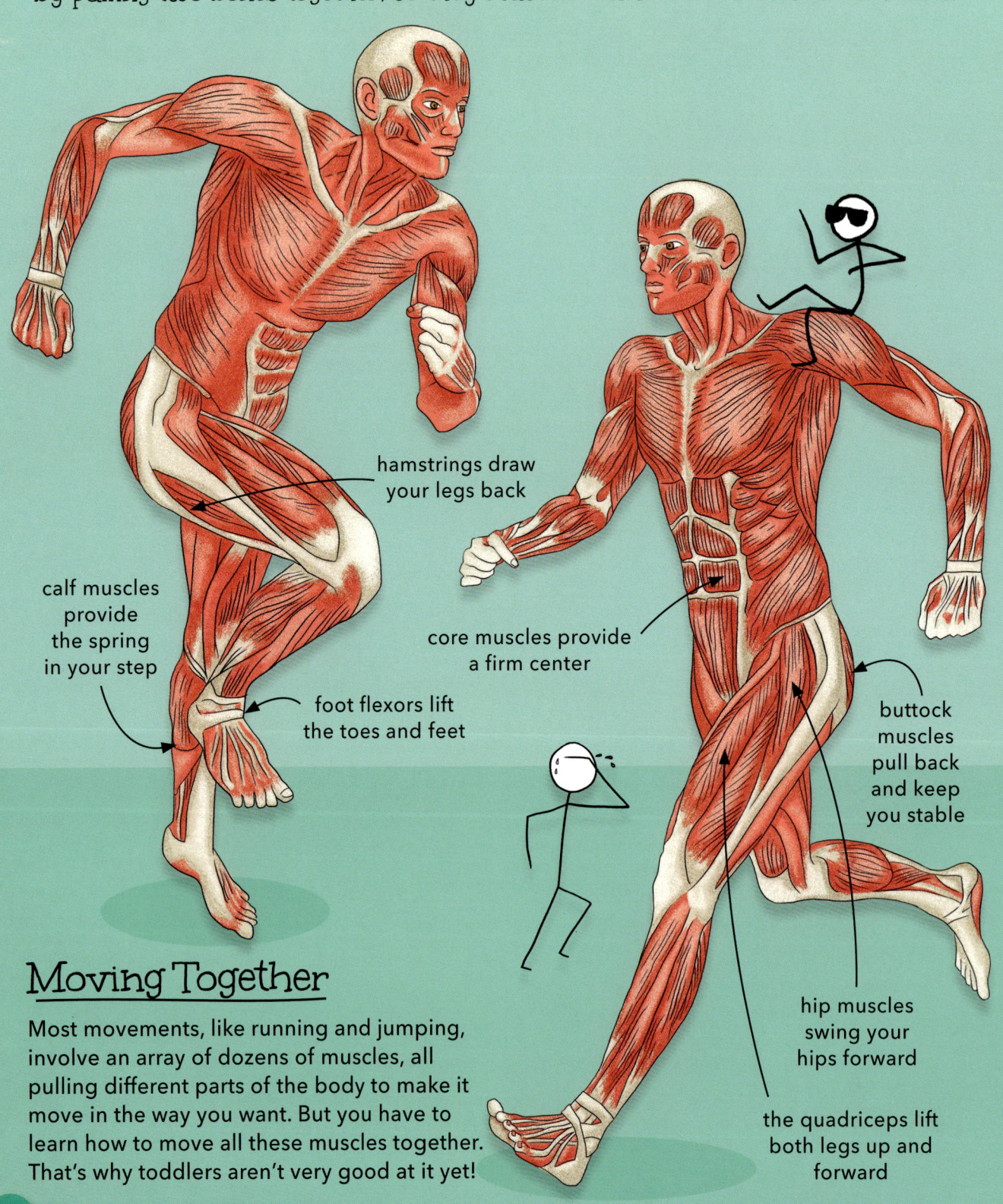

hamstrings draw your legs back

calf muscles provide the spring in your step

foot flexors lift the toes and feet

core muscles provide a firm center

buttock muscles pull back and keep you stable

hip muscles swing your hips forward

the quadriceps lift both legs up and forward

Moving Together

Most movements, like running and jumping, involve an array of dozens of muscles, all pulling different parts of the body to make it move in the way you want. But you have to learn how to move all these muscles together. That's why toddlers aren't very good at it yet!

Muscle Pairs

Muscles can make themselves shorter, but they cannot make themselves longer. So each time a muscle pulls shorter, it must be pulled back by another muscle shortening in the opposite direction. That's why muscles are arranged in pairs, with a flexor to bend a joint and an extensor to straighten it out.

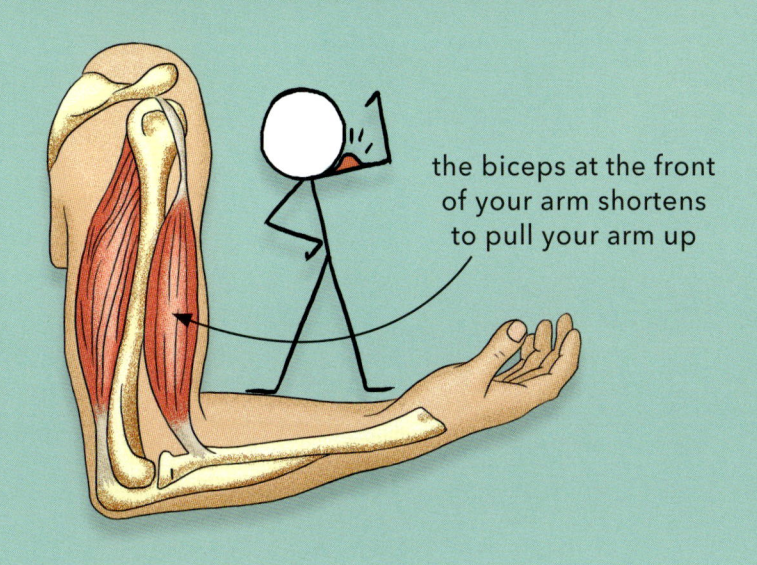

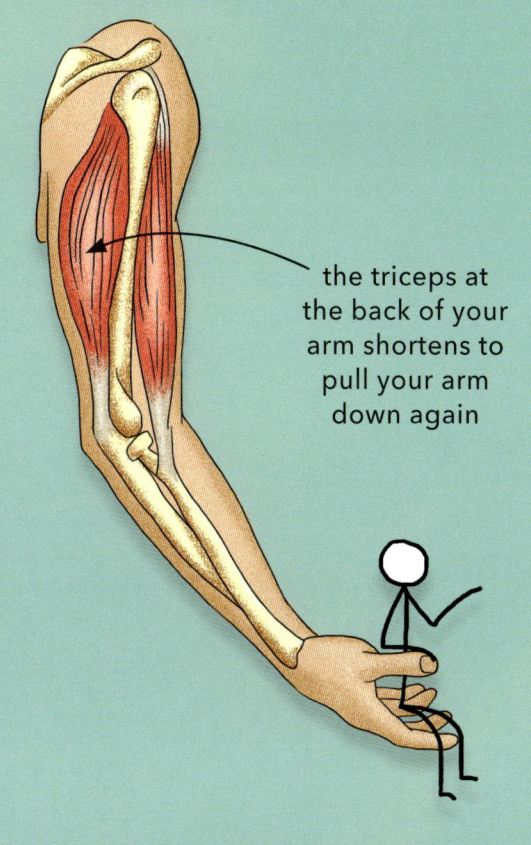

the biceps at the front of your arm shortens to pull your arm up

the triceps at the back of your arm shortens to pull your arm down again

Push-up

Push-ups are one of the simplest and most effective forms of exercise, which is why they are very popular with people who want to stay fit. They involve most of the muscles in the upper body, including those in the arms, chest, and abdomen.

deltoids are the shoulder muscles that provide a firm base for the arms

pectorals are the large upper chest muscles that really take the strain

abdominal muscles help to hold the body steady

Inside a Muscle

Skeletal muscles get their strength from bundles of fibers that stretch from one end of the muscle to the other. Some muscles are made from just a few hundred fibers. Others are made from hundreds of thousands. But their superpower is getting shorter!

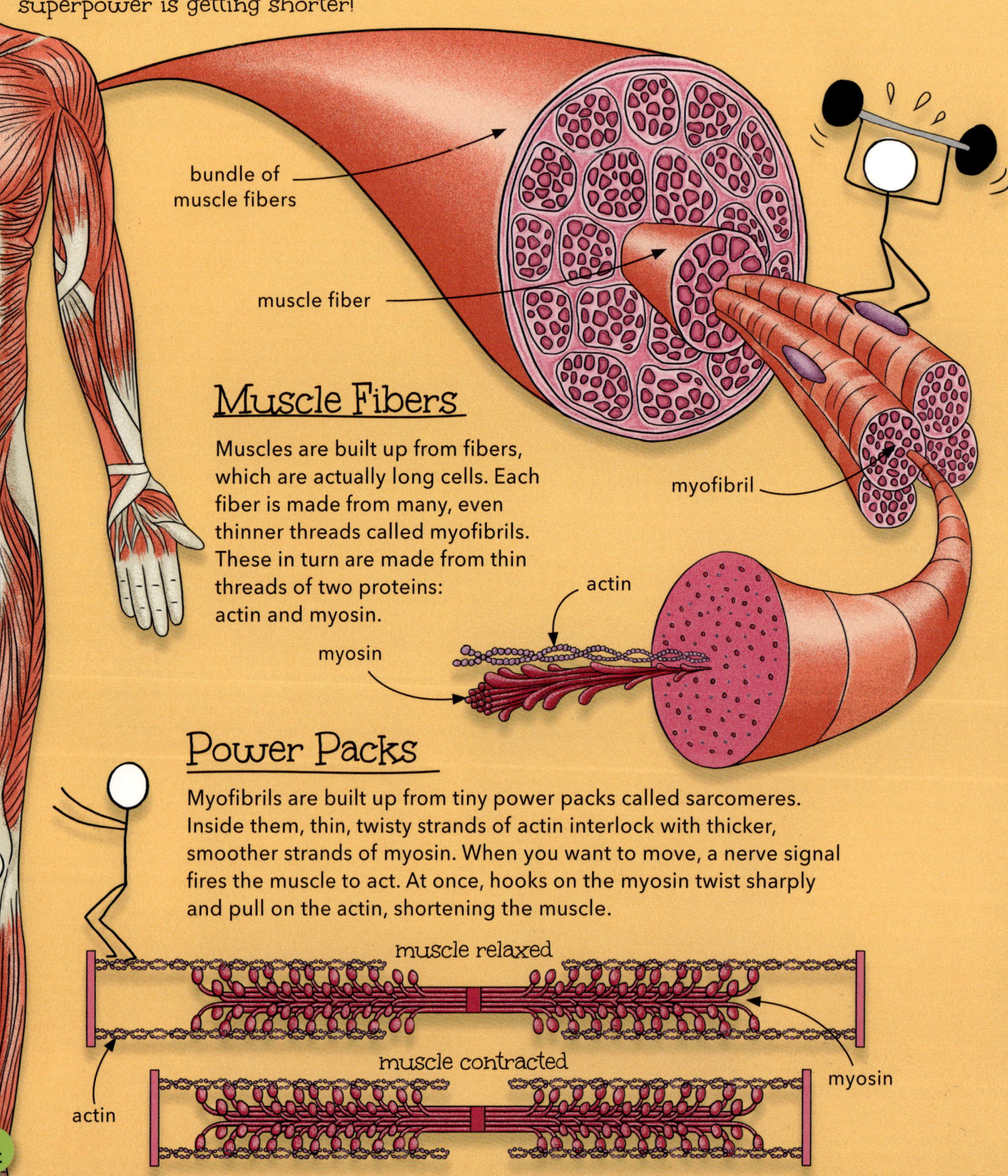

bundle of muscle fibers

muscle fiber

Muscle Fibers

Muscles are built up from fibers, which are actually long cells. Each fiber is made from many, even thinner threads called myofibrils. These in turn are made from thin threads of two proteins: actin and myosin.

myofibril

actin

myosin

Power Packs

Myofibrils are built up from tiny power packs called sarcomeres. Inside them, thin, twisty strands of actin interlock with thicker, smoother strands of myosin. When you want to move, a nerve signal fires the muscle to act. At once, hooks on the myosin twist sharply and pull on the actin, shortening the muscle.

muscle relaxed

muscle contracted

actin

myosin

Pulling or Holding

When a muscle moves part of the body, it shortens. This happens when you run, for example, and is called an isotonic contraction. Sometimes, though, the muscles can pull to hold the body in place without getting shorter. This is an isometric contraction.

Pulling
(isotonic contraction)

Holding
(isometric contraction)

tendon

muscle contracts and shortens

muscle contracts but does not shorten

Holding Weight

When muscles contract, they can shorten by almost half their length. When muscles work isometrically, however, they simply get fatter and stay the same length. This happens when weight lifters hold the bar still overhead.

15

How to Get Strong

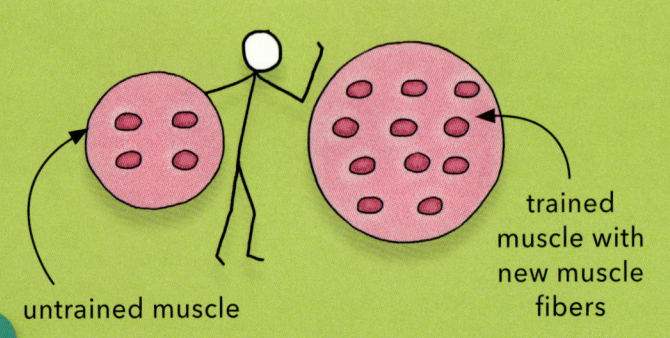

Top athletes train hard to get strong. They work hard at exercises that make their muscles grow and become better able to keep pulling. If muscles aren't used, they gradually become weaker.

Weight training

When you exercise, you get fitter and stronger. Regular exercise improves fitness by bulking up your muscles, strengthening your heart, and building up your body's ability to pump blood and supply muscles with oxygen. Weight lifters concentrate on building up their muscles for maximum strength. Marathon runners focus on endurance.

How a weightlifter's body shape changes as the muscles grow

untrained muscle

trained muscle with new muscle fibers

Muscle growth

When you exercise, your muscles grow larger. At first, the fibers just get fatter. But if you go on exercising regularly, you grow new fibers, so your muscles become stronger. The blood supply to the muscles improves, so they can work for longer.

16

Fast or Slow?

Muscle fibers come in two kinds: white and red. Each kind pulls, or twitches at different rates. Sprinters have lots of white fibers that twitch rapidly to give a burst of action. Marathon runners develop slow-twitch red fibers that keep working longer.

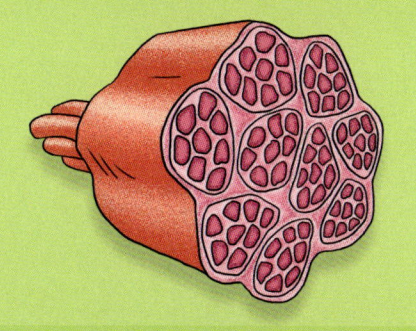

slow reds for marathons

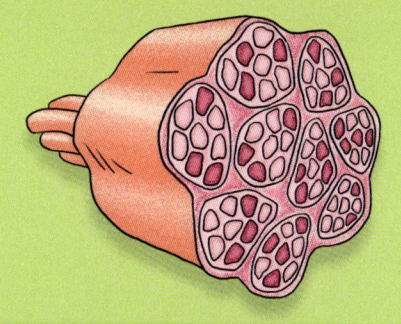

mix of whites and reds for middle distance

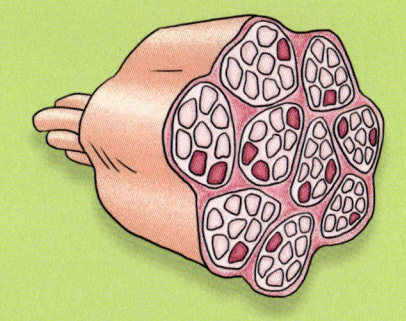

fast whites for sprints

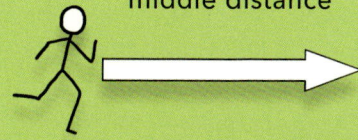

Air Power

Muscle cells get their power from sugar in your food and the oxygen you breathe. On a long bike ride, they work slowly and aerobically. That means they work gently enough to take in air as they go. But when you sprint, your muscles work so fast your body can't deliver enough fresh oxygen. So they briefly work anaerobically (without air).

Cramps

If you're out of shape, your muscles go on working anaerobically longer. Lactic acid builds up, making your muscles feel sore. You might also get cramps. A cramp is a painful twinge in your muscles. It is set off when the nerves that trigger them fire erratically. This is usually because of a temporary shortage of the minerals your nerves need to work properly.

Your Framework of Bones

Under your skin and muscles, you have a strong framework of bones called a skeleton. It holds your body together; provides anchor points for the muscles you use to move; supports your skin and other tissues; and protects your heart, brain, and other organs.

Human skeleton

Your skeleton is made of over 200 bones. Your skull, spine and ribcage make the 'axial' skeleton. Your shoulders, arms, hands, hips, legs and feet are attached to this and form the 'appendicular' skeleton.

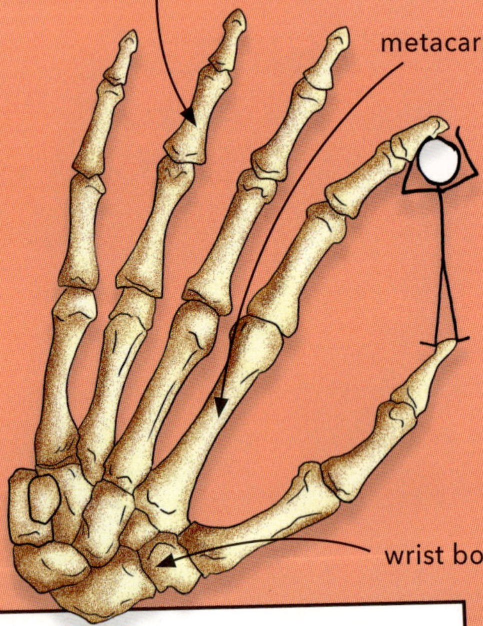

cheekbone

collarbone

finger bones or phalanges

metacarpals

breastbone or sternum

Hand Bones

The hands each have 27 bones, making almost a quarter of all your bones. That's why hands can move in more ways than any other part of your body. The hand bones form joints at the knuckles.

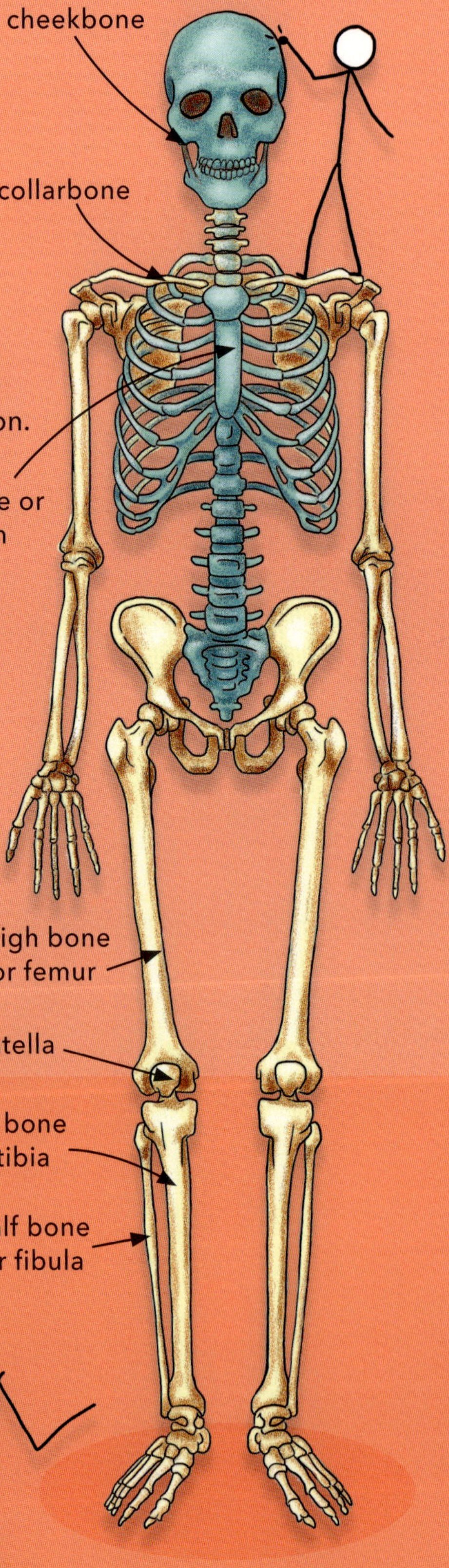

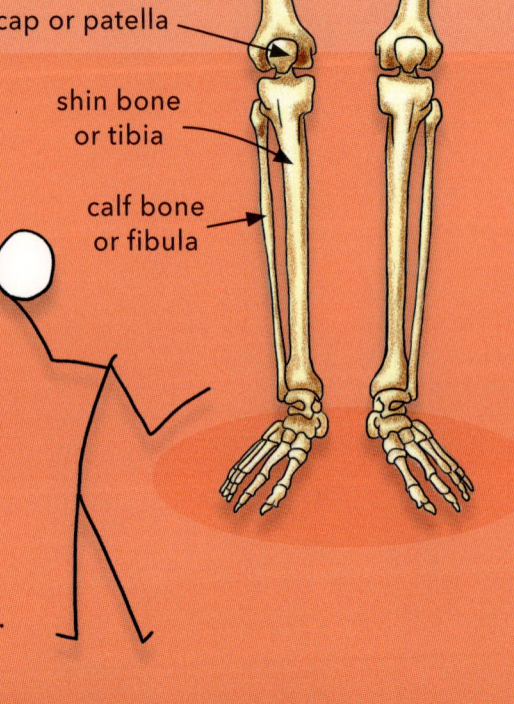

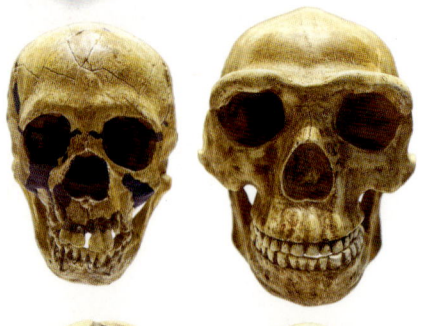

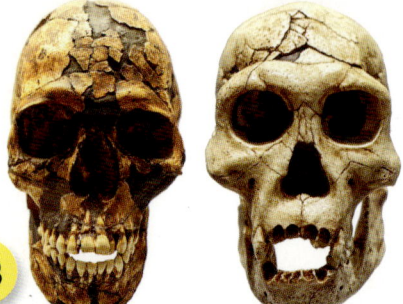

wrist bones or carpals

thigh bone or femur

kneecap or patella

Head Office

Humans have rounded skulls like no other animals. Experts can track how humans developed in the distant past from the changing shape of ancient skulls they have found. They can see how the top, or cranium, grew to allow room for a bigger brain.

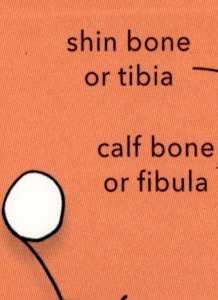

shin bone or tibia

calf bone or fibula

18

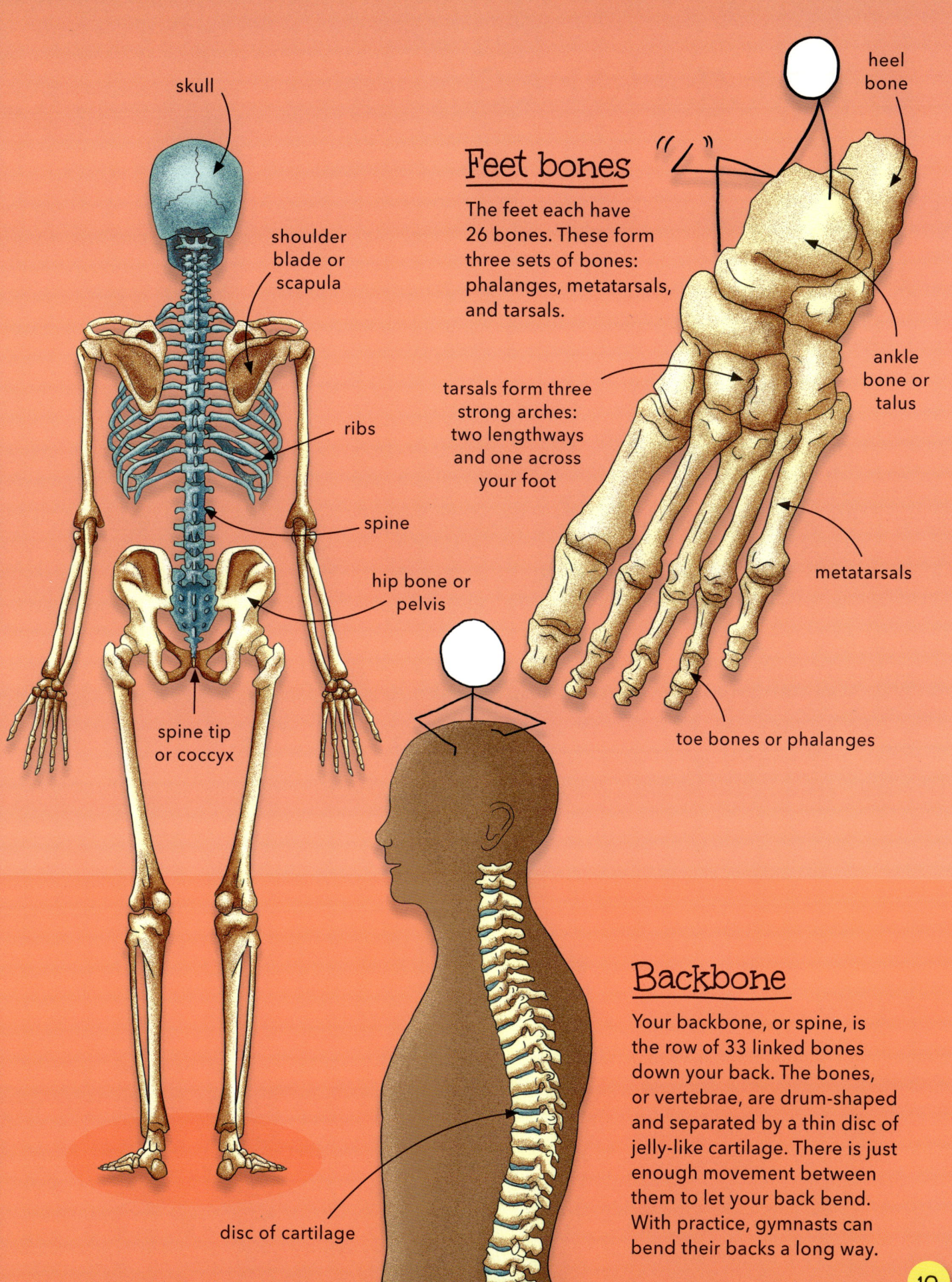

- skull
- shoulder blade or scapula
- ribs
- spine
- hip bone or pelvis
- spine tip or coccyx

Feet bones

The feet each have 26 bones. These form three sets of bones: phalanges, metatarsals, and tarsals.

- heel bone
- ankle bone or talus
- tarsals form three strong arches: two lengthways and one across your foot
- metatarsals
- toe bones or phalanges

Backbone

Your backbone, or spine, is the row of 33 linked bones down your back. The bones, or vertebrae, are drum-shaped and separated by a thin disc of jelly-like cartilage. There is just enough movement between them to let your back bend. With practice, gymnasts can bend their backs a long way.

- disc of cartilage

Strong Bones

Bones are really light because they're partly hollow. But they're superstrong too because they're made of both hard minerals and stretchy fibers that stop them snapping.

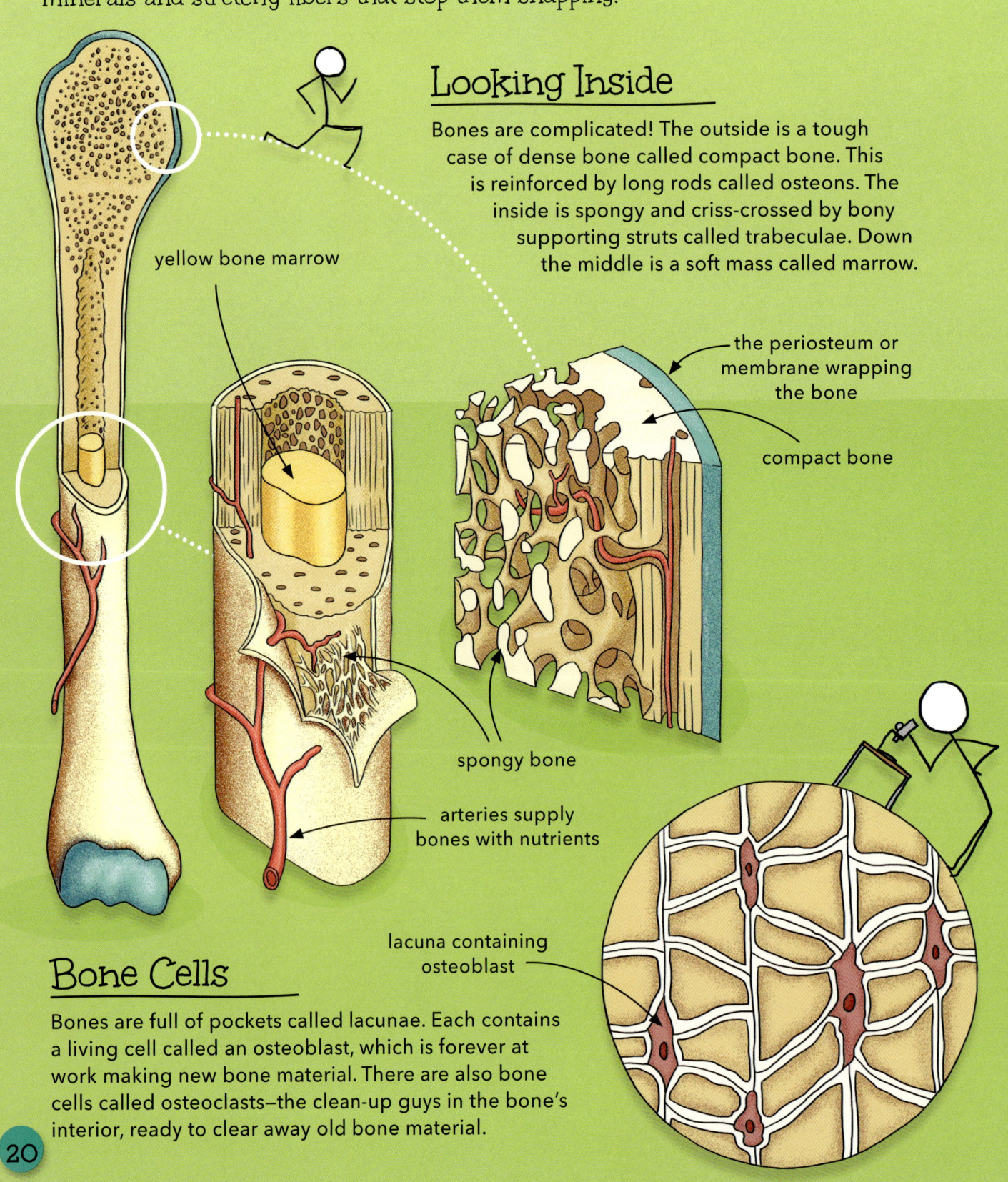

Looking Inside

Bones are complicated! The outside is a tough case of dense bone called compact bone. This is reinforced by long rods called osteons. The inside is spongy and criss-crossed by bony supporting struts called trabeculae. Down the middle is a soft mass called marrow.

- yellow bone marrow
- the periosteum or membrane wrapping the bone
- compact bone
- spongy bone
- arteries supply bones with nutrients
- lacuna containing osteoblast

Bone Cells

Bones are full of pockets called lacunae. Each contains a living cell called an osteoblast, which is forever at work making new bone material. There are also bone cells called osteoclasts—the clean-up guys in the bone's interior, ready to clear away old bone material.

red blood cells

white blood cells

marrow

platelets

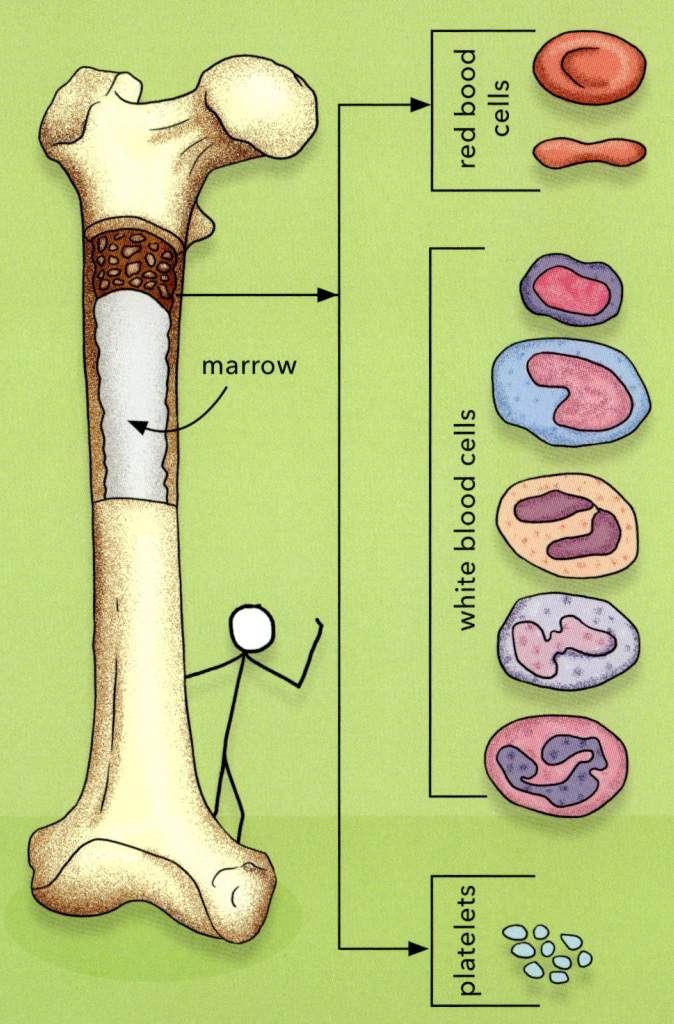

Blood Factory

The hollow center of your bones contains a soft, spongy substance called marrow. Some is red and bloody, some yellow and fatty. Red marrow is the body's blood factory, churning out new blood cells nonstop.

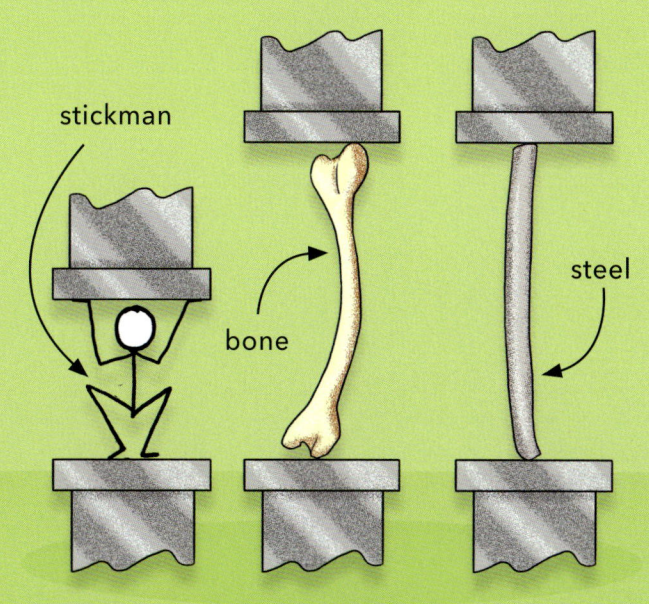

stickman

bone

steel

Bone v. Steel

People sometimes say that bone is stronger than steel, weight for weight! That's not quite true: steel is stronger and bone is also very light, so a rod of steel the same size would be much stronger than bone. All the same, bone is both strong and very light—just what you need for moving around.

Broken Bones

Bones are strong, but sometimes they do get broken. Amazingly, though, most fractures heal. First the body stops any bleeding. Then proteins bring in osteoclasts to clear away the debris, so the osteoblasts can begin to create new bone material to heal the fracture.

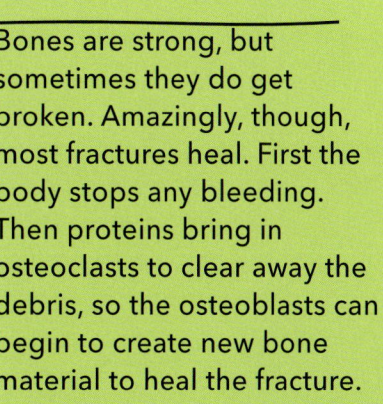

21

Moving Parts

Even though it is incredibly strong, your skeleton can bend and move in almost any direction thanks to its joints. Joints are where bones meet. All your bones, except one in your throat, form a joint with another bone.

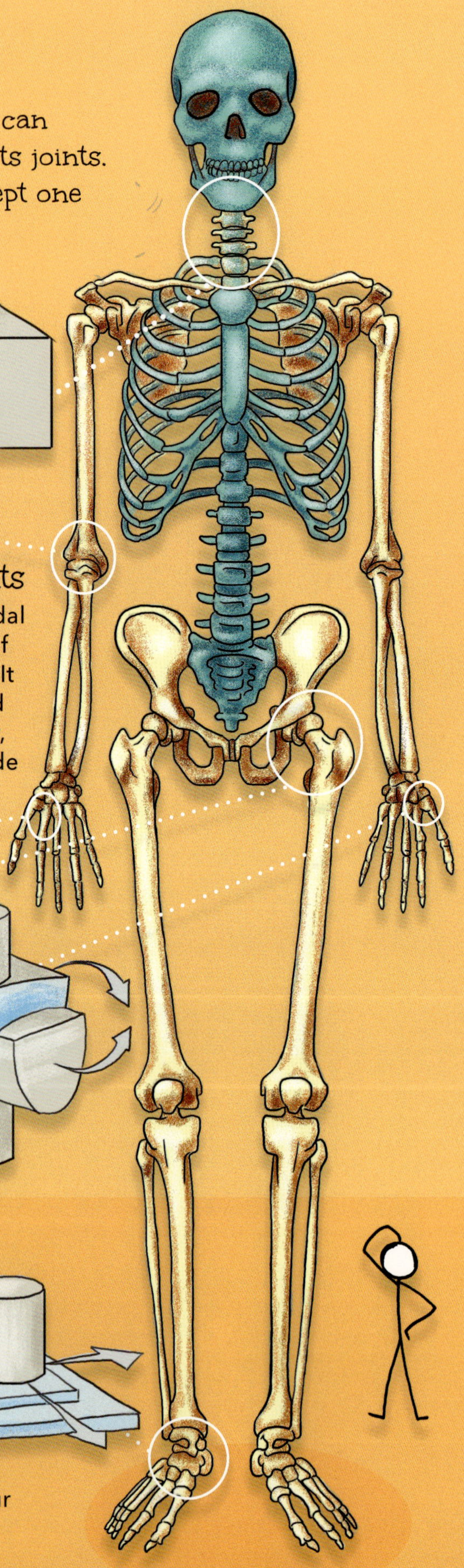

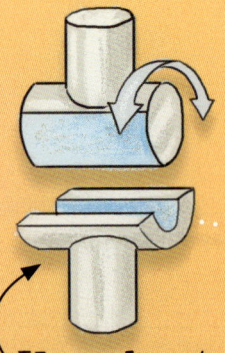

Swivel Joint
The swivel joint in your neck allows you to turn your head to the left and right.

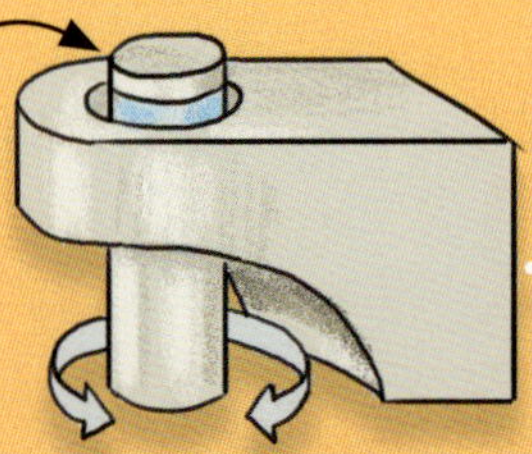

Hinge Joints
The hinge joints in your fingers, elbows, ankles, and toes swing in only two directions, just like a door on hinges—but they are very strong. You use hinge joints when you make a fist or curl your toes.

Ellipsoidal Joints
There is an ellipsoidal joint at the base of each index finger. It lets you bend and extend this finger, and rock it from side to side.

Ball and Socket Joints
Your hip and shoulder joints are your most flexible joints. They are ball-and-socket joints which let you swing your arms and legs in lots of different directions.

Saddle Joints
The joints at the base of your thumbs are saddle joints. In these, two saddle-shaped bones fit togethr snugly and can rock back and forth and from side to side. They are strong but can't rotate much.

Gliding Joints
Where two flat bones are held together by ligaments just loosely enough to glide past each other, it's called a gliding joint. Some of the bones in your wrists and ankles move like this.

22

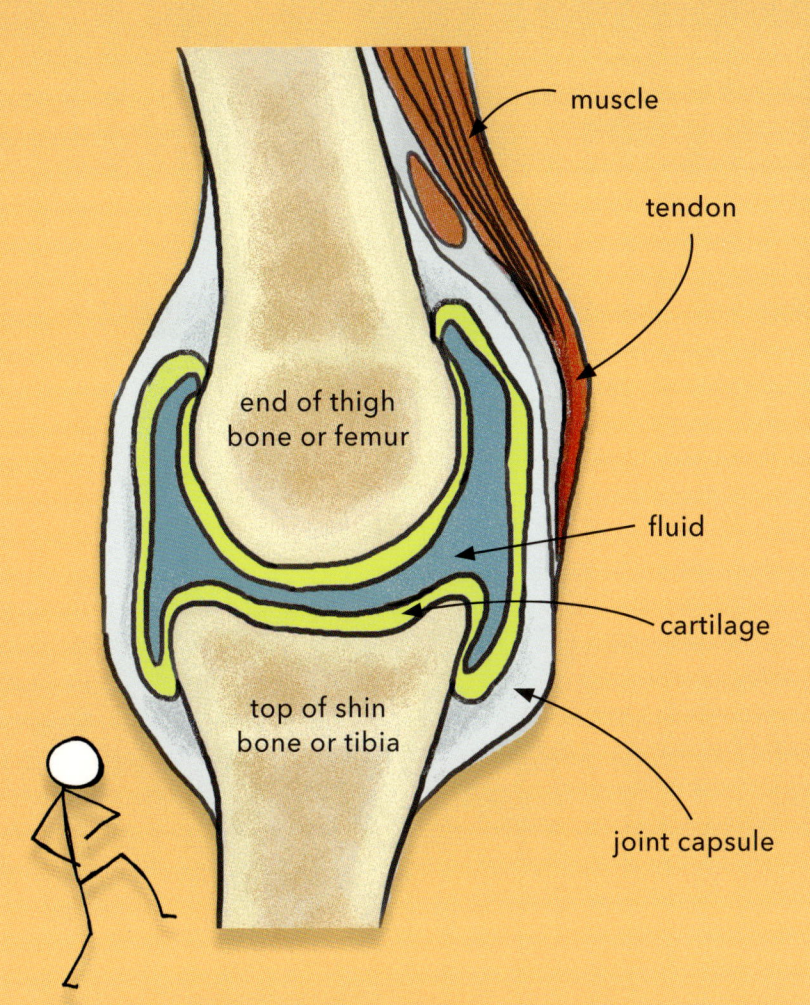

Diagram labels: muscle, tendon, end of thigh bone or femur, fluid, cartilage, top of shin bone or tibia, joint capsule

Knee Joint

Your knee is a special hinge joint. It can bend like all hinge joints, but it can also rotate slightly. It's protected by a little shield of bone called the kneecap and surrounded by a capsule of rubbery cartilage and fluid to cushion and lubricate it.

Knee Injury

Knee joints are particularly vulnerable to damage. Many athletes suffer knee injuries that bring about major career setbacks. One of the most common is ligament injury caused by turning the knee sharply.

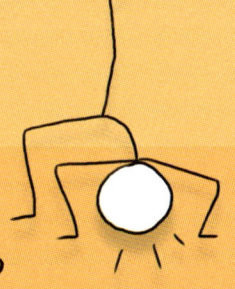

Bending Bones?

Ligaments usually restrict the movement of your skeleton. But with practice, some contortionists are able to stretch them and bend their bodies into all kinds of strange shapes. But the bones are not bending—it is just the joints moving further than normal.

Binders

Bones are tied together and muscles are tied to bones with short, strong fibers called ligaments and tendons. Ligaments are attached to the bones on either side of a joint and bind them together. Tendons anchor muscles to bones.

Hand Holding

Your hand contains lots of strong ligaments and tendons to give you a strong grip. The muscles that move your fingers are not in your hand at all—they're in your arm and connected by tendons. If you spread your fingers out, you can see these tendons clearly as ridges in the back of your hand.

- pretendinous bands pull your fingers up
- abductor muscles in the palm spread your hands
- the palmaris longus tendon runs from a muscle in your arm to your hand

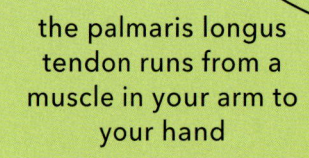

- shoulder blade
- triceps
- tendon
- biceps
- radial tuberosity
- radius bone

Arm Bands

The muscles in your arm are attached to bones via tendons at either end. The biceps is attached with a tendon to a part of the radius bone called the radial tuberosity, a small bump on the bone near your elbow joint.

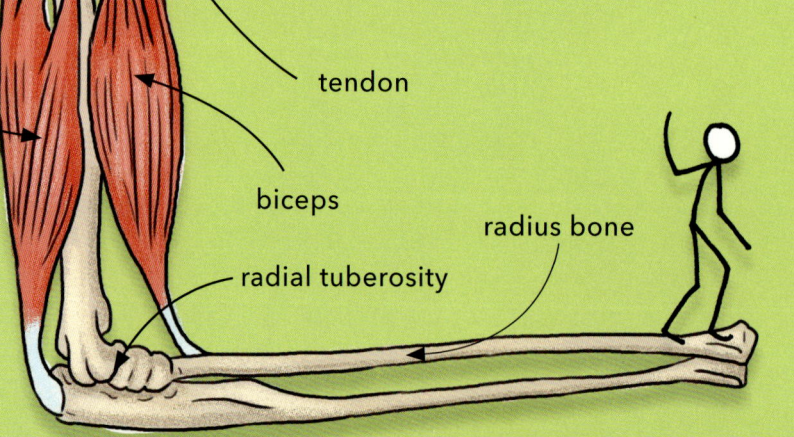

24

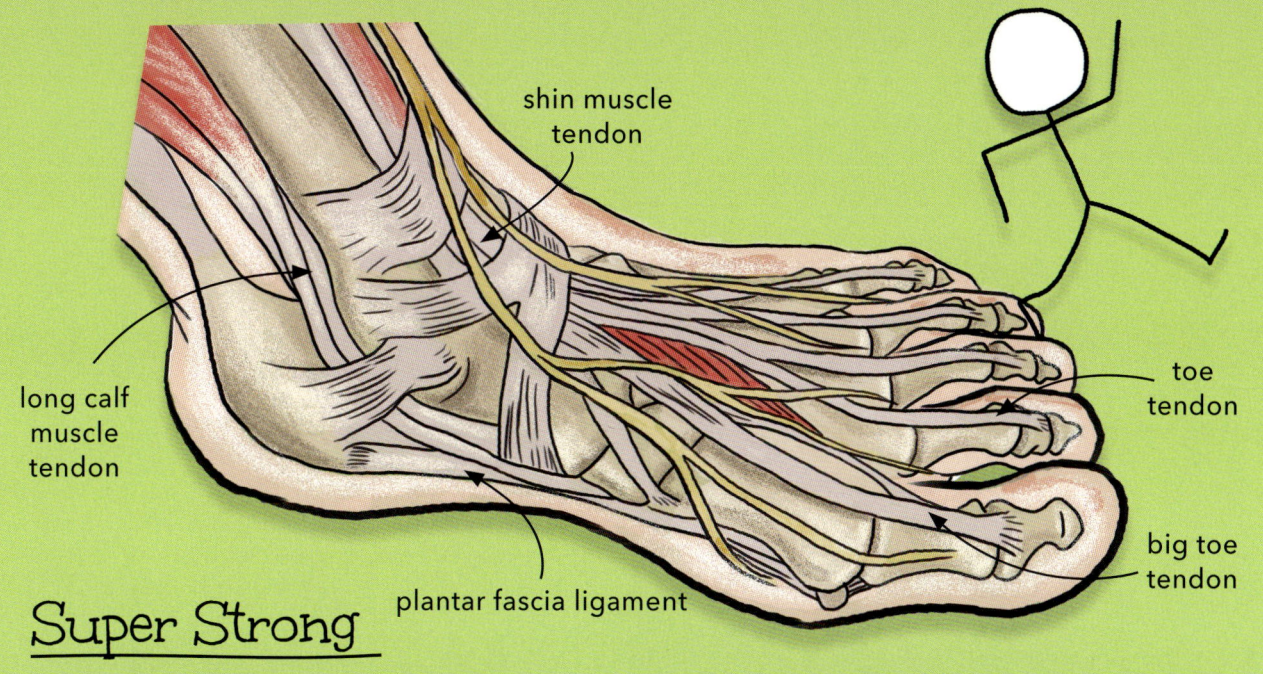

shin muscle tendon

long calf muscle tendon

toe tendon

big toe tendon

plantar fascia ligament

Super Strong

The tendons and ligaments in your feet have to be especially strong since they must bear your entire weight and provide the spring in your foot for running and jumping. The key ligament is the plantar fascia, which gives your foot its arch. By stretching and contracting, it allows the arch to curve or flatten, so you can balance and walk.

Achilles Heel

When Ancient Greek hero Achilles was a baby, his mother dipped him in a magic river to make him invulnerable. But the water never reached the place on his heel where she held him. Later, he died in battle from a wound inflicted there. That's why the tendon holding your foot is called the Achilles tendon—but it is actually pretty strong!

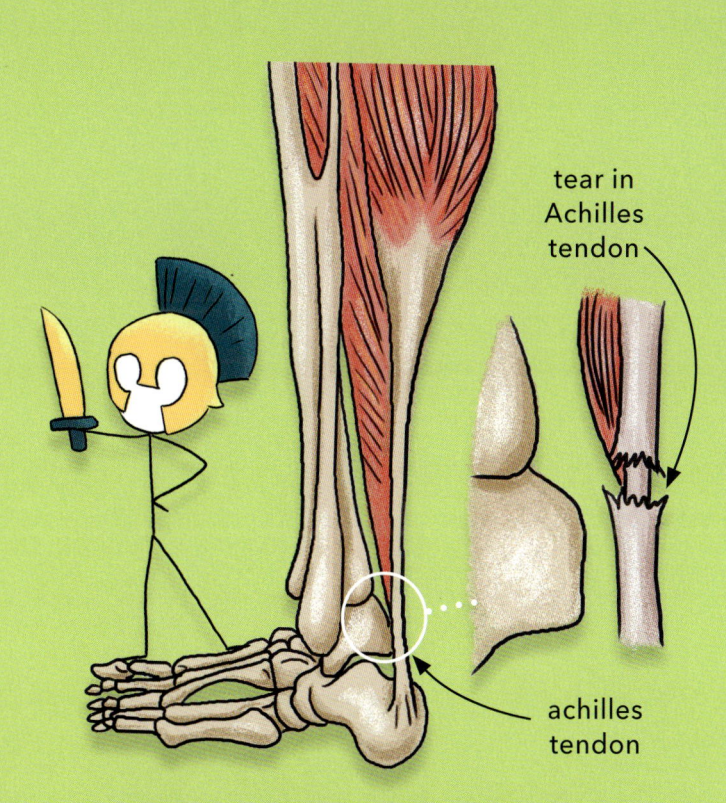

tear in Achilles tendon

achilles tendon

Cartilaginous Joints

Cartilage is the amazing rubbery material that cushions the ends of bones and stops them being damaged. And under your skin, your ears and nose are made of a special kind of extra bendy cartilage called elastic cartilage.

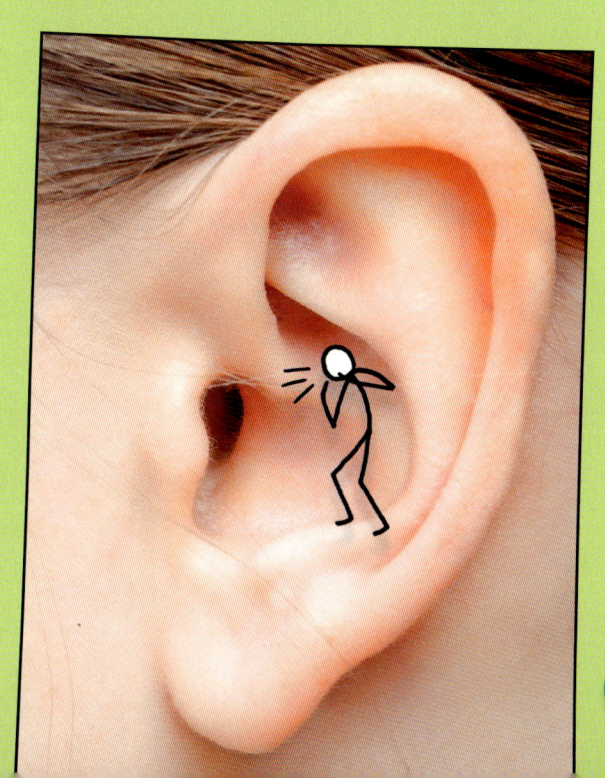

25

Bonehead

Your skull is the tough dome of bone that protects your brain. It looks like a single bone, but it is actually made from 22 bones cemented together by rigid joints called sutures.

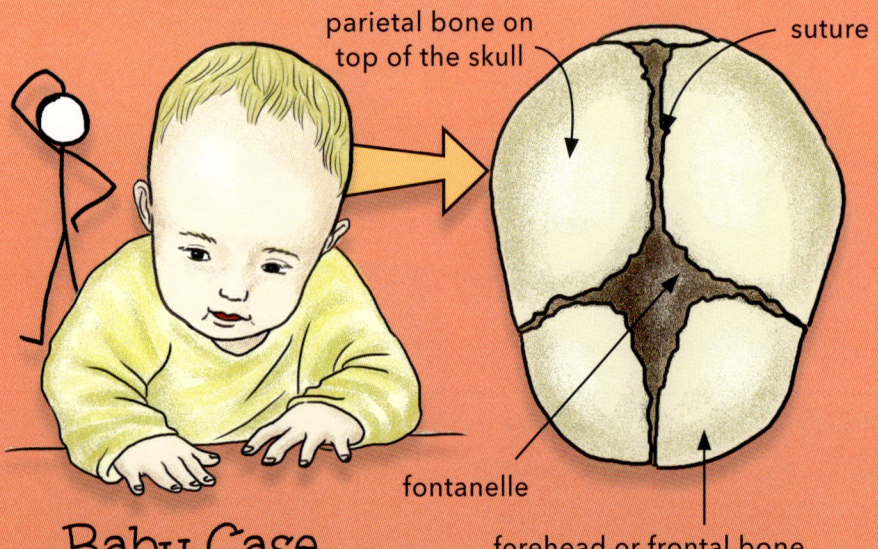

parietal bone on top of the skull

suture

Cranium

fontanelle

forehead or frontal bone

two parietal bones form the sides and top of the cranium

Baby Case

When you're born, the bones of your skull are not fixed together. That way they can slide over each other and overlap to let your head squeeze through your mother's birth canal. For a while after you're born, your skull has soft spots called fontanelles. These spots gradually fuse and harden.

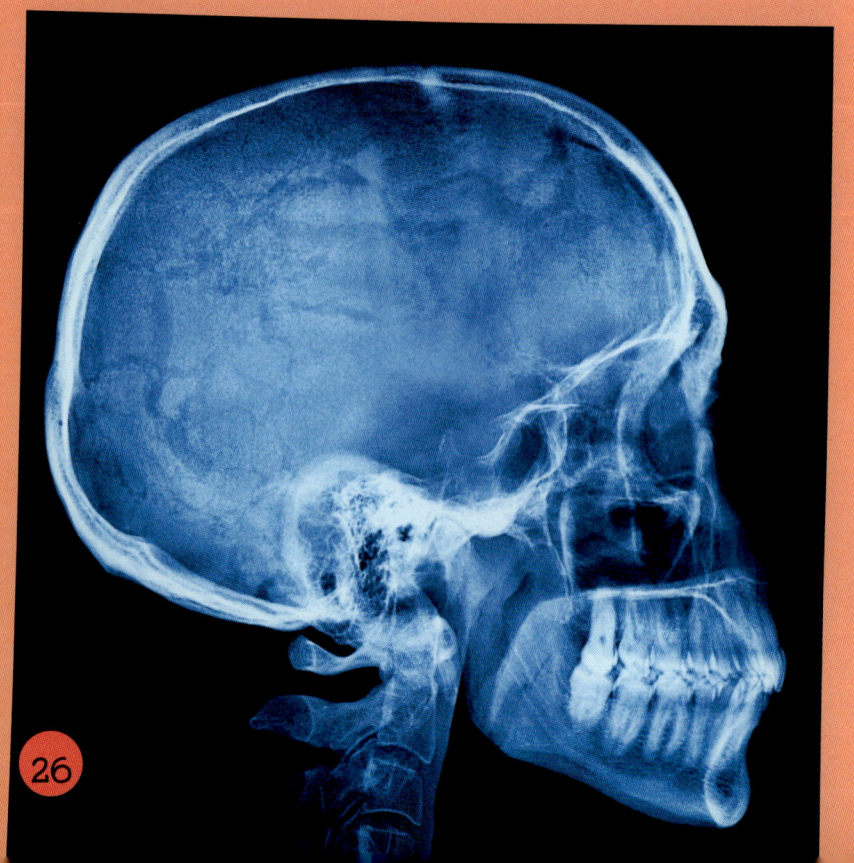

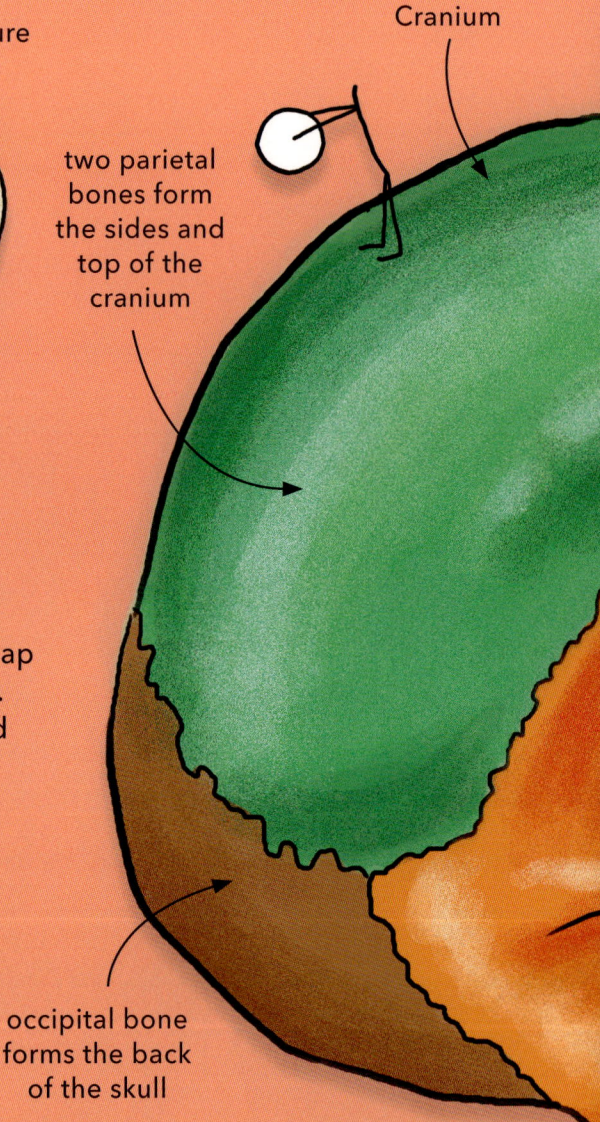

occipital bone forms the back of the skull

Inside Your Head

Your skull provides such effective protection for your head that it's hard to know what's happening inside. That's why X-rays and brain scans are so important. They allow doctors and scientists to see inside, check for damag,e and learn more about what's going on.

Nut Case

The dome at the top of your head that holds your brain is called the cranium. It's made of eight curved pieces of bone fused together along sutures. The rest of the skull comprises the 14 bones of your face. This includes your lower jaw, the only bone in your skull that moves.

Hole in the Head

In ancient times, many people were trepanned. Trepanning meant drilling a large hole in your skull. It was very dangerous and must have been incredibly painful. No one knows just why they did it. Maybe they thought it would stop seizures or let evil spirits out.

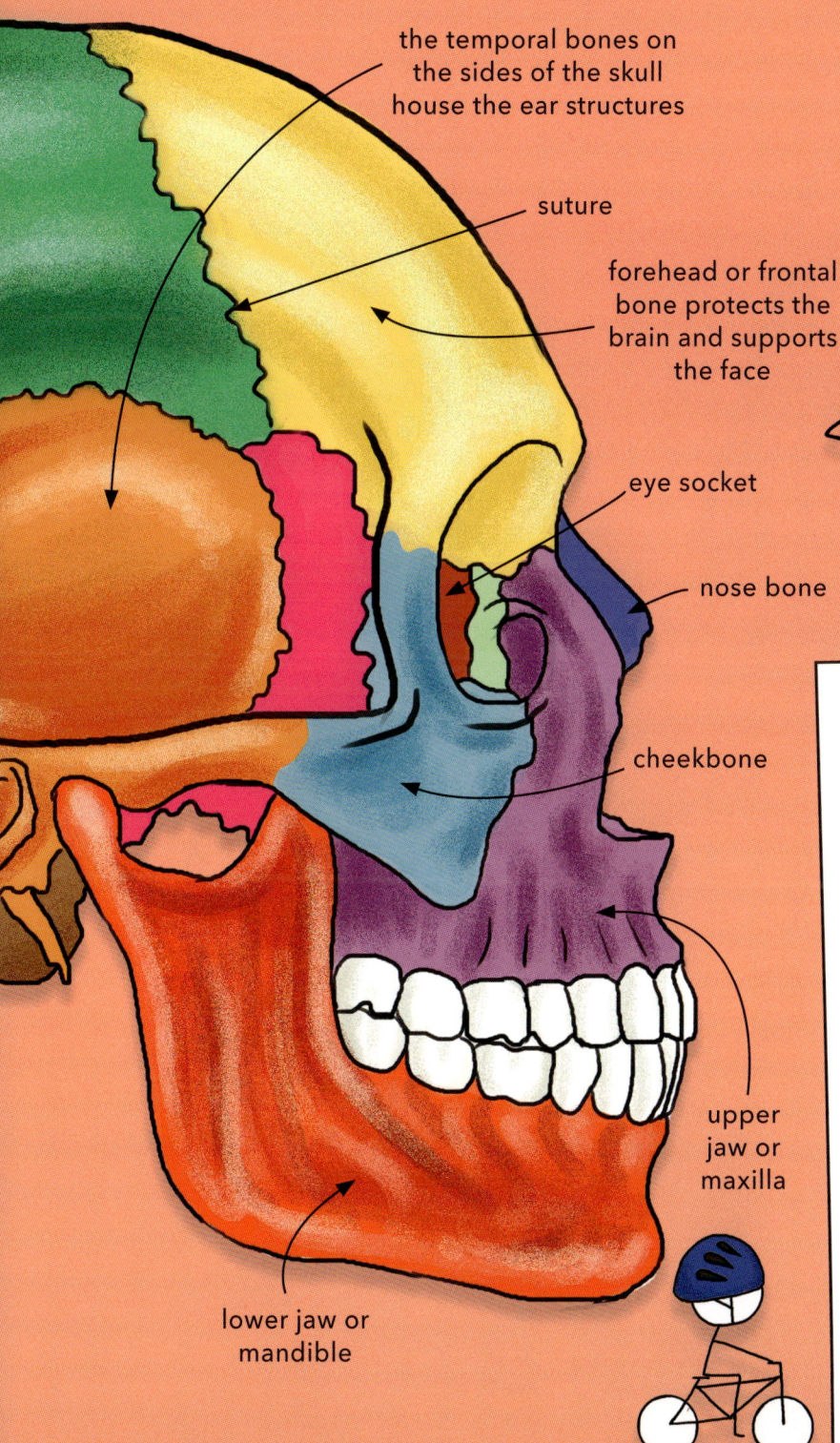

the temporal bones on the sides of the skull house the ear structures

suture

forehead or frontal bone protects the brain and supports the face

eye socket

nose bone

cheekbone

upper jaw or maxilla

lower jaw or mandible

Helmet

Your skull provides very strong protection for your vulnerable and delicate brain. Yet even your skull may not be enough if you hit your head hard. That's why safety helmets are important when you ride a bike or play sports where you can fall hard.

27

Your Brilliant Brain

Every creature has a brain, but we humans have especially clever ones. The human brain is a living supercomputer! But like a computer, it needs inputs and outputs, and that's where nerves come in. Nerves provide input by sending signals to the brain from sensors all over the body, and output by sending signals to tell the body what to do. Your brain and nerves make up the nervous system.

Brainy Neanderthals

We humans like to think we've got big brains. Well, our brains are quite big. But Neanderthal people had even bigger brains. Neanderthal people lived 160,000 to 40,000 years ago in Eurasia. Their brains were about 30 percent bigger than ours. Mind you, an elephant has a brain three times as big as ours!

Intelligence Quotient

An IQ (Intelligence Quotient) test features a series of questions designed to test your brainpower. Most people get an IQ score between 85 and 115. Some very clever people get higher scores. But IQ scores don't really show how clever you are; they only show how good at IQ tests you are. The more you practice, the better you do!

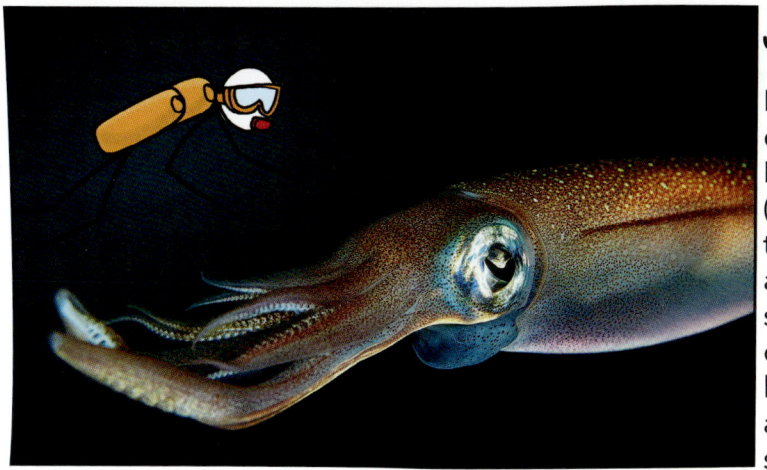

Just Squidding

Most nerves are far too small to see, except under a powerful microscope. But the squid has a nerve with an axon (tail) that is over 0.04 inches (1 mm) thick—thicker than cotton thread. The axon sends the signal that fires the squid's jet propulsion system—the jet of water it shoots out to give it a quick burst of speed. Scientists have learned a lot about how our nerves work by studying the squid's giant nerve.

Mind Your Brain

Scientists and other thinkers often argue about whether you think with your brain or your mind. Your brain is the mass of nerves inside your head that does your thinking. Your mind is all your thoughts. If your brain were a computer, your mind would be all the things a computer does.

Sigmund Freud, the world's best-known psychologist

Brain Science

Different sciences involve different aspects of the brain and how it works. Neuroscientists study how the brain and nerves work physically. Cognitive neuroscientists study how the nerves in your brain make you think. Psychologists study people's minds and how they behave..

29

Central Control

Your nervous system is like a busy internet, wired to every part of your body and whizzing messages back and forth. It's a two-way system. Sensory nerves send signals in toward the brain from sense receptors all around the body, such as the touch sensors in the skin. Motor nerves send signals in the other direction, out from the brain, telling the muscles to move.

Branching Out

The core of the nervous system is the brain and the bundle of nerves running down through the backbone known as the spinal cord. Together, the brain and spinal cord are known as the central nervous system (*shown in green*). From this system, nerves branch out to the whole body through what is called the peripheral nervous system (*shown in pink*). The main branches of the peripheral nervous system are the 12 pairs of cranial nerves (in the brain) and the 31 pairs of spinal nerves. All other nerves branch off these.

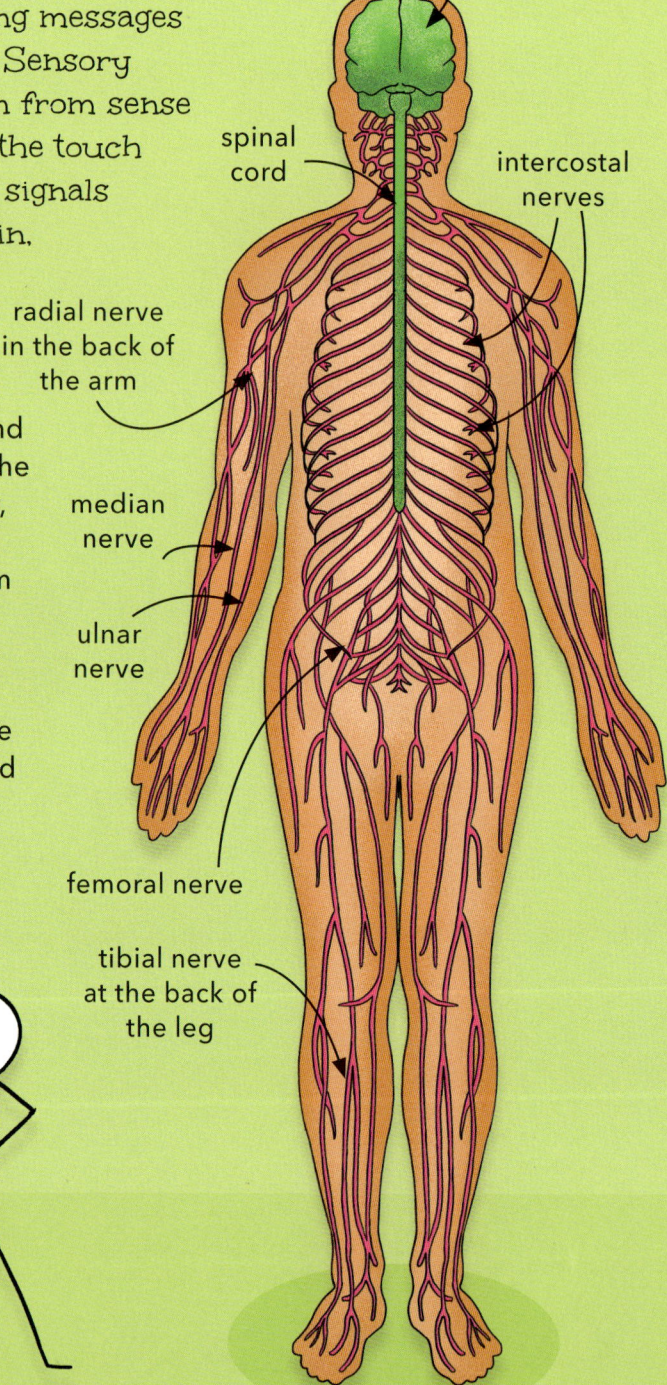

- brain
- spinal cord
- intercostal nerves
- radial nerve in the back of the arm
- median nerve
- ulnar nerve
- femoral nerve
- tibial nerve at the back of the leg

- eight cervical nerves in the neck
- 12 thoracic nerves in the upper back
- five lumbar nerves in the lower back
- six sacral nerves at the base of the spine

Spinal Cord

The spinal cord is the motorway that carries all nerve signals to and from the brain. It is protected by cerebrospinal fluid. The 31 pairs of major nerves that branch off the spinal cord form four groups: the cervical, thoracic, lumbar, and sacral nerves.

Automatic Nerves

Besides the central and peripheral systems, you have a third system, the autonomic nervous system. This controls automatic tasks such as heartbeat and digestion. It has two parts: the parasympathetic, which deals with everyday tasks; and the sympathetic, which prepares your body for action if you are ever in danger.

Fight or Flight

The autonomic nervous system gets your body ready for action in times of danger when you have to stand and fight or run away: the fight or flight reflex.

The Wandering Nerve

The vagus nerve gets its name from the Latin for wandering—and that's just what it does. It wanders from the brain stem, all the way down from the base of your brain to the gut. On its way, it controls lots of things, from your breathing and heartbeat to the way you digest food.

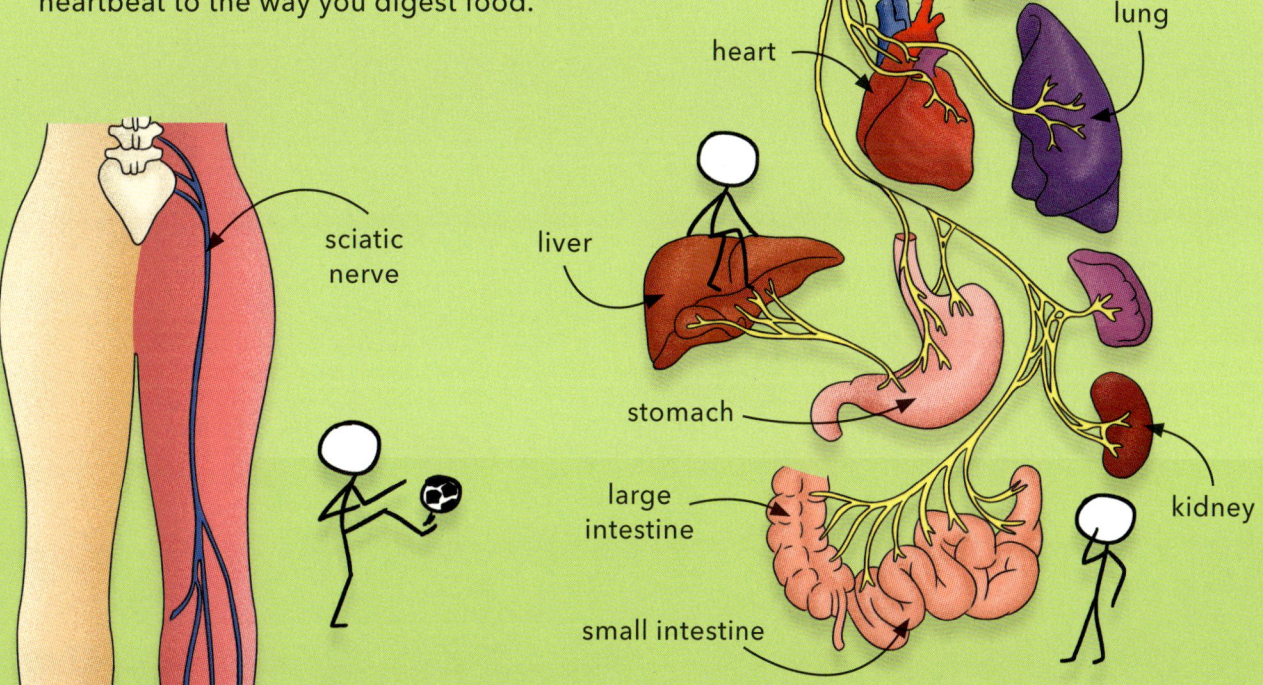

Sciatic Nerve

The sciatic nerve is the largest single nerve in your body. It runs down from your lower spine into your buttocks and thighs, then all the way down to your feet. It plays a vital role in linking the spinal cord to the muscles in your legs and feet. It can sometimes cause a pain known as sciatica.

You've Got a Nerve

Your nervous system is made of lots of nerve cells strung together. Nerve cells, known as neurons, are unusual cells. While most cells are like little parcels, neurons are a spidery shape with threads branching out in all directions to connect with other nerves, sense organs, or muscles.

A Nerve Cell

Nerve signals enter a neuron through any one of a bunch of spidery threads called dendrites. They then pass through the cell's nucleus and out the other side through a long tail, or axon, to connect to other neurons. Axons from several cells bunch together like threads in a string to make nerve fibers.

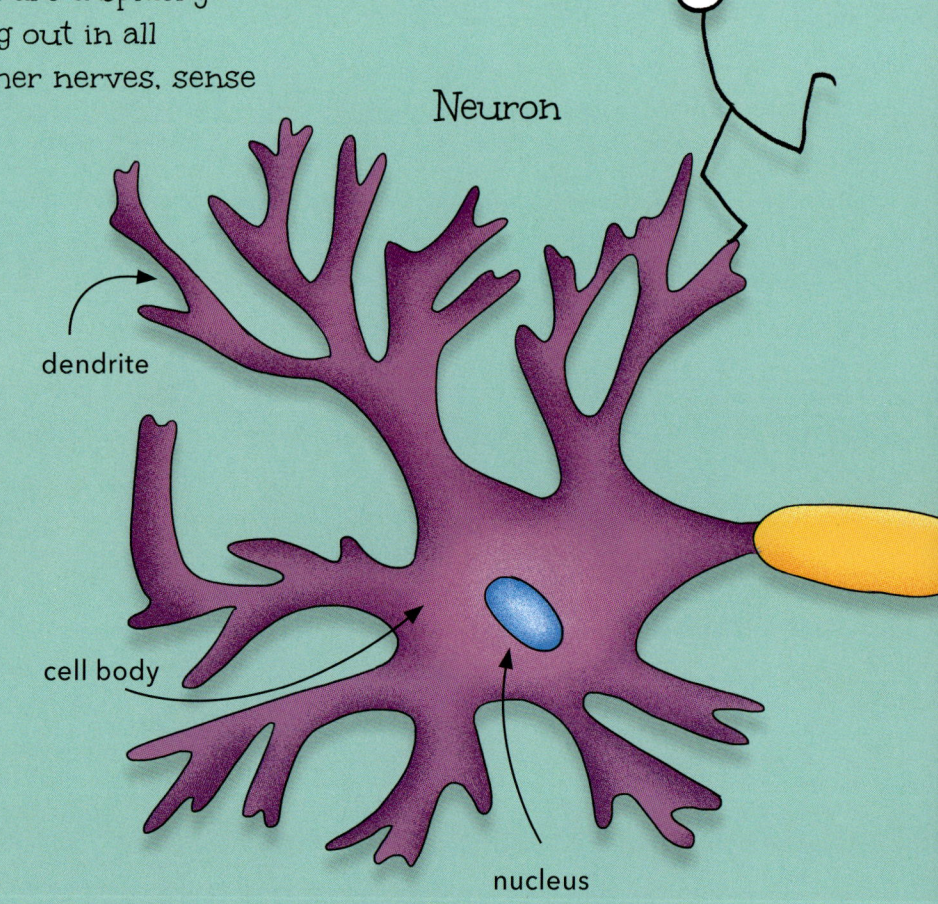

Neuron

dendrite

cell body

nucleus

How Nerve Signals Move

Nerve signals are sent with a mix of chemistry and electricity. When a nerve is resting, there are lots of little particles (chemical ions) with negative electricity on the inside. Nerve signals start by opening "gates" in the nerve walls. This lets positive particles, or sodium ions, in. The positive particles are attracted toward the negative particles farther up the nerve.

1. A nerve signal starts as gates open to let particles with positive electricity in.

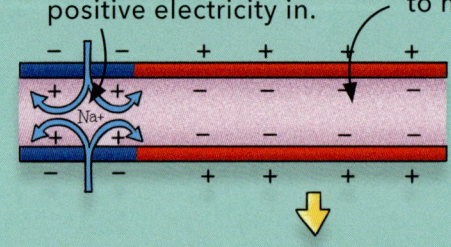

Positive ions are drawn to negative ions farther up the nerve.

segment of axon

2. The signal sweeps up the nerve, as more gates open farther up to let positive particles flood in.

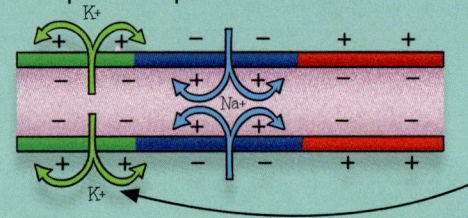

Other gates close behind the signal to let out positive particles (potassium (K) ions) and keep the signal brief.

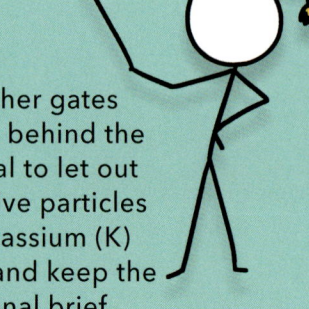

Mind the Gap

No two neurons ever touch because there is a tiny gap between them called a synapse. When a nerve signal reaches a nerve end, tiny droplets of chemicals called neurotransmitters are released into the synapse. These chemicals lock onto matching receptor sites on the neighboring cell, starting a new signal.

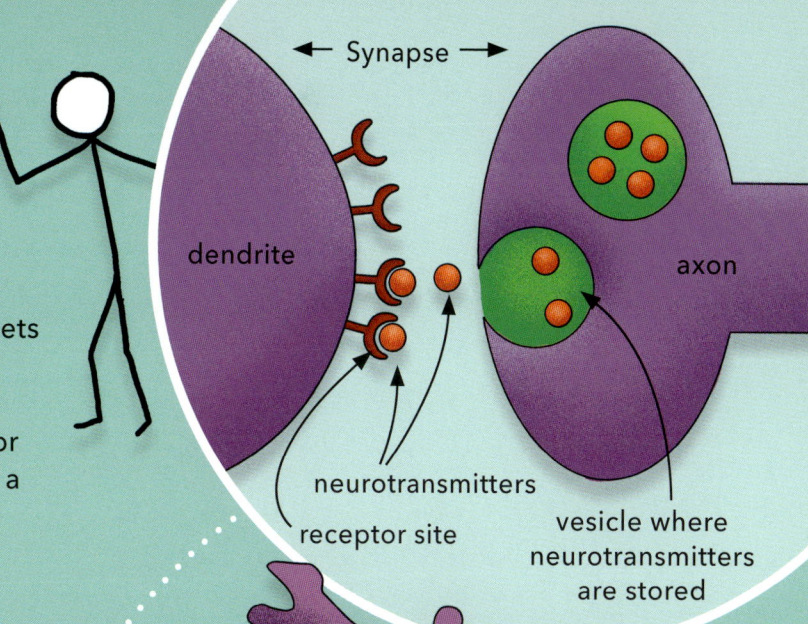

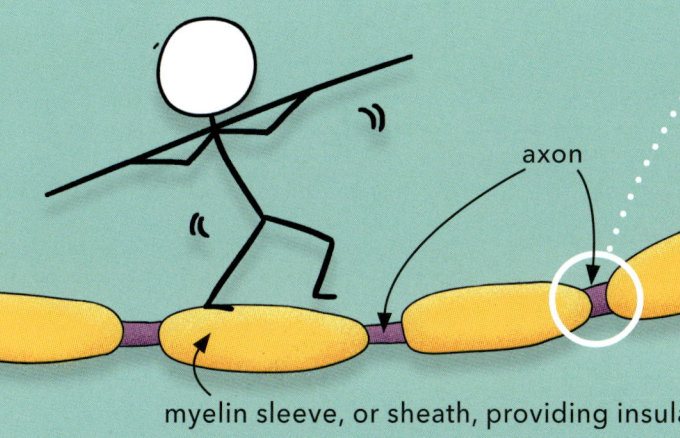

Synapse

dendrite

axon

neurotransmitters

receptor site

vesicle where neurotransmitters are stored

axon

axon terminal

myelin sleeve, or sheath, providing insulation

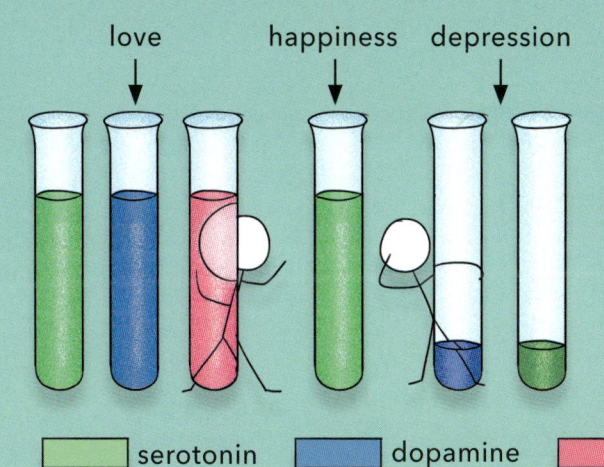

love   happiness   depression

Mood Makers

Different combinations of neurotransmitters have different effects on your mood. Having lots of the neurotransmitter serotonin puts you in a good mood. Combine it with a lot of dopamine and oxytocin, and you're in love. The less serotonin and dopamine you have, the worse your mood.

serotonin   dopamine   oxytocin

Love It

When people first fall in love, their brains flood with dopamine, which makes them feel excited, energetic, and focused—perfect for dancing or talking all night! If they couple stays together and becomes affectionate, they get lots of oxytocin too. This is triggered when you cuddle.

33

Brainy

Inside your head is an amazing computer: your brain. It is made from over 100 billion neurons, each connected to 10,000–20,000 other neurons. That means there are over a thousand trillion connections to help you think. No wonder you're so clever!

In Your Head

Your brain fills the inside of the top of your skull. The wrinkled outer layers are know as gray matter, which is made of the bodies of nerve cells, along with dendrites and synapses. The inside is mostly white matter, which is made of axons, the long tails of nerve cells.

If you're a girl, your brain weighs 2.5 percent of your body weight, on average; if you're a boy, it weighs 2 percent—but boys' brains are heavier on average.

A Brain of Two Halves

Your brain is divided into two halves or hemispheres, linked by a huge bundle of nerves called the corpus callosum. Surprisingly, the left half of your brain controls the right side of your body, and the right half of your brain controls the left side. Each side of your brain was once thought to have very different skills (*shown below*), but many scientists now believe it is not as simple as this.

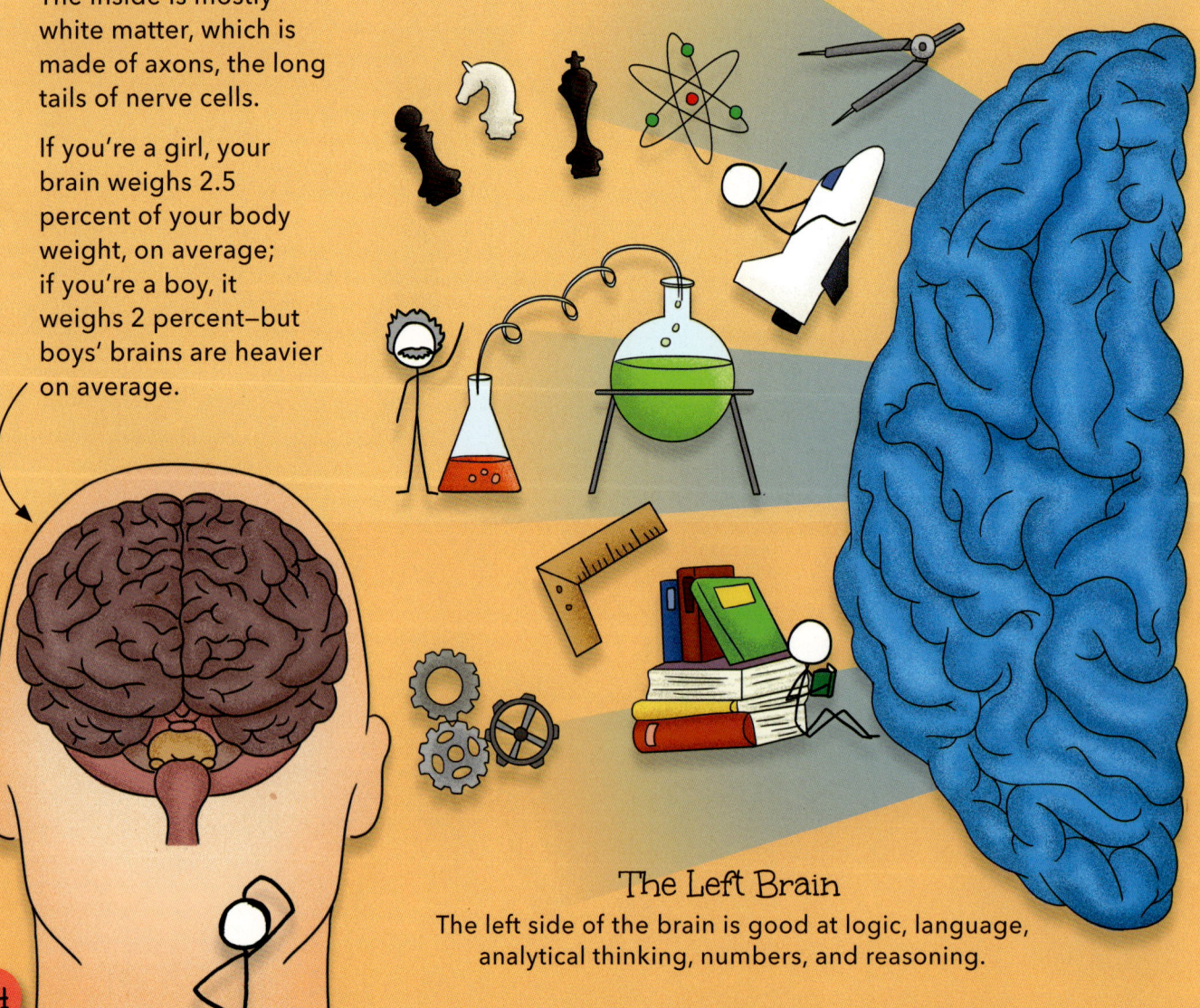

The Left Brain
The left side of the brain is good at logic, language, analytical thinking, numbers, and reasoning.

Making Up Your Mind

Your brain is actually 85 percent water and quite a lot of fat. But what really matters is all the nerve cells, which are held in tight bundles by supporting cells called glial cells. All your thoughts come as signals whizzing through this amazing network.

glial cell
glial cell
nerve cell

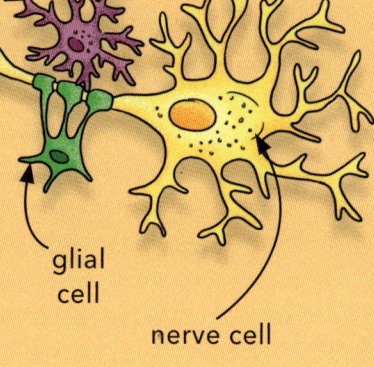

The Right Brain

The right side of the brain is best at expressing and reading emotions, recognizing faces, intuition, and creative tasks related to music, color, and images.

There's a Thought!

Thoughts are nerve signals that buzz through the brain between nerve cells, making billions of connections in a fraction of a second. What you're thinking depends on which nerve pathways fire up. Pathways that are used a lot get stronger and quicker. Those that are little used tend to get lost.

Hungry Brain!

All those cells in your brain need a lot of energy—and a lot of oxygen! If the blood supply to your brain were cut off, you'd lose consciousness in just 10 seconds, and die in minutes.

Inside Your Brain

The wrinkled outer layer of your brain is where conscious thoughts go on. Conscious thoughts are thoughts you know about. But there are also subconscious thoughts occurring deep inside your brain that you know very little about!

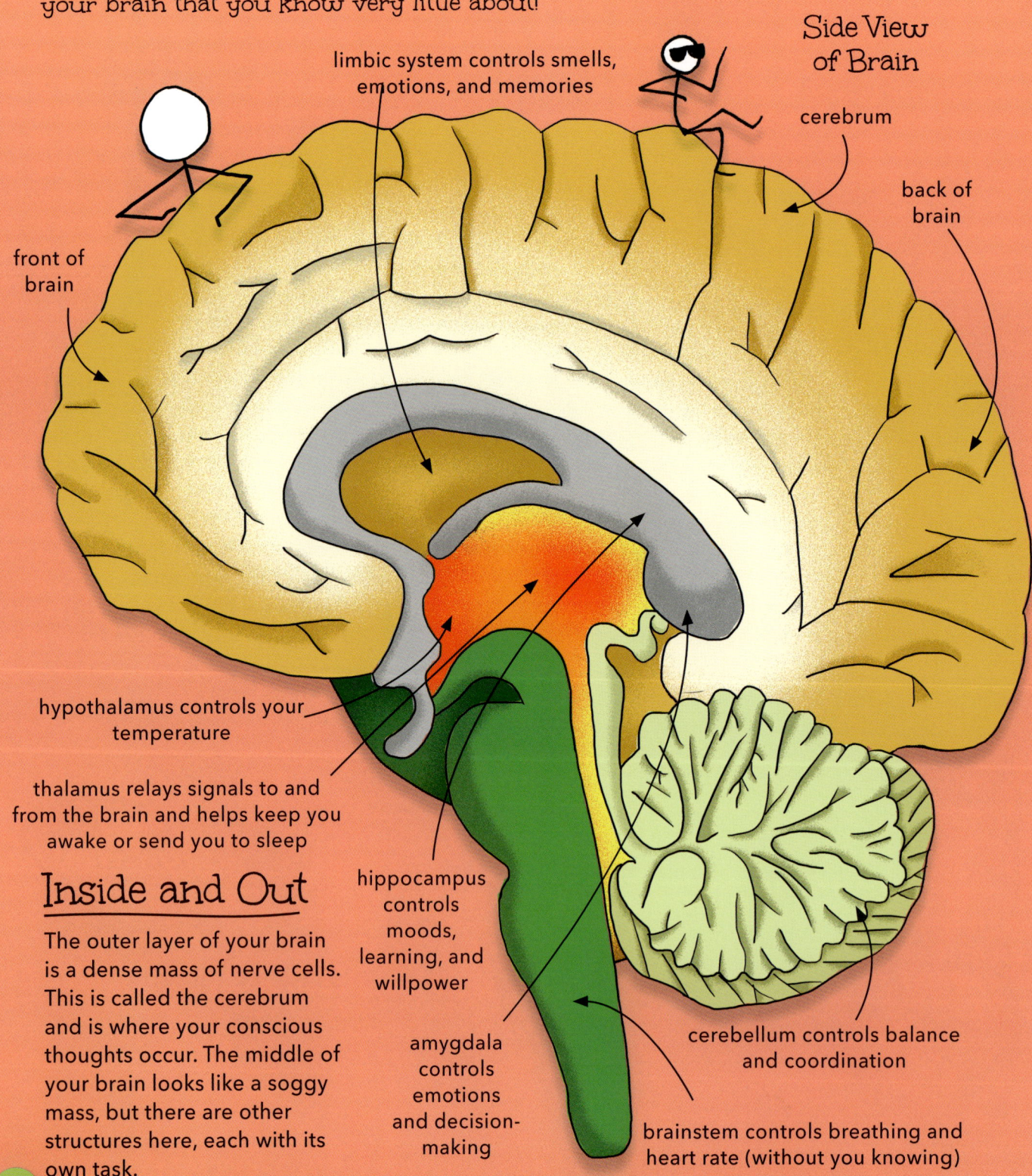

Side View of Brain

- limbic system controls smells, emotions, and memories
- cerebrum
- back of brain
- front of brain
- hypothalamus controls your temperature
- thalamus relays signals to and from the brain and helps keep you awake or send you to sleep
- hippocampus controls moods, learning, and willpower
- amygdala controls emotions and decision-making
- cerebellum controls balance and coordination
- brainstem controls breathing and heart rate (without you knowing)

Inside and Out

The outer layer of your brain is a dense mass of nerve cells. This is called the cerebrum and is where your conscious thoughts occur. The middle of your brain looks like a soggy mass, but there are other structures here, each with its own task.

On Balance

For your body to make even a simple move, your brain has to issue precise controls to different muscles. It needs continual feedback from sensors in the muscles called proprioceptors, which tell you where every part of your body is. All these signals are coordinated in the cerebellum at the back of the brain, which then sends signals out to the correct muscles.

Brain Base

The brainstem is the stalk at the base of your brain where it runs into your spine. It's the main pathway from your brain to the rest of your body, including your face and head. It controls your breathing and heart rate and tells you when to go to sleep and when to eat.

Chess Problem

When you play chess or similar games, you use the conscious part of your brain, the cerebral cortex, to figure out the problem. All the same, you get better with practice as certain routines become established in your subconscious brain deep inside.

Seahorse Brain

Right in the middle of your brain is a structure shaped like a seahorse. It's called the hippocampus, named after the Greek for "horse" (hippo) and "sea monster" (campus). It's linked with your moods, and is thought to play a key part in memory.

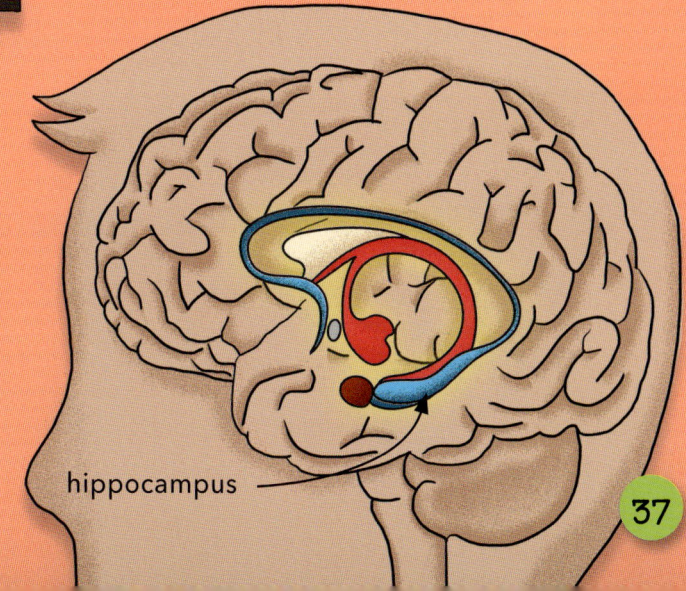

hippocampus

37

Brain Map

The cerebrum is the large, walnut-shaped bit of your brain that wraps round the inner brain like a peach around its pit. The outside of this is called the cerebral cortex. This is where all the brain's clever activities go on. It receives messages from your senses and issues commands to your muscles.

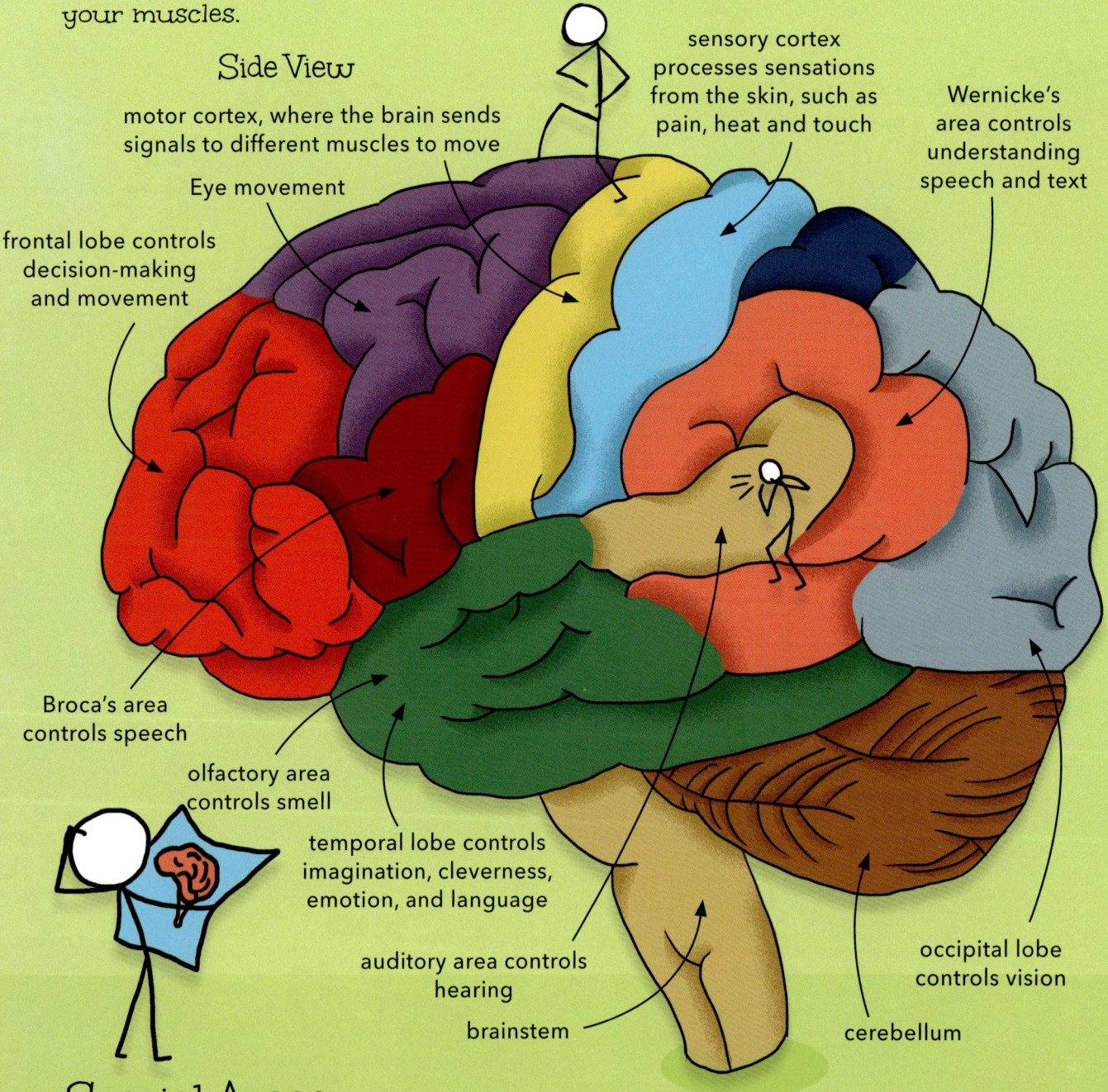

Side View

- motor cortex, where the brain sends signals to different muscles to move
- Eye movement
- sensory cortex processes sensations from the skin, such as pain, heat and touch
- Wernicke's area controls understanding speech and text
- frontal lobe controls decision-making and movement
- Broca's area controls speech
- olfactory area controls smell
- temporal lobe controls imagination, cleverness, emotion, and language
- auditory area controls hearing
- brainstem
- occipital lobe controls vision
- cerebellum

Special Areas

Each half of your brain has four ends, called lobes. A large, very prominent one at the front, called the frontal lobe, is where all your bright ideas happen. Lots of thoughts seem to take up the whole of your brain. Yet certain places in the brain, called association areas, seem to become especially active when you're doing certain things.

38

Top view
The left and right side of the cerebrum mirror each other.

frontal lobe

motor cortex

sensory cortex

wernicke's area

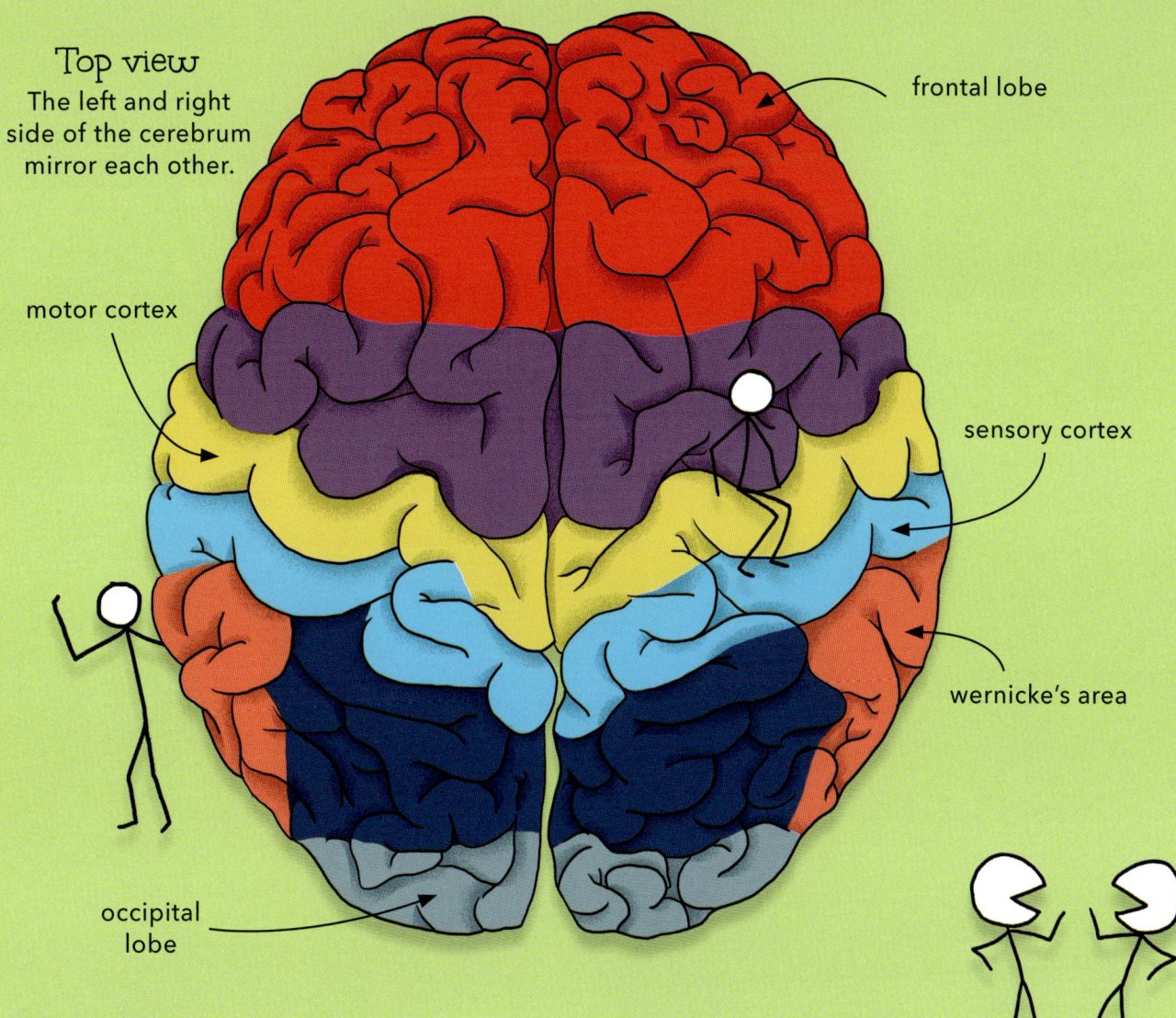

occipital lobe

The Meaning Spot

When you're reading, an area near the back of the brain called Wernicke's area seems to get excited. Wernicke's area seems to be the area where you work out what you're reading, and where you decide what you're going to say. It then sends instructions to Broca's area to work out how you say it.

Chatter Spot

When you speak, an area of the brain near the front called Broca's area seems to be involved. Scientists are not quite sure how it works. They used to think that its role was just to put words together into proper sentences. Now they think it may help you understand what someone else is saying too.

39

Moving and Feeling

There are two kinds of nerve that branch throughout your body away from your spine. Motor neurons trigger muscles to make your body move. Sensory neurons send signals from your senses to your brain to tell it what's going on.

Motor and sensory nerves are involved in whatever you're doing, whether it's writing a letter or playing football. Here's what happens when you're holding a pen:

1. Sensors in the tips of your finger and thumb trigger signals in the sensory nerve.
2. The signal travels to your spine and up to your brain.
3. In the brain, the signal is registered in the sensory cortex, a band running round the top of the brain, a bit like the strap on a set of headphones.
4. The brain responds in the neighboring motor cortex to send out a signal.
5. The signal travels through the motor neuron back down through your spine.
6. The motor neuron triggers muscles in your hand to move your finger and thumb.

Feedback

Whenever you're doing something, such as playing electronic games, there is a nonstop interaction between sensory and motor nerves. The sensory nerves continually take in data from the screen and from the world around you. The motor nerves in your hands control the screen.

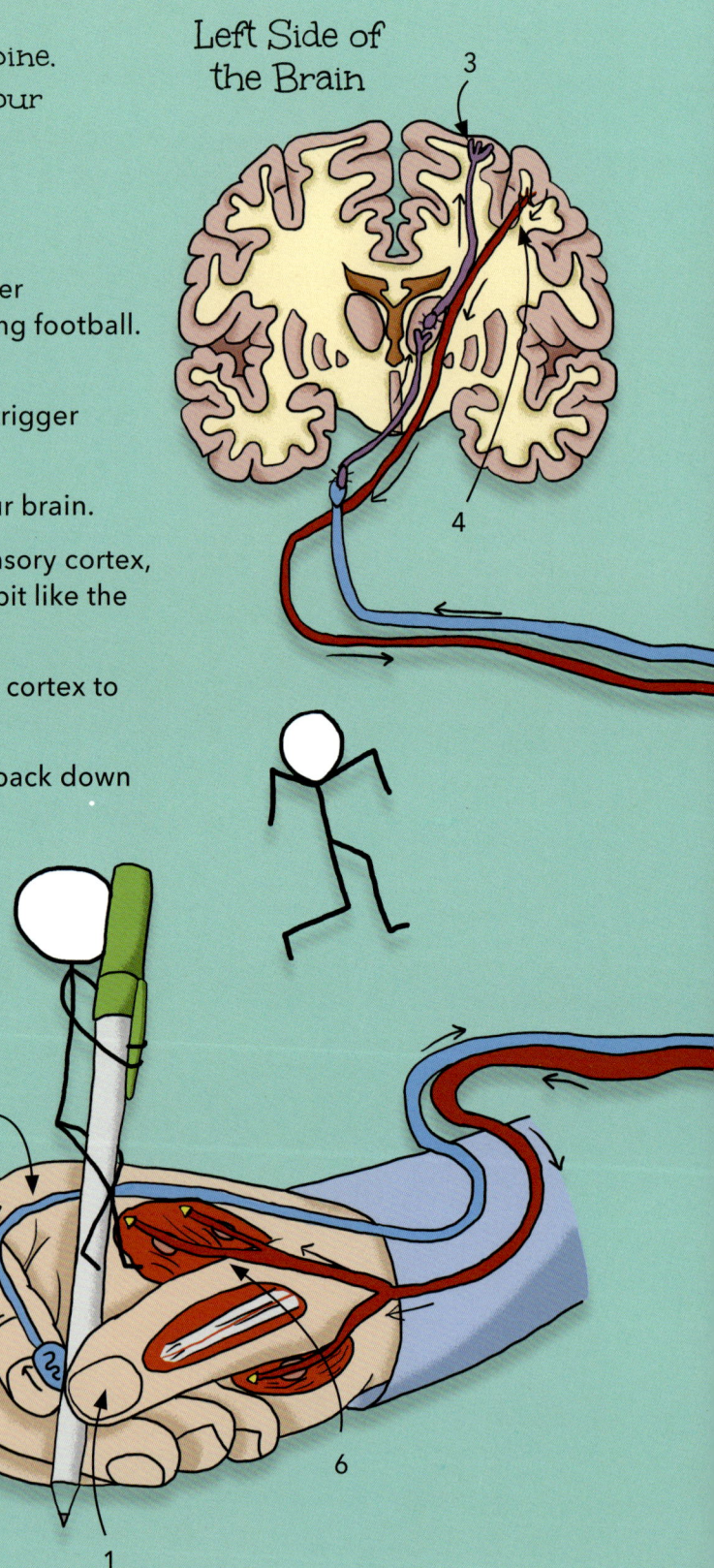

Left Side of the Brain

A Pain in the Elbow

Whenever you suffer a sharp pain, such as hitting your elbow, pain receptors send an alarm signal to your brain. You experience this alarm signal as pain. The pain is telling your body not to ignore the damage.

Reflexes

Reflexes are automatic reactions in your body over which you have no control. A reflex gives your body a way to respond to emergencies at lightning speed—before the danger signal has even reached your brain. It works like this:

7   You accidentally put your finger in a candle flame.

8   The sensory nerve from your finger sends a signal to your spine.

9   When the signal reaches your spine, it not only travels on to your brain, it also crosses through a link called an interneuron to the motor neuron.

10 The interneuron fires a signal down the motor neuron.

11 The motor neuron triggers the muscles in your arm to jerk your finger away from the flame.

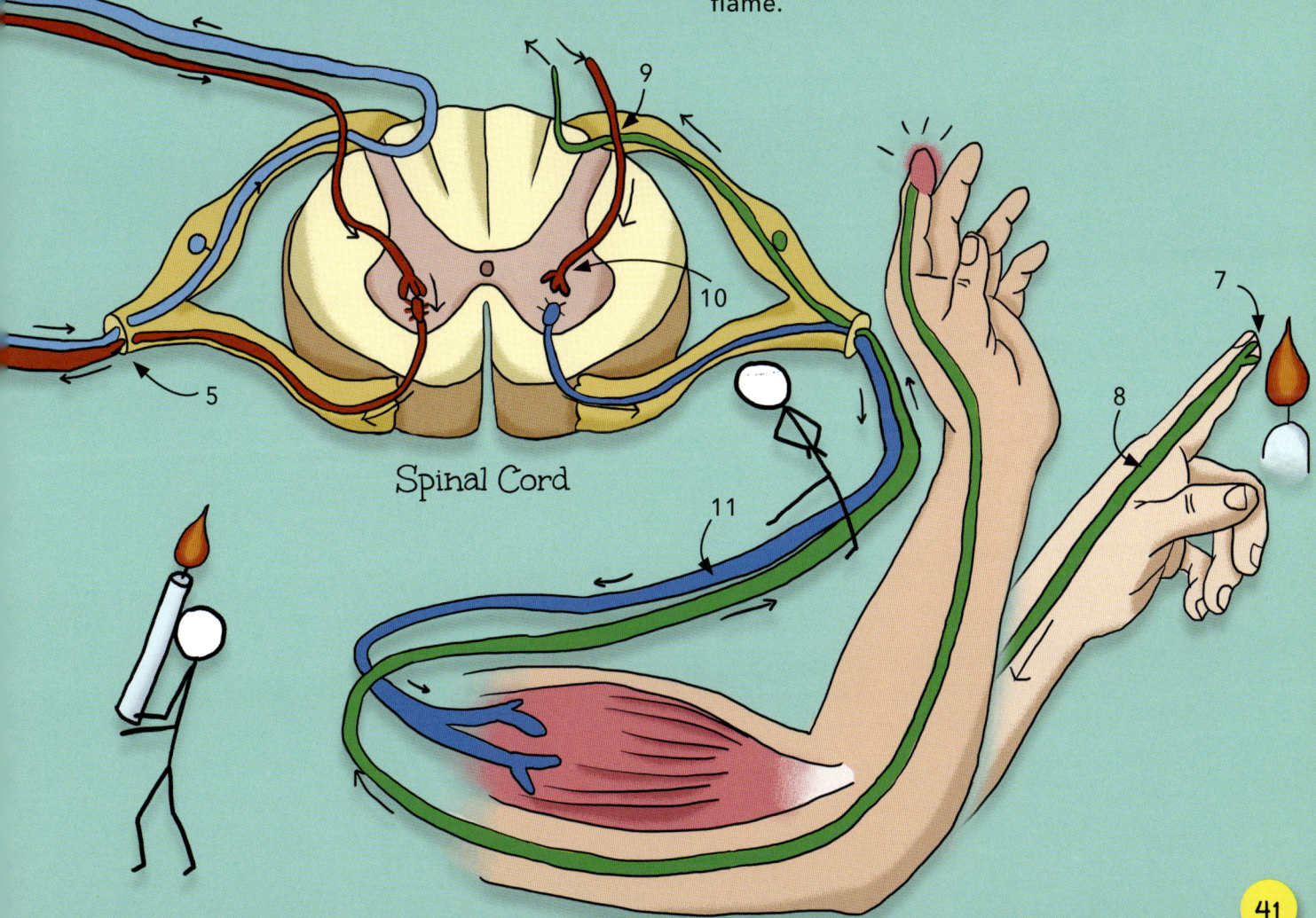

Spinal Cord

Seeing Things

Each of your eyes is an amazing camera with a powerful built-in lens that gives you an extraordinarily clear picture of the world. And behind your eyes, your brain has a visual processing system to make instant sense of the picture.

Cross Section of Eye

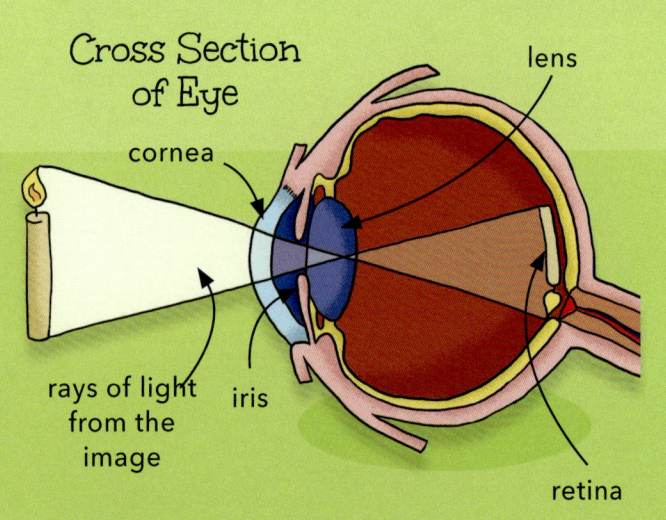

lens
cornea
rays of light from the image
iris
retina

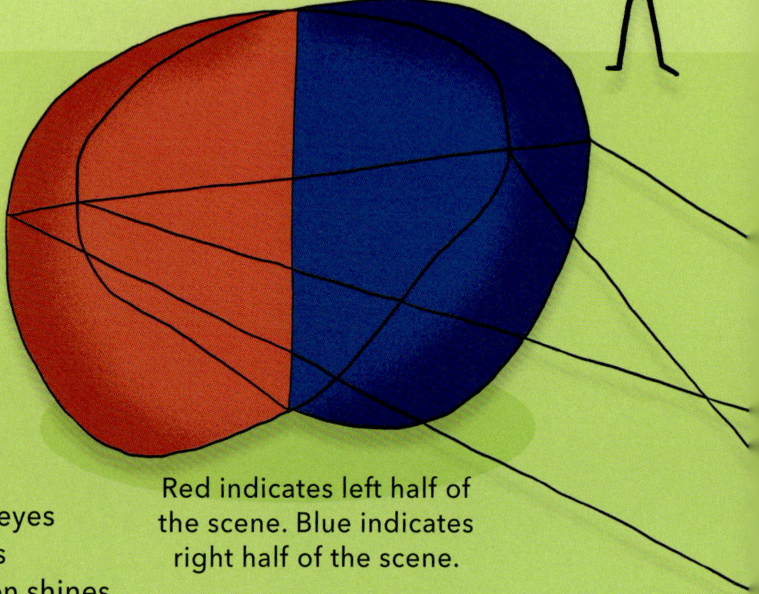

Red indicates left half of the scene. Blue indicates right half of the scene.

Making a Picture

Light from a scene you're looking at enters your eyes through the cornea, the main lens in the eye. This focuses the light to create a picture. The light then shines through a smaller lens that adjusts the focus to give a sharp picture, whether you are looking close-up or far away. The picture is upside down, but that doesn't bother your brain.

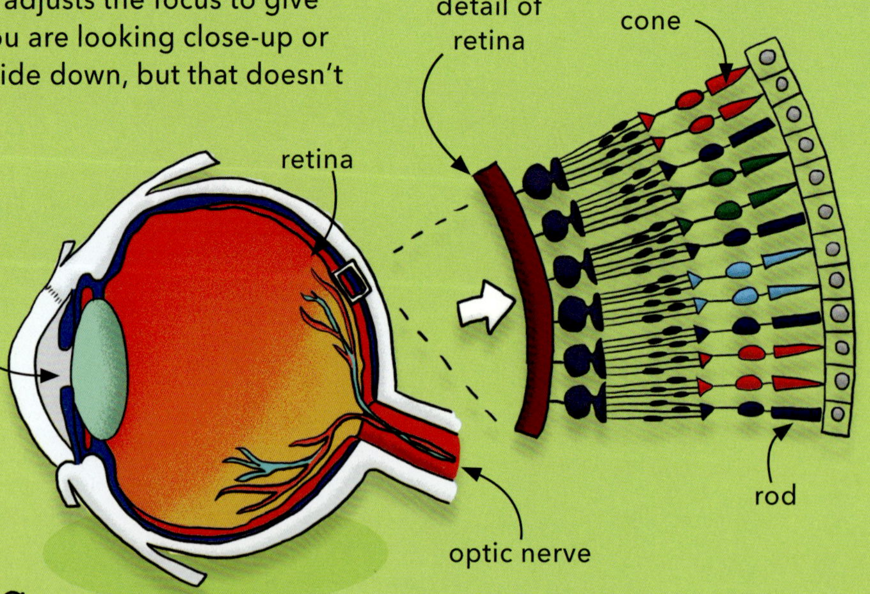

detail of retina
cone
retina
pupil
optic nerve
rod

Rods and Cones

The lenses project the picture onto the back of the eye, known as the retina. Here, there are two kinds of light-sensitive cells to record the picture. There are 150 million rods that detect if it's dark or light, and they work even in very low light. And there are eight million cones that identify colors and work best in daylight.

Light or Dark

Between the lenses, light passes through the pupil, the dark circle in the center of your eyes. It looks black because your eye is dark inside. The colored fringe around it is the iris. In bright light, tiny muscles in the iris constrict the pupil, making it small. In dim light, the iris opens the pupil wider to let in more light.

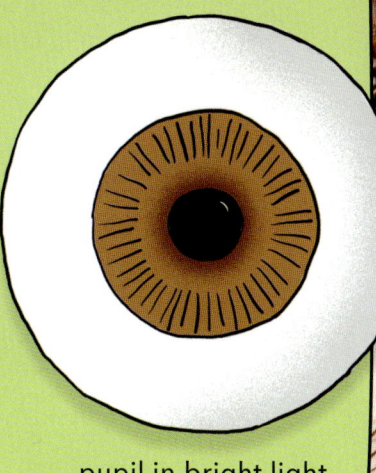

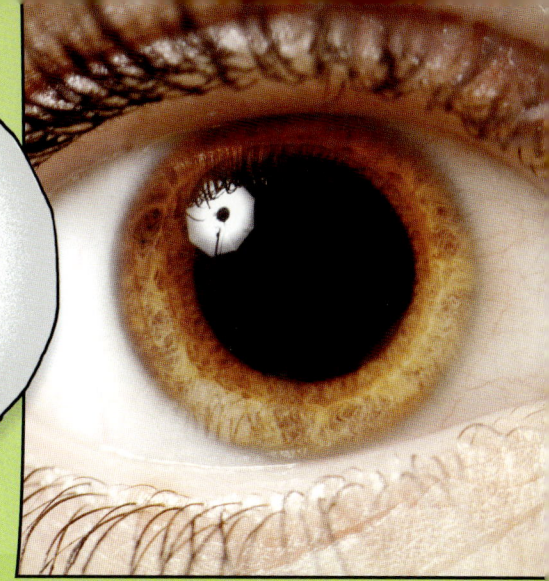

pupil in bright light (above) and in dim light (right)

Your seeing brain

From the retina, signals zoom off to your brain down the optic nerve. The optic nerves from both eyes meet and cross at the optic chiasma. Here, the signals split: half from each eye go right and half go left, then travel to a sorting office called the LGN. The LGN analyzes what kind of picture you're seeing—moving, strongly lined, dark, light, and so on. It sends each aspect of the picture to the right place in your brain to be interpreted. Finally, your brain sees the pictures, right side up, on the screens of its own cinema, the visual cortex.

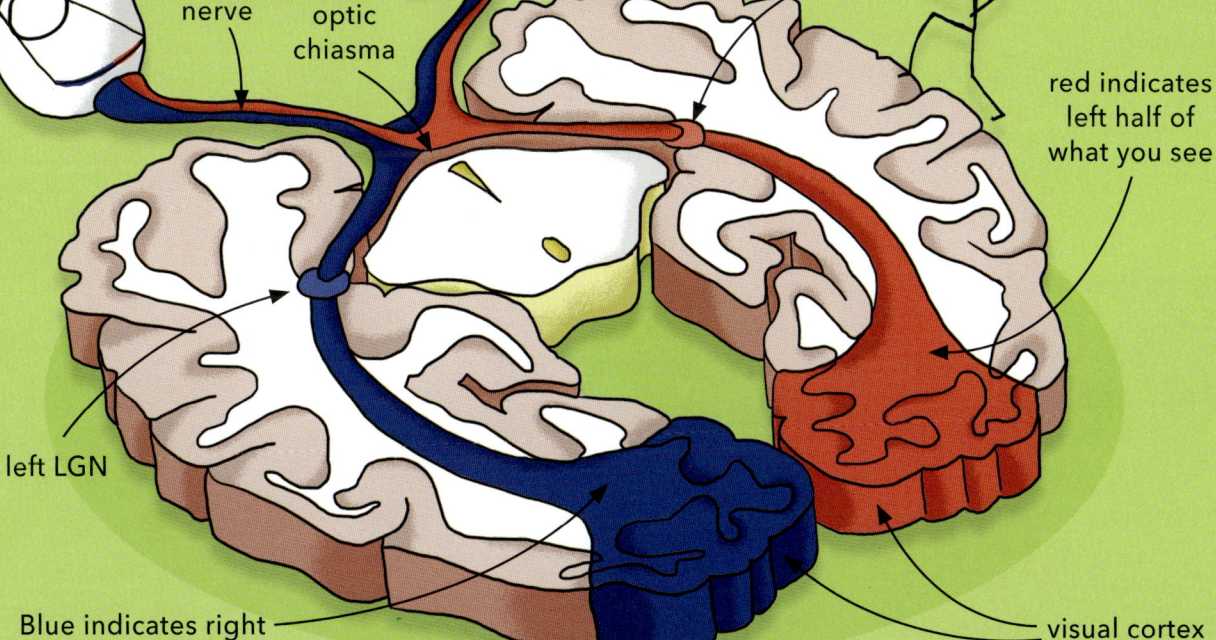

direction of light traveling to your eyes

left eye

right eye

optic nerve

optic chiasma

right LGN

red indicates left half of what you see

left LGN

Blue indicates right half of what you see.

visual cortex

43

Hear, Hear

Sounds are just vibrations in the air, and your ears are clever devices for picking these vibrations up. The flaps of skin on the sides of your head that you call ears are just the entrances. The ears funnel in sounds to supersensitive detectors deep inside your brain.

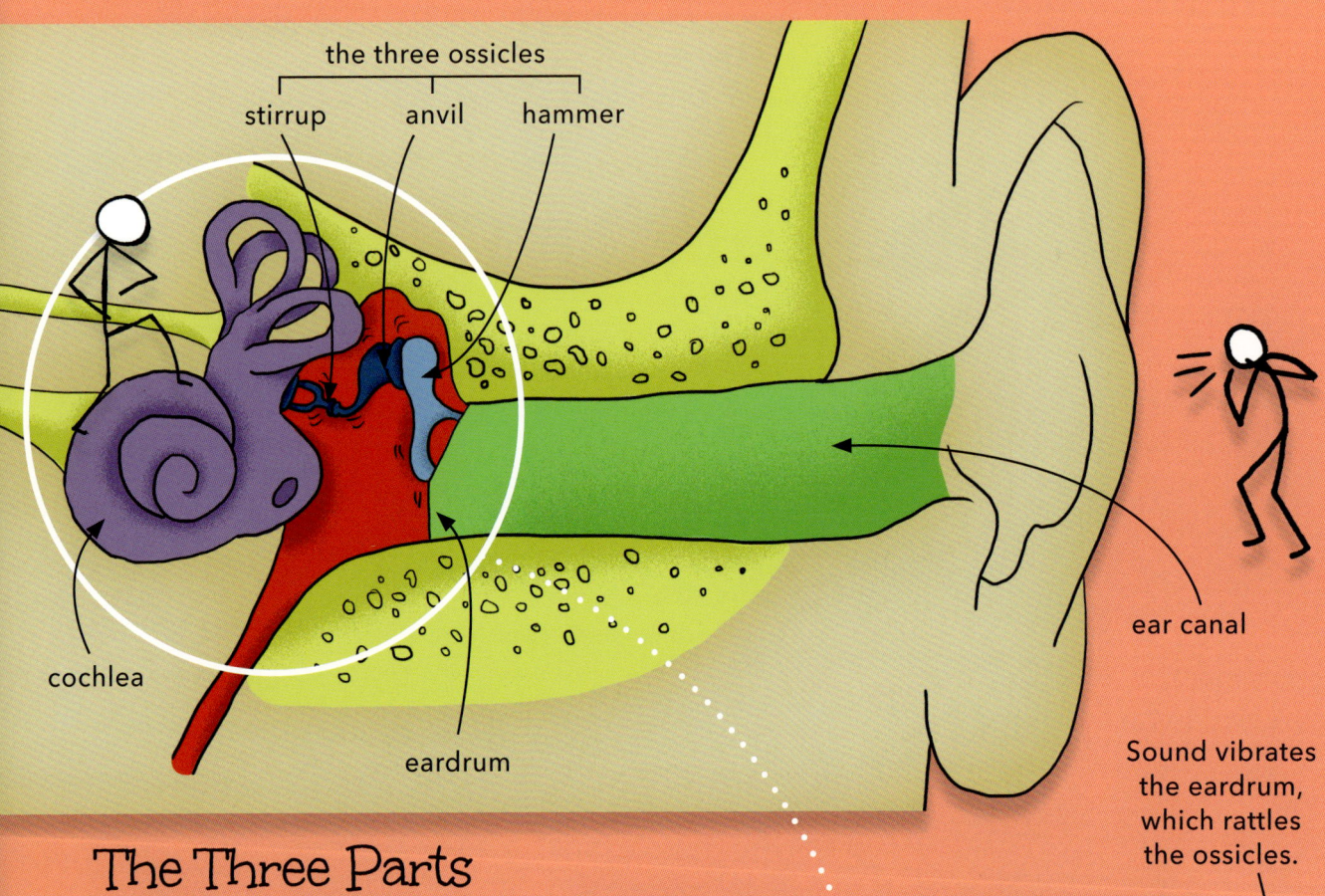

the three ossicles
stirrup   anvil   hammer

cochlea

eardrum

ear canal

The Three Parts of Your Ears

The earflap and funnel into your head is the outer ear. Inside your head is the middle ear, where sound hits a wall of skin called the eardrum, shaking it rapidly. As the eardrum shakes, it rattles three tiny bones, or ossicles. These in turn tap on a window in a curly, fluid-filled tube called the cochlea, which makes up the inner ear. The rattling creates waves in the cochlea fluid, which wiggle minute hairs so that they send signals to the brain.

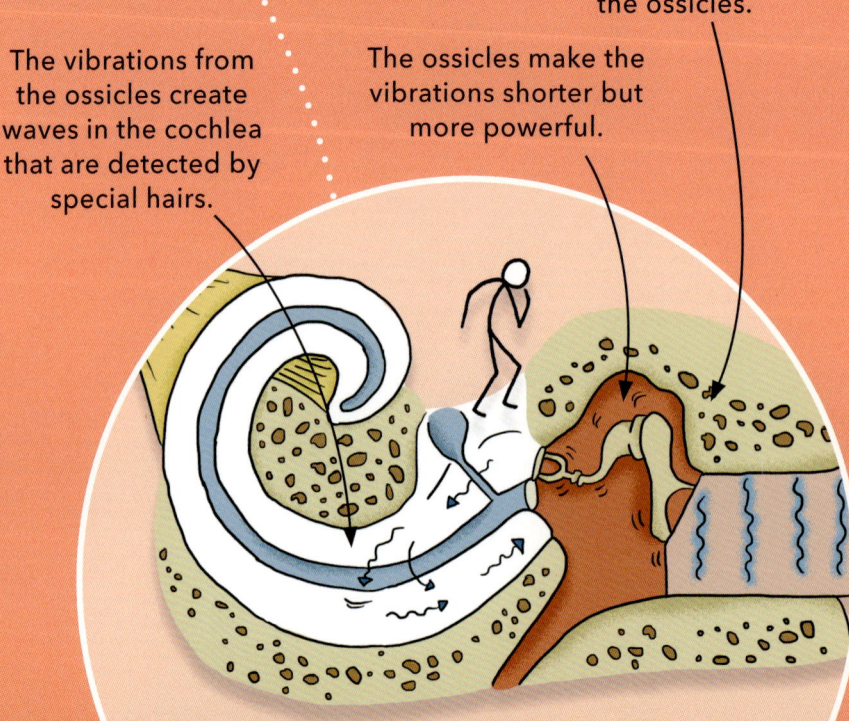

The vibrations from the ossicles create waves in the cochlea that are detected by special hairs.

The ossicles make the vibrations shorter but more powerful.

Sound vibrates the eardrum, which rattles the ossicles.

44

Loud or Soft?

Some sounds are loud. Some are very quiet. Loudness can be measured in decibels (dB), the force of sound waves against the ear. The louder the sound, the more decibels it is.

- 130 dB — jet engine
- 110 dB — chainsaw
- 95 dB — lawnmower
- 80 dB — alarm clock
- 60 dB — chatter
- 20 dB — ticking watch

Two Ears

There's a reason you have two ears. It helps you pinpoint the distance and direction of sounds. Ears are so sensitive that they can hear the very slight difference in the time that sounds take to reach each one. Your brain analyzes the difference and tells you where the sound is coming from. Some headphones can fool the brain into thinking the sounds really are coming from different places.

Smell That, Taste That

Your nose may not be as sensitive as a dog's, but it can identify more than 3,000 different chemicals from their vapor alone. And it can detect just a few tiny particles from among billions in the air. And by working with smell, your taste is pretty sensitive, too.

2 When a smell sensor detects its molecule, it buzzes a signal to the nose's smell reception area, the olfactory bulb.

3 Each kind of sensor sends its message to a structure called a glomerulus.

4 When a glomerulus is triggered, it sends a message to the brain.

5 The brain identifies the smell from the messages it receives.

1 Vapor molecules travel up the nose.

What is Smell?

Things smell because they give off a vapor. You can detect them when just a few vapor molecules drift up your nose to the top and reach hair-like smell sensors on a patch called the olfactory epithelium. There are 400 or so kinds of sensor, each on the lookout for its own favorite smell molecule.

olfactory bulb

taste signal sent to brain

What is Taste?

Your tongue's chemical receptors are called taste buds. There are 10,000, located in tiny pits all over your tongue. The tiny bumps, or papillae, on your tongue show where they are. There are five kinds of taste bud, each sensitive to a different flavor. There are taste buds for salty, sweet, sour, and bitter tastes. There are also buds for a savory taste called umami, which is the strong taste you get from meaty dishes and soy sauce. People once thought the taste buds for each taste were in different parts of the tongue, but now it seems they are all evenly spread.

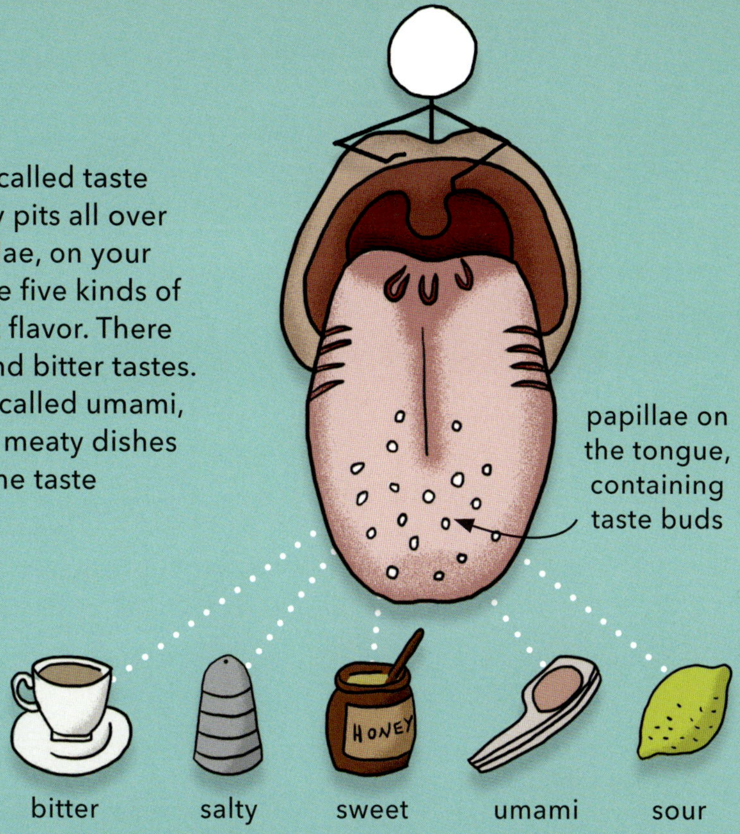

papillae on the tongue, containing taste buds

6 In each taste bud there is a cluster of cells with tiny hairs on the end.

bitter   salty   sweet   umami   sour

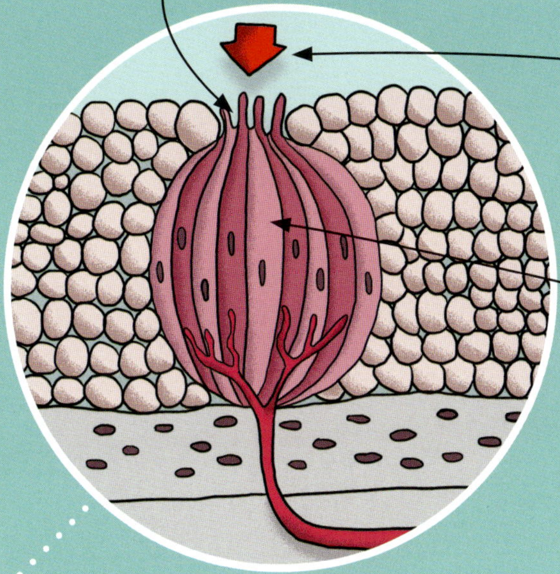

7 Saliva containing the food taste washes over these hairs

8 If the taste is right for the bud, the hairs trigger sensor cells beneath to send a signal.

Dog on the Scent

If you ever catch a bad smell, be thankful you don't have a dog's acute sense of smell. A dog has over 50 times as many smell receptors as humans and an olfactory area in its brain 40 times as large (in proportion to its brain). That means a dog's nose is up to ten million times as sensitive as yours!

47

Remember, Remember

If anyone tells you you're forgetful, they're wrong! The human brain has a fantastic ability to remember. There are billions of neurons in your brain, each connecting with thousands of others. When you remember something, your brain makes a new pathway of nerve connections, called a memory trace. You forget only when connections weaken through lack of use.

Will it Last?

Memories are stored in your brain in three stages:

1. In sensory memory, new data arrives through your senses, and your senses go on seeing, hearing, or feeling something momentarily.

2. In short-term memory, the brain stores data just long enough to pass it on—like remembering a phone number while you key it in.

3. In long-term memory, your brain makes strong connections so you remember things for a long time

Get It Into Your Head

Your brain stores long-term memories in two ways. Explicit memories are tucked away in your head quickly, and you only need to experience them a few times to remember them. But implicit memories only stick when you go over them again and again, such as when you learn to play the piano or football. Memories like these are stored by making nerve connections throughout your body, not just in your brain.

What a Moment!
Some explicit memories are episodic. These are dramatic episodes, such as a memorable Christmas. You remember every sensation and may be able to recall them years later.

It's a Fact
Facts such as the tallest mountain (Mount Everest) are called semantic memories. Your brain seems to store these in the temporal lobe in the left of your brain.

Practice Makes Perfect
You teach your body skills and procedures, such as playing a musical instrument, by practicing them, so that the correct nerve connections are slowly reinforced.

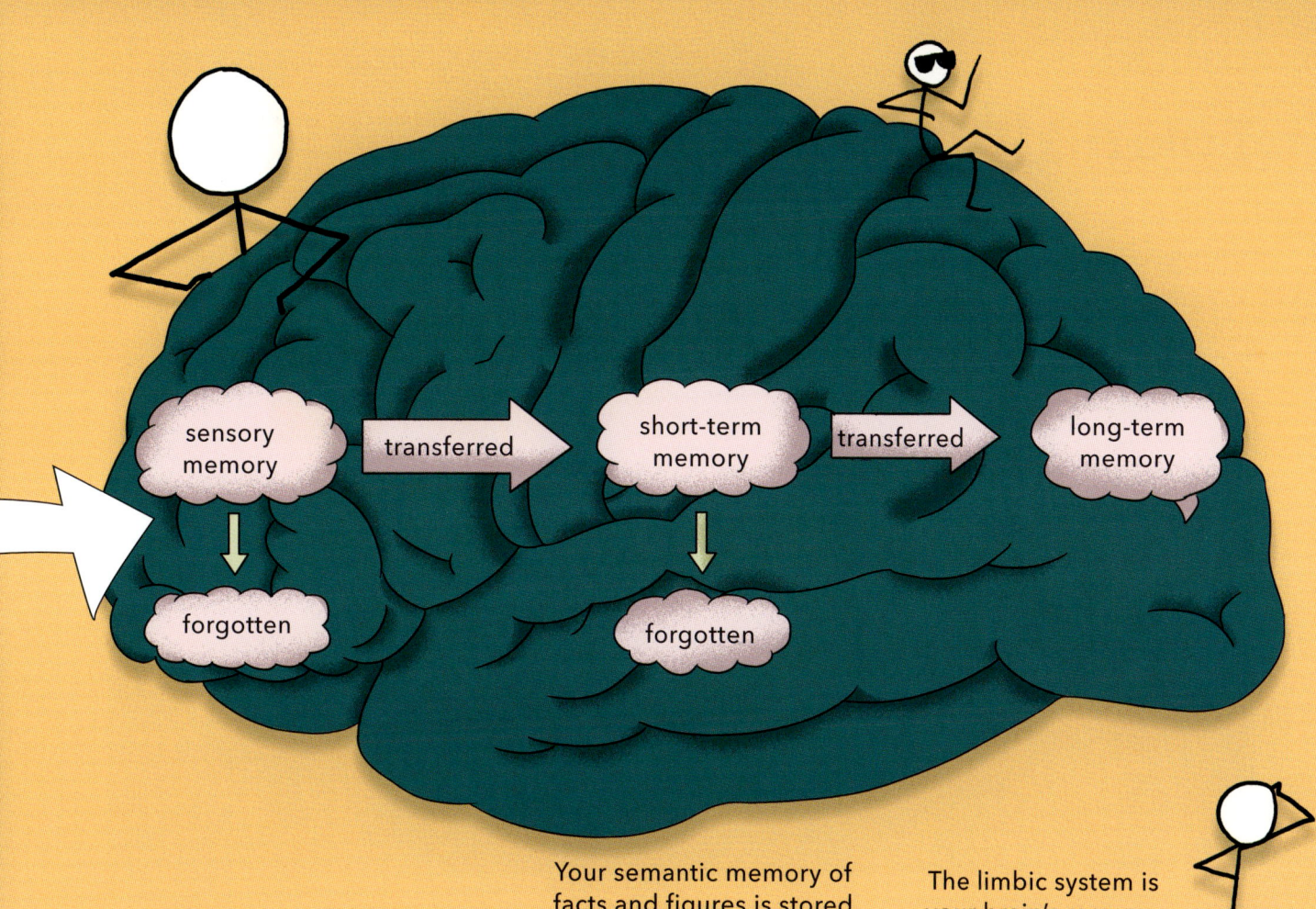

Flow diagram: sensory memory → (transferred) → short-term memory → (transferred) → long-term memory; with "forgotten" branches from sensory memory and short-term memory.

Where Memories are Stored

Sensations and experiences arrive in the brain via what is called the limbic system, which sits right in the middle of the brain. From there, they are sent to various parts of the brain for storage.

Your semantic memory of facts and figures is stored in the temporal lobe at the front left of your brain.

The limbic system is your brain's memory arrival lounge.

The wrinkly cortex stores all kinds of memories.

The hippocampus makes sure dramatic episodes are sent off to various places in your cortex for remembering long-term.

The cerebellum works on procedural memories—the coordination of physical skills that you build up through practice.

Your Beating Heart

Every cell in your body needs a nonstop supply of oxygen from the air. Without it, cells in your brain die in minutes! To keep up this vital supply, your body has two interlocking systems. Scientists call them the respiratory and cardiovascular systems—but they just mean breathing and blood circulation.

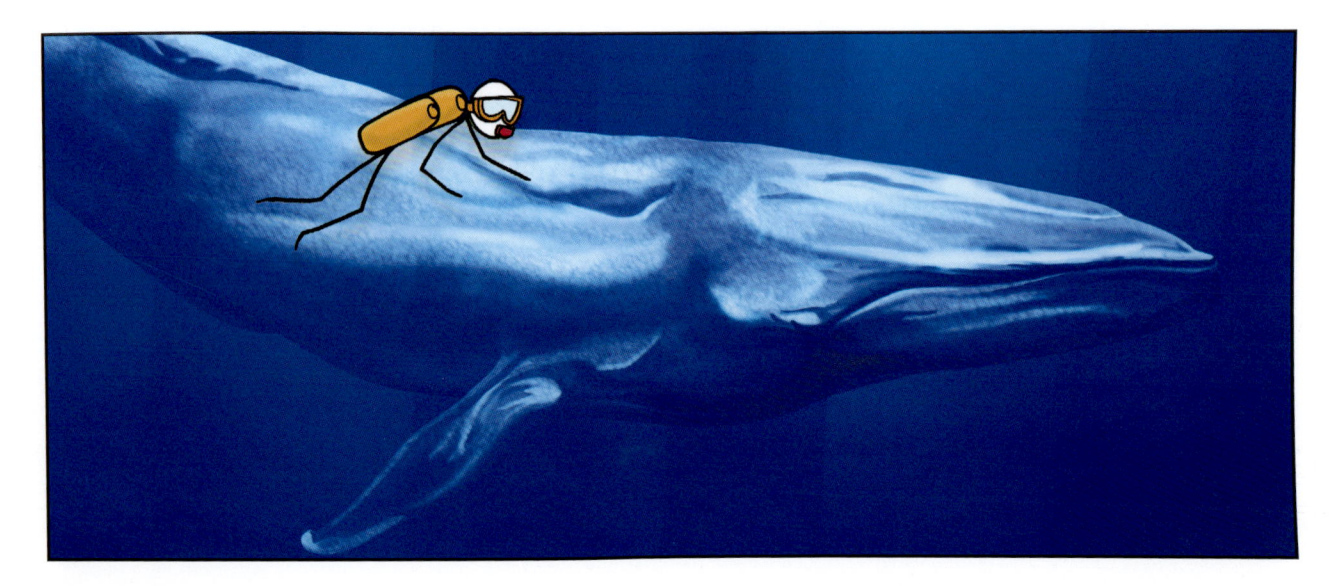

Big-hearted

The biggest heart in the world belongs to the blue whale. It's about the size of a bumper car at the fair and weighs 440 lb (200 kg) or so. If you're very small, you might even squeeze inside its main outflow pipe (the aorta) and into the pumping chamber inside! Your heart is about the size of an apple. Yet apart from its size, the whale's heart is pretty much like yours.

Breathing Air

The average human being breathes in about 145 gallons (550 liters) of oxygen per day. So around the world, people breathe in nearly 1 trillion gallons (4 trillion L) of oxygen: about 4 km³ (0.9 cubic miles). We breathe out about 800 billion gallons (3 trillion L) of carbon dioxide.

Faint-hearted

Diseases related to the heart are now the biggest cause of early death around the world. And they are going up rapidly. In 1990, over 12 million people died of heart disease. In 2013, it was over 17 million. It is thought that this may be because more people are living to the age when heart disease is a risk.

Love Hearts

The heart has been associated with love since ancient times. And we often tag internet posts we love with a heart symbol. Yet the heart symbol is nothing like the shape of your own heart, which has no particular shape at all. Scholars think the heart symbol was developed in the late Middle Ages.

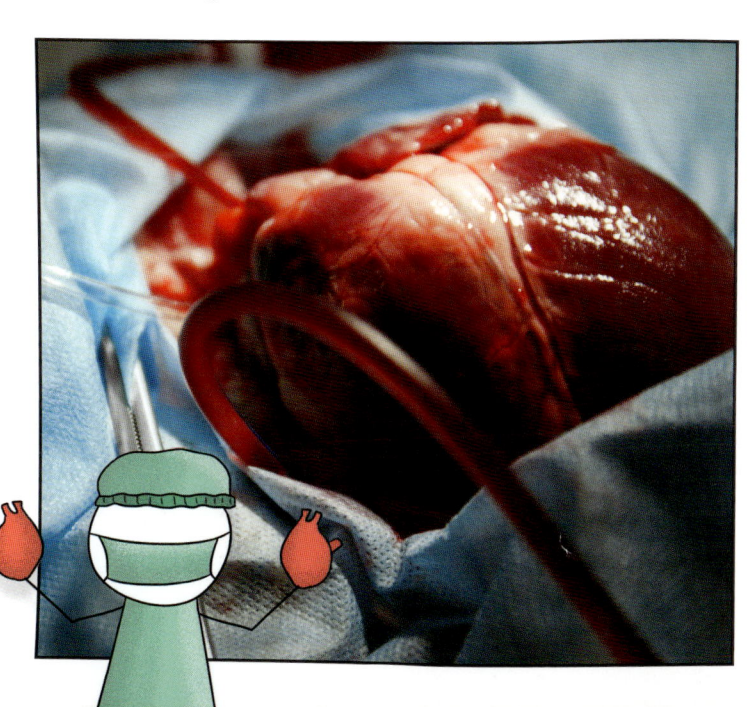

Heart Memories

In the past, people thought memories were stored in the heart as well as the brain. And it may be that heart cells have some kind of memory. The evidence is thin, but a few patients who received a heart transplant sometimes seem to develop the same odd tastes in food as the donors who gave them their new hearts.

Breathing

Your lungs are amazingly good at extracting lots of oxygen from the air every few seconds. They contain a vast network of airways that allows the oxygen you breathe in to pass into the bloodstream, so it can then be carried all around the body.

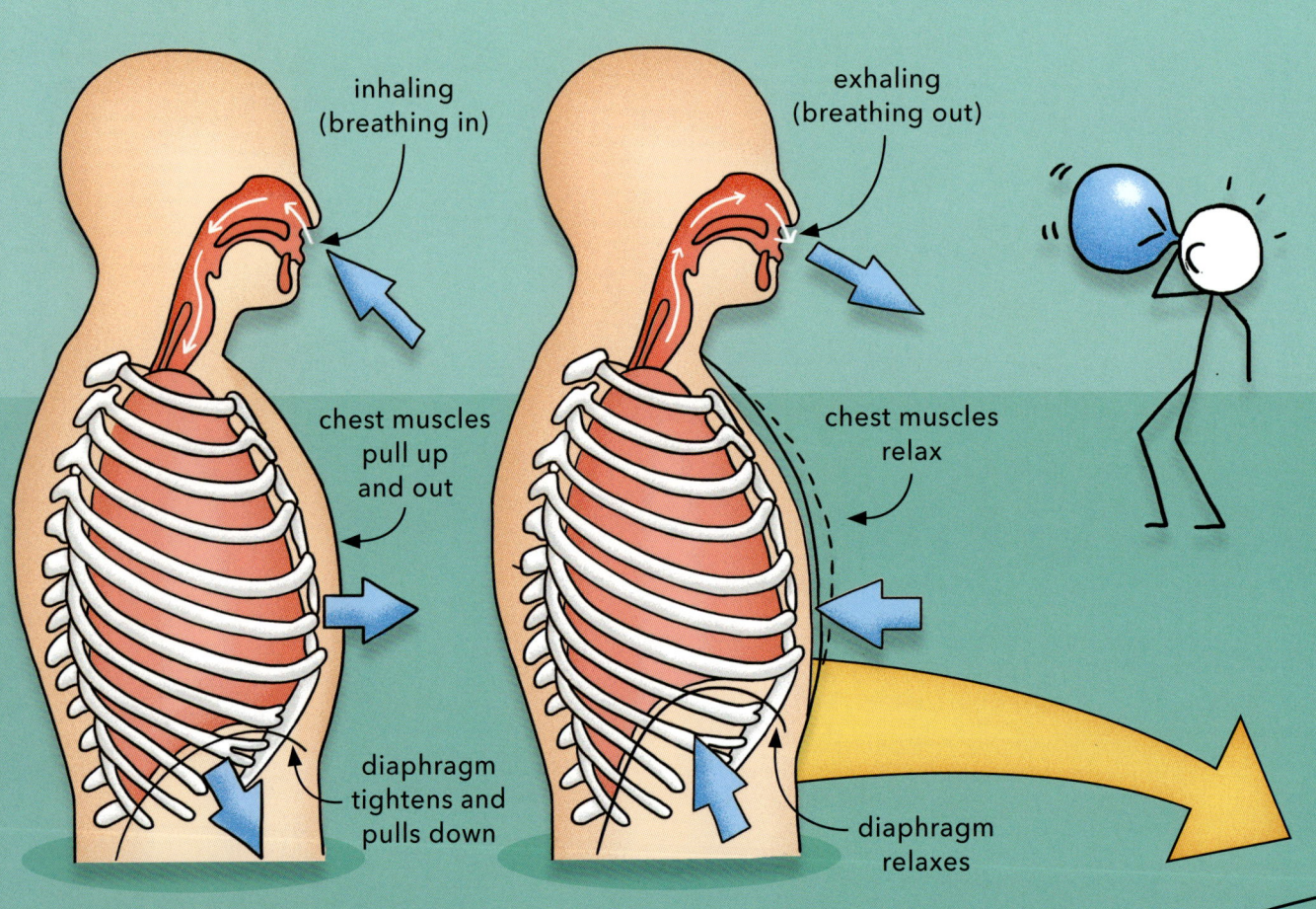

inhaling (breathing in)

exhaling (breathing out)

chest muscles pull up and out

chest muscles relax

diaphragm tightens and pulls down

diaphragm relaxes

Breathe!

Breathing starts with the diaphragm. This is a sheet of muscle that domes up under the lungs. When you breathe in, it tightens and flattens downwards, making more space for your lungs. At the same time, muscles between your ribs, known as intercostal muscles, pull your chest outwards and upwards. When you breathe out, the opposite happens.

Air Bags

Your lungs are a pair of organs inside your chest that are filled with tiny branching airways. When you breathe in, air is sucked in through your mouth or nose and rushes down your trachea (the windpipe in your neck). Deep inside your chest, the trachea forks into two airways or bronchi (plural of bronchus), one leading to each lung. Inside the lungs, the bronchi branch into millions of smaller airways called bronchioles.

alveoli

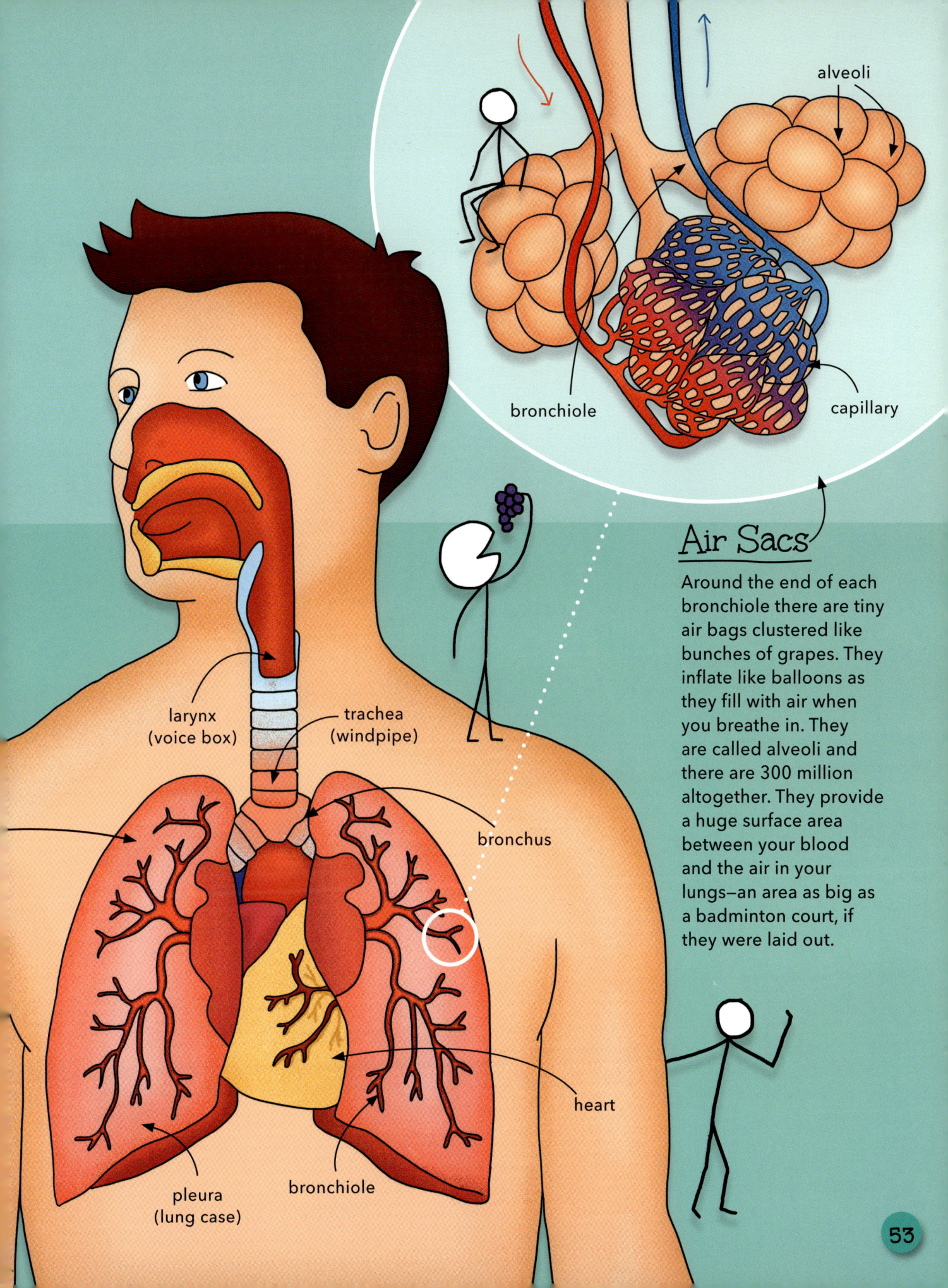

bronchiole

capillary

larynx (voice box)

trachea (windpipe)

bronchus

heart

pleura (lung case)

bronchiole

Air Sacs

Around the end of each bronchiole there are tiny air bags clustered like bunches of grapes. They inflate like balloons as they fill with air when you breathe in. They are called alveoli and there are 300 million altogether. They provide a huge surface area between your blood and the air in your lungs—an area as big as a badminton court, if they were laid out.

Blood Circulation

Your body cells really need their oxygen, and it's the blood's task to supply it. Pumped by the heart, blood picks up fresh oxygen from your lungs, carries it around the body through a network of pipes, then goes back to the lungs for more. At the same time, it carries waste carbon dioxide to the lungs for breathing out.

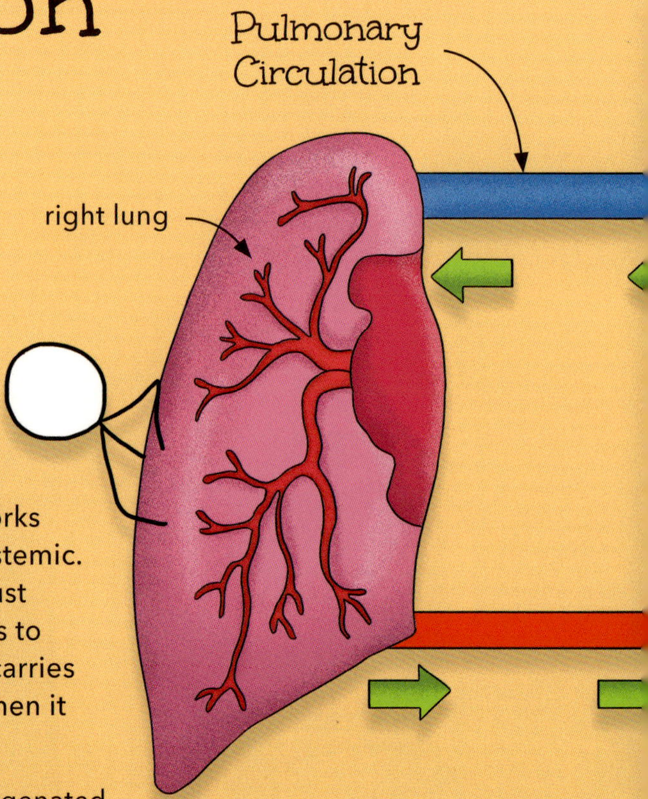

Pulmonary Circulation

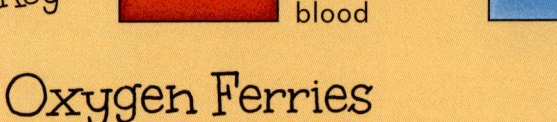

right lung

Two Circulations

The blood circulation is divided into two separate networks that come together in your heart: the pulmonary and systemic. Pulmonary means "related to lungs." The pulmonary is just a short network that brings fresh oxygen from your lungs to your heart. The systemic goes right round your body. It carries oxygen-rich blood out from the left side of your heart. Then it distributes this blood all around the body.

Key — oxygenated blood — deoxygenated blood

Oxygen Ferries

Oxygen is ferried around the body by 25 trillion button-shaped red blood cells. They contain tangly molecules called hemoglobin. Hemoglobin glows red when it takes on a load of oxygen. That's what makes your blood bright red. Once the cells have delivered their oxygen, they lose their glow, and your blood goes a darker red.

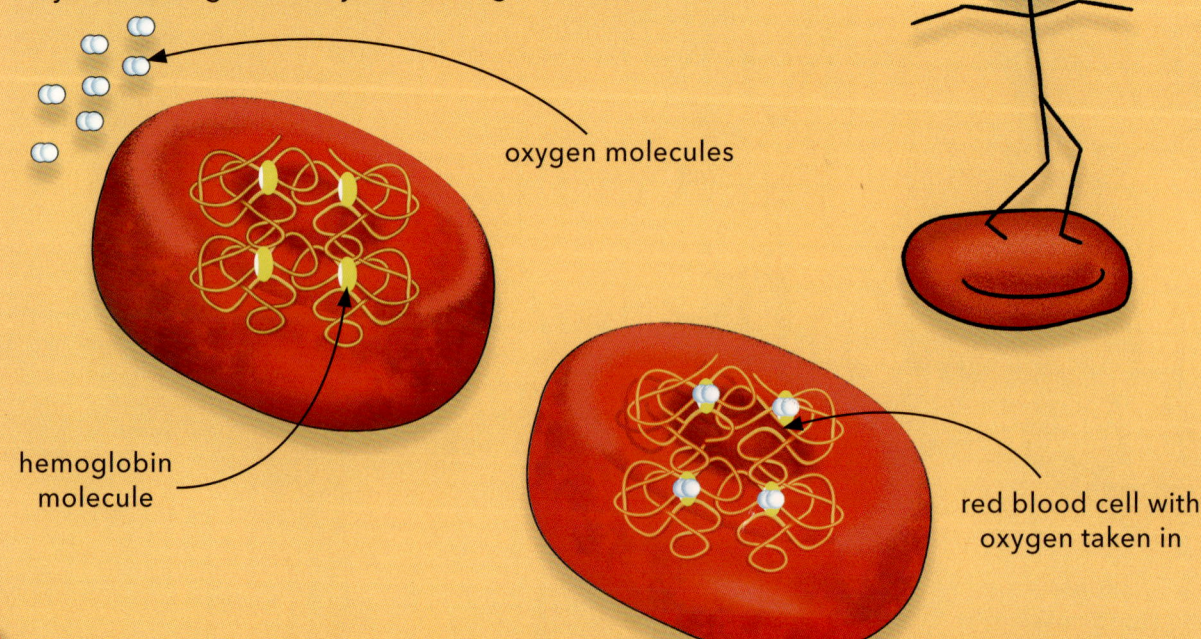

oxygen molecules

hemoglobin molecule

red blood cell with oxygen taken in

54

upper body and brain

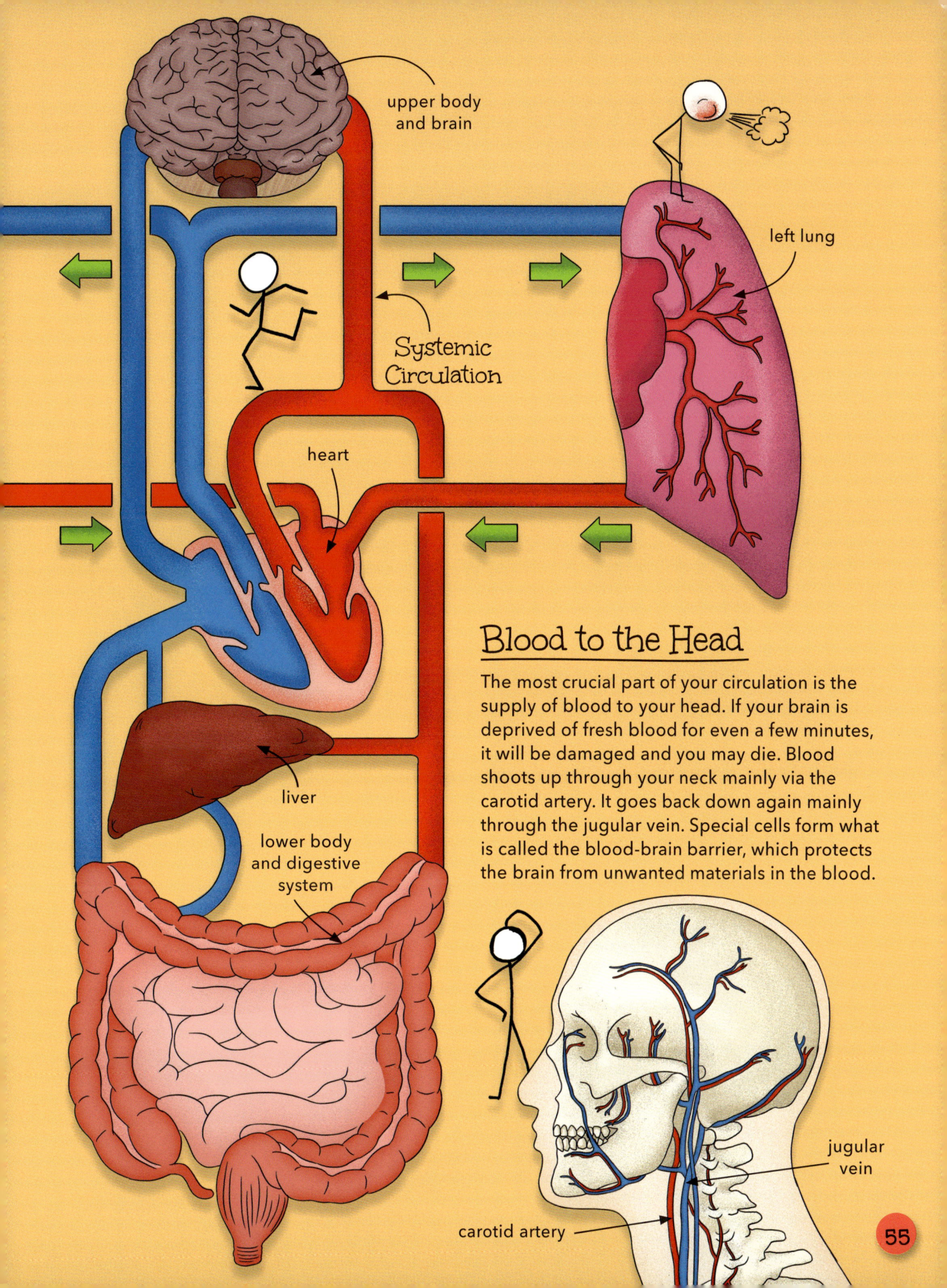

left lung

Systemic Circulation

heart

liver

lower body and digestive system

Blood to the Head

The most crucial part of your circulation is the supply of blood to your head. If your brain is deprived of fresh blood for even a few minutes, it will be damaged and you may die. Blood shoots up through your neck mainly via the carotid artery. It goes back down again mainly through the jugular vein. Special cells form what is called the blood-brain barrier, which protects the brain from unwanted materials in the blood.

jugular vein

carotid artery

55

Heartbeat

Your heart is an amazing little pump made of pure muscle. Every second of your life, it is squeezing away, pushing blood round your body. It owes its steady beat to the special muscle it is made from, called cardiac muscle, which contracts and relaxes rhythmically by itself.

Double Heart

Your heart is not just one pump but two, set side by side and separated by a wall of muscle. The left side is the stronger, driving oxygen-rich blood all the way around the body. The right sends blood to the lungs and back again. Each side has two chambers, separated by a one-way valve. The atrium at the top is where blood gathers. The ventricle below is the main pumping chamber.

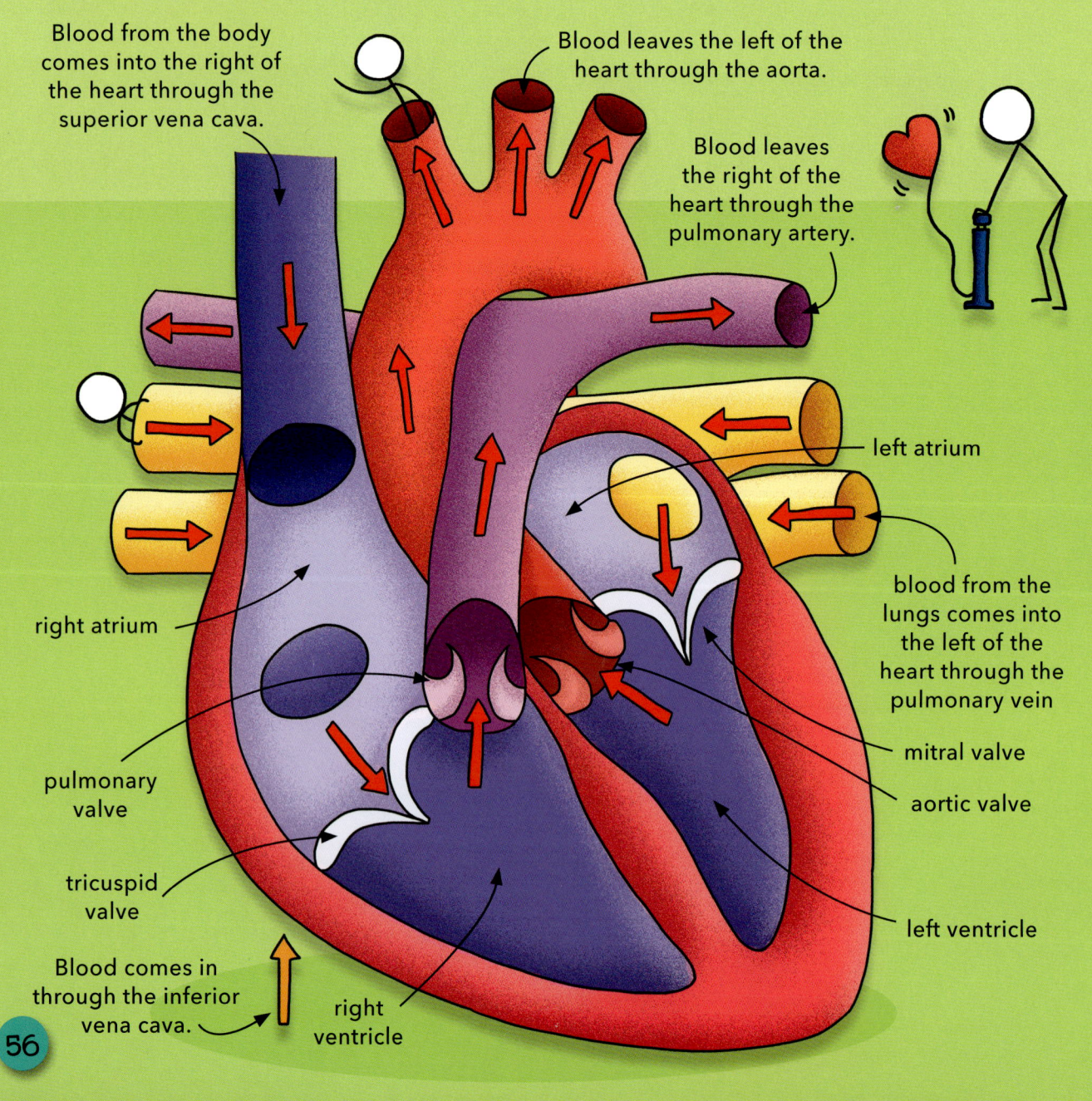

Blood from the body comes into the right of the heart through the superior vena cava.

Blood leaves the left of the heart through the aorta.

Blood leaves the right of the heart through the pulmonary artery.

left atrium

blood from the lungs comes into the left of the heart through the pulmonary vein

right atrium

mitral valve

aortic valve

pulmonary valve

tricuspid valve

left ventricle

Blood comes in through the inferior vena cava.

right ventricle

56

Heart Cycle

Every time your heart beats, it goes through the same sequence, called the cardiac cycle. This has two phases—systole (contraction) and diastole (relaxation)—that sweep in a wave across the heart. In systole, first the atria (plural of atrium) squeeze to drive blood into the ventricles, then the ventricles squeeze to drive blood out through the arteries. In diastole, first the atria, then the ventricles relax to allow them to fill up again.

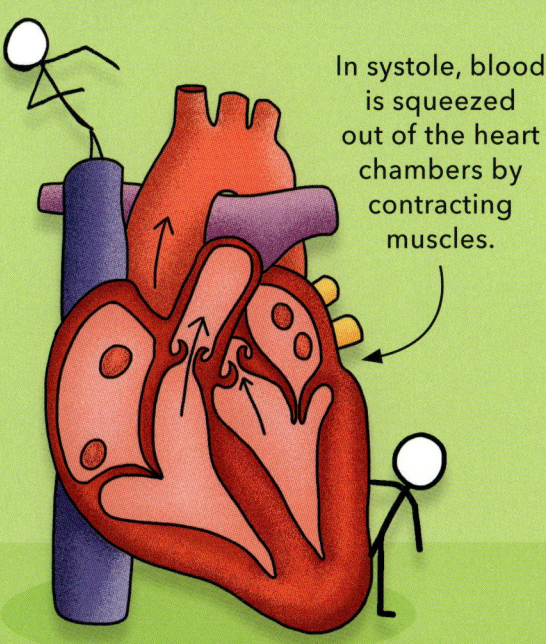

In systole, blood is squeezed out of the heart chambers by contracting muscles.

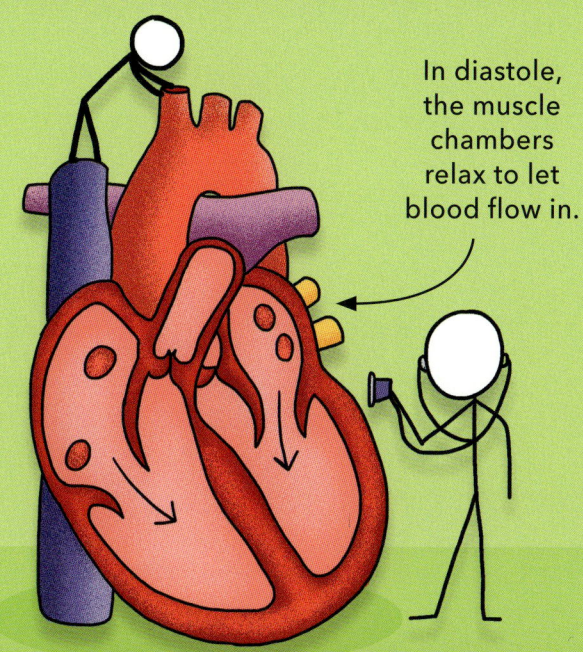

In diastole, the muscle chambers relax to let blood flow in.

Steady Beat

An electrocardiogram (ECG or EKG) can monitor the heart by picking up the tiny electrical signals it sends out every time it beats. Typically, your heart beats about 75 times a minute. But this can more than double when you exercise hard. The ECG here shows regular spikes for each beat. Erratic spikes show there's a problem with the heart.

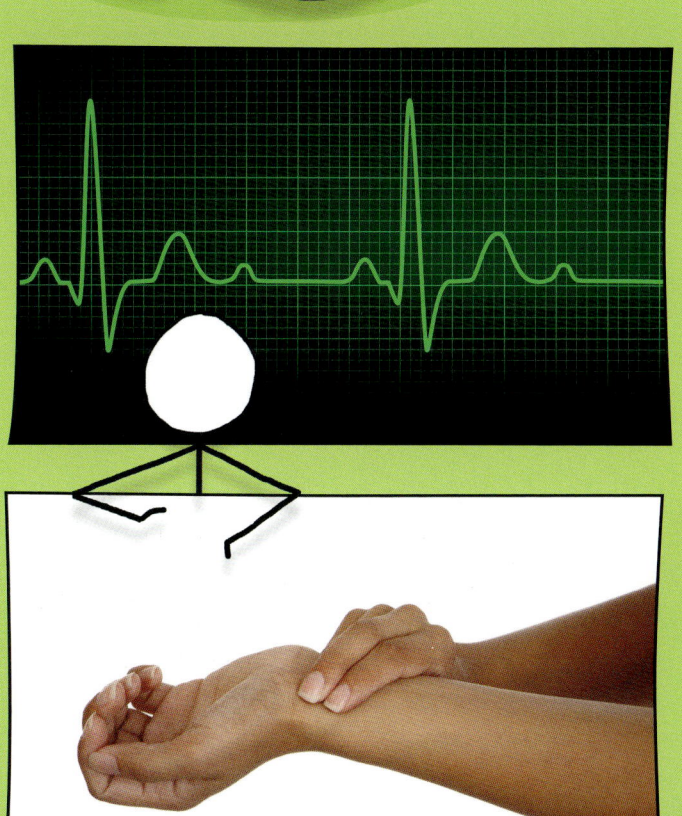

Feeling Your Pulse

When the valves of the heart snap shut, they send a shock wave or pulse running through your arteries. Doctors can hear this pulse with a special device called a stethoscope. You can also feel it yourself by gently laying two fingers on the inside of your wrist, where your radial artery comes close to the surface.

Arteries and Veins

You have millions of blood vessels—pipes that carry blood—threading through your body. Some are as wide as a pencil. Others are thinner than a hair. The largest blood vessels carrying oxygen-rich blood away from the heart are called arteries. The largest blood vessels carrying oxygen-poor blood back to the heart are called veins.

Running in Parallel

The body's branching networks of blood vessels are like two intertwined rivers. Throughout the body, bright red arteries carrying blood away from the heart run alongside blue veins carrying it back again. The largest blood vessels are those linked directly to the heart: the ascending and descending aorta (arteries) and the superior and inferior vena cava (veins).

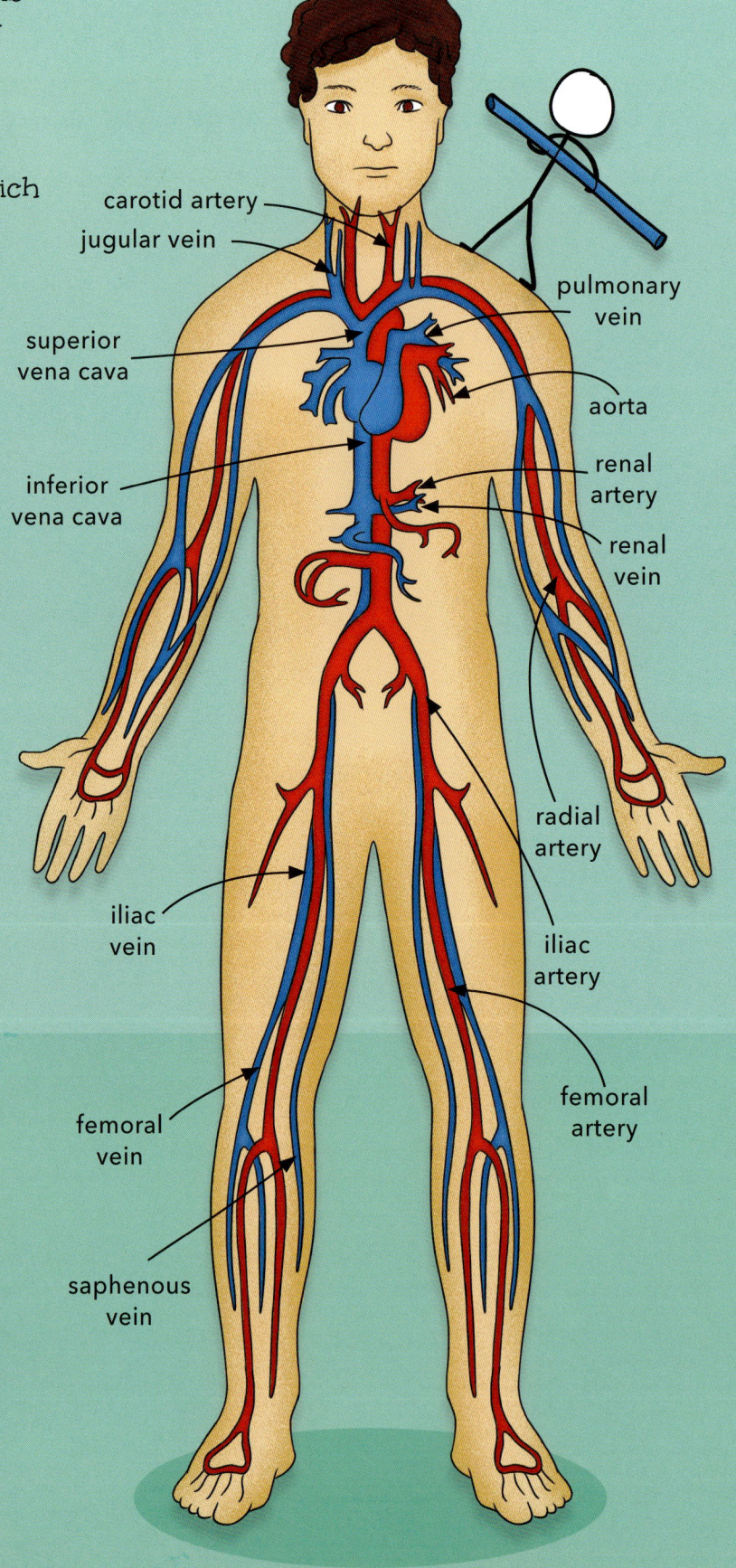

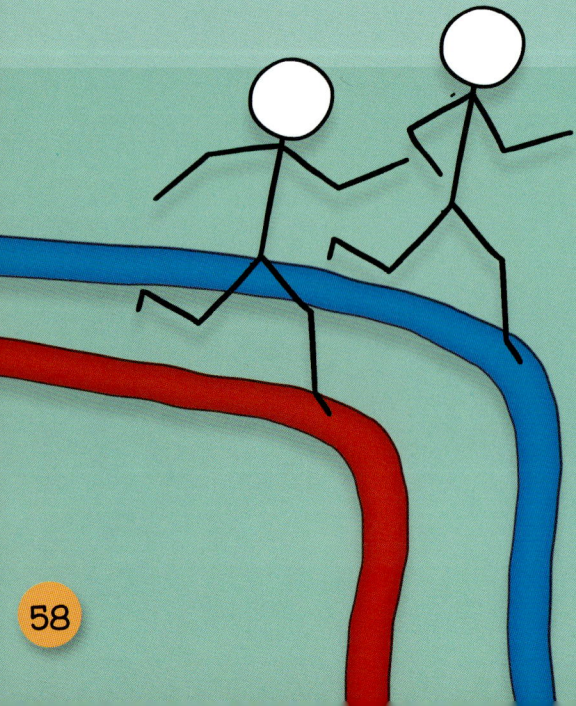

- carotid artery
- jugular vein
- pulmonary vein
- superior vena cava
- aorta
- renal artery
- inferior vena cava
- renal vein
- radial artery
- iliac vein
- iliac artery
- femoral vein
- femoral artery
- saphenous vein

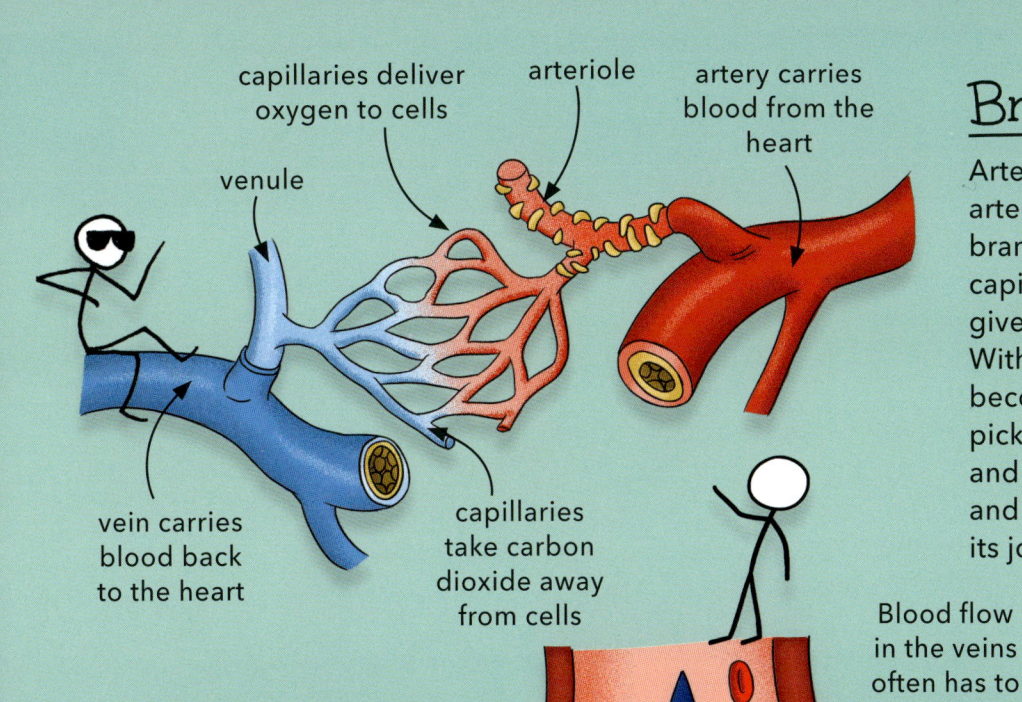

capillaries deliver oxygen to cells

arteriole

artery carries blood from the heart

venule

vein carries blood back to the heart

capillaries take carbon dioxide away from cells

Branching Pipes

Arteries branch into narrower arterioles and arterioles branch into even narrower capillaries, where the blood gives up its oxygen to cells. Without its oxygen, the blood becomes dark red and is picked up by more capillaries and returned to wider venules, and even wider veins, to make its journey back to the heart.

Active Pipes

Blood vessels are not simply stiff pipes. They have valves and muscular walls that control the flow of blood. They may widen when you're hot, to allow more blood to get near the surface to cool off—which is why you may look red when you're hot. Or they may narrow when it's cold to keep blood warm inside, which is why you can look white or even blue with cold.

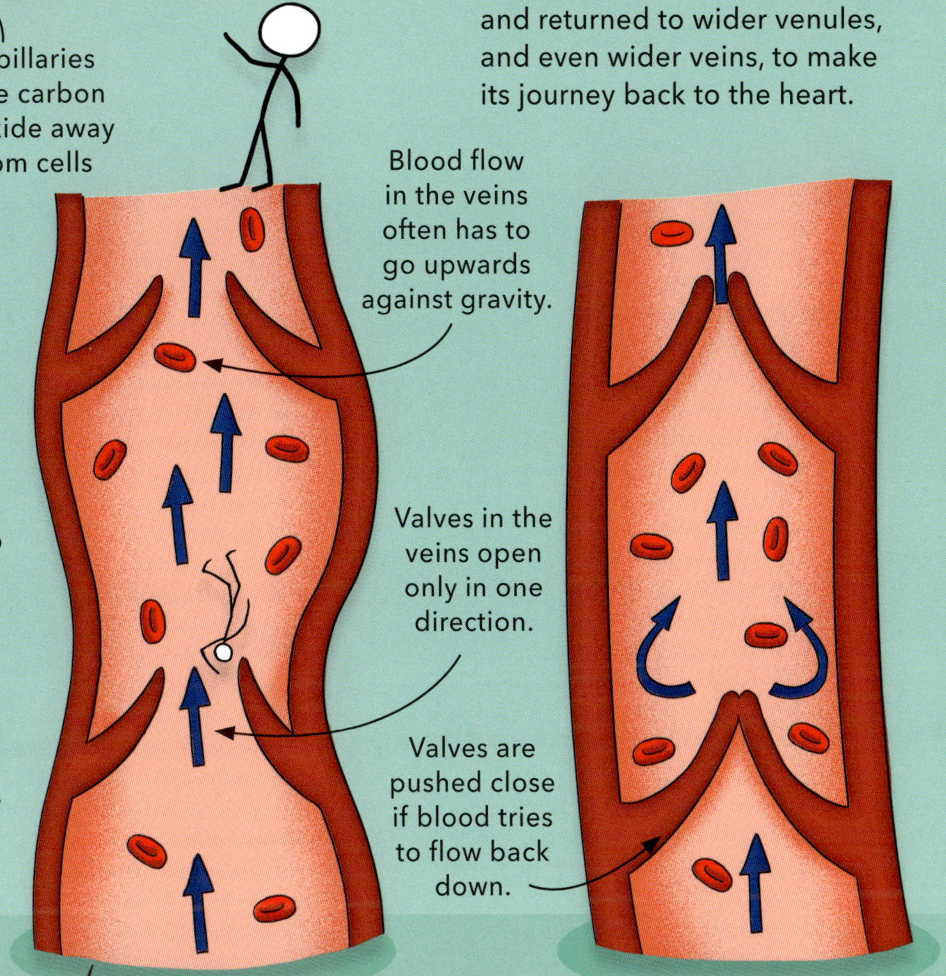

Blood flow in the veins often has to go upwards against gravity.

Valves in the veins open only in one direction.

Valves are pushed close if blood tries to flow back down.

Under Pressure

The muscles of the walls of blood vessels squeeze or relax to control the pressure of blood. The pressure must be strong enough to push oxygen-rich blood to every cell, yet not so strong that its bursts the delicate capillaries. Doctors can check your blood pressure with a simple 'cuff' that squeezes your arm to reveal how much it affects the blood flow.

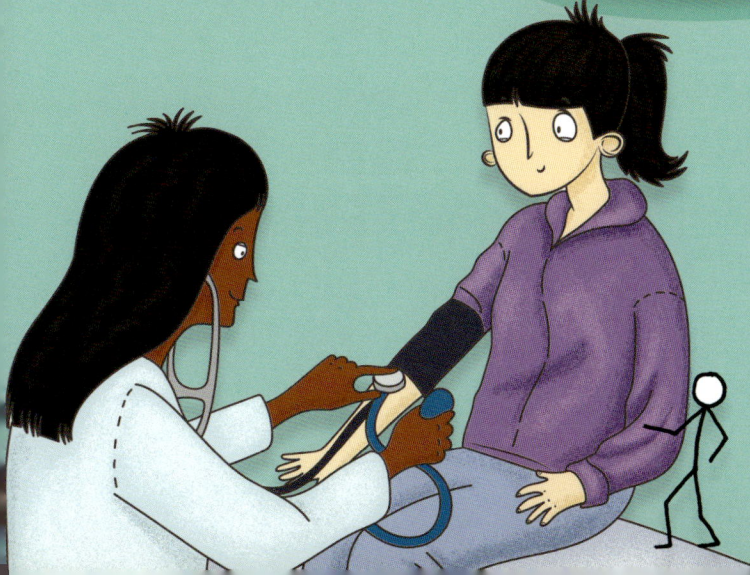

How Cells Breathe

Like a machine, your body cells need a constant supply of fuel to keep them going. Their fuel is glucose, a kind of energy-rich sugar that your body makes by breaking down the food you eat. But just as fire needs air to burn, so your cells need oxygen to use glucose. That's why you need to breathe as well as eat!

Mini Power Stations

Inside every one of your body cells there are microscopic furnaces called mitochondria (plural of mitochondrion). Mitochondria break down glucose to release tiny bursts of energy with the help of oxygen supplied in your blood. This generates heat, just like a fire. It's called cellular respiration.

Cellular respiration packs energy into millions of tiny molecules of a special chemical called ATP (adenosine triphosphate). The energy is released when needed.

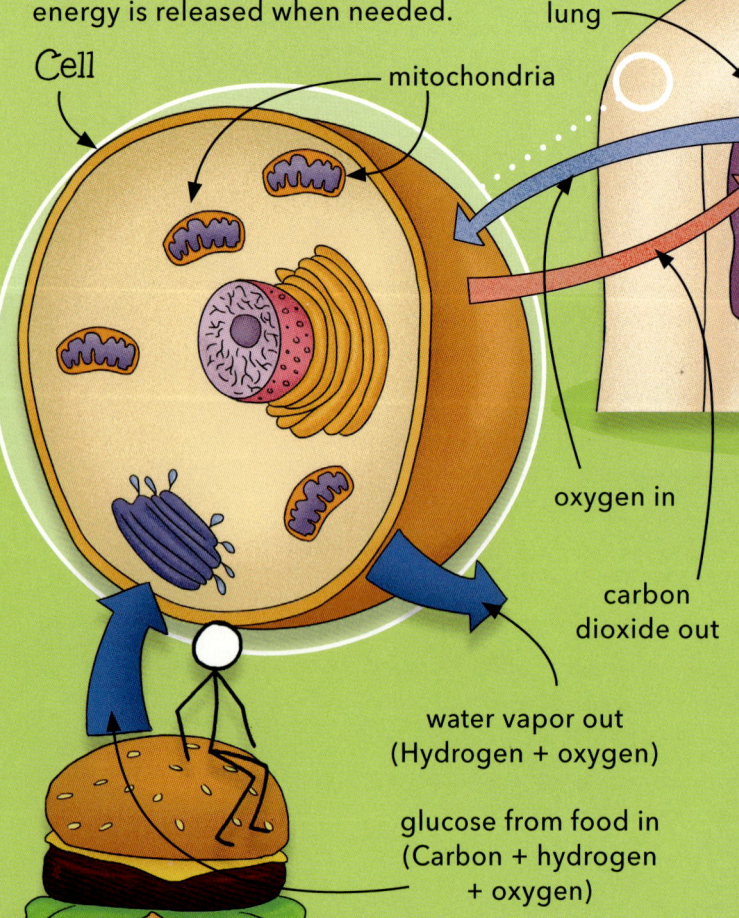

oxygen in

carbon dioxide out

lung

Cell

mitochondria

oxygen in

carbon dioxide out

water vapor out (Hydrogen + oxygen)

glucose from food in (Carbon + hydrogen + oxygen)

Sugar Power

Glucose is made mainly from carbon and hydrogen. When your cells break up glucose to release its energy, the hydrogen bonds with oxygen to make water, and the carbon bonds with oxygen to make carbon dioxide. Carbon dioxide is poisonous, so the body must get rid of it. This is what happens when you breathe out.

60

Heat Control

For body processes to work well, your body must stay at a steady 98.6°F (37°C). So you have a temperature control in your brain called the hypothalamus to monitor how hot you are. If you're too hot, the hypothalamus tells your body to lose heat by sweating. Sweating takes warm water out of your body and cools your skin as moisture evaporates.

Too Cold

If you're too cold, the hypothalamus alerts your thyroid, which sends chemical messages to stoke up cellular respiration. It also tells muscles to move rapidly (which is why you shiver) and sends signals to restrict the supply of blood to your skin and cut heat loss.

We are Family

Mitochondria are almost like independent organisms trapped inside your body cells. The genes of mitochondria are known as mDNA (mitochondrial DNA). They are passed on through mothers for generations. They remain almost unchanged, so using mDNA you can trace your family history far back in time. Amazingly, mDNA shows that we all have very mixed ancestors, no matter where we were born.

What is Blood?

Blood might look a little like red ink. But if you viewed it through a powerful microscope, you'd see it has lots of different ingredients. It's full of a whole zoo of different kinds of cell and other ingredients. It is the body's transportation system, carrying not only oxygen to the cells but food too. And it helps defend the body against disease.

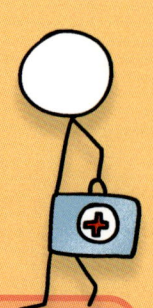

Blood Cells

Your blood is populated by three kinds of cell: platelets, red blood cells, and white blood cells. Red blood cells, or erythrocytes, are the button-shaped cells that carry oxygen. White blood cells, also known as leucocytes, are your body's main defence against germs.

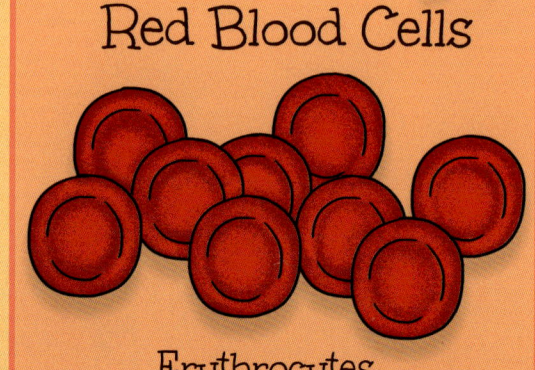

Red Blood Cells

Erythrocytes

The body makes 2 million new red blood cells every second. They are much smaller than most white cells.

First Aid Kit

Platelets are the blood's emergency repair team, made of scraps that break off other cells. When you cut yourself, platelets instantly gather to deal with the damage. They send out an alarm in chemicals called clotting factors. These encourage a protein called fibrin to grow and plug the leak. The fibrin dries out to form a scab, protecting the wound until it has healed.

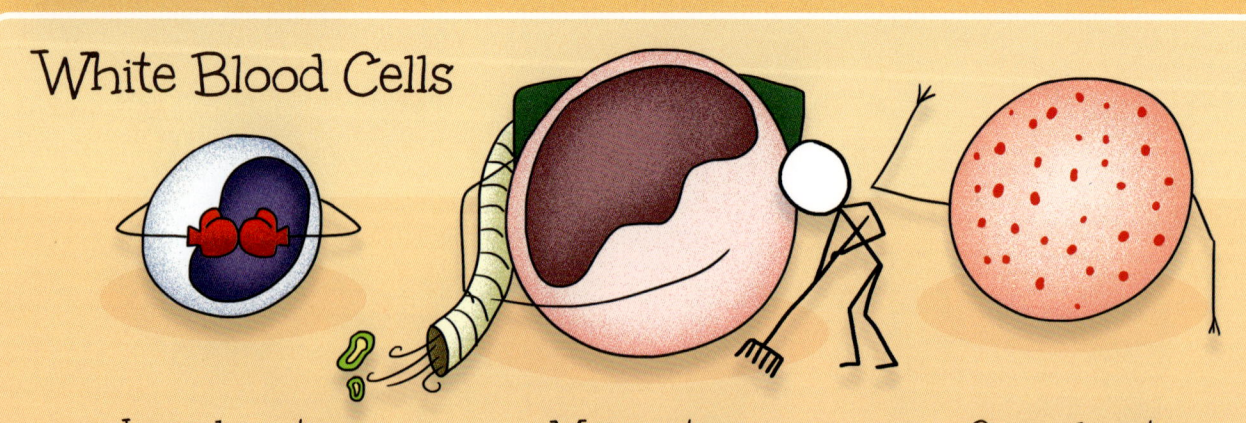

White Blood Cells

Lymphocytes
are cells that fight germs. There are at least five different kinds, including B cells, T cells, and Natural Killers.

Monocytes
are the biggest white blood cells and act like street sweepers, sucking up debris.

Granulocytes
have colored grains and come in three kinds: neutrophils, eosinophils, and basophils (*right*).

The Watery Bit

All the blood's ingredients float in a fluid called plasma. Plasma makes up just over half your blood. It's pale yellow in color and mostly water, but contains many dissolved chemicals, such as salts and glucose, that it brings to your cells for food.

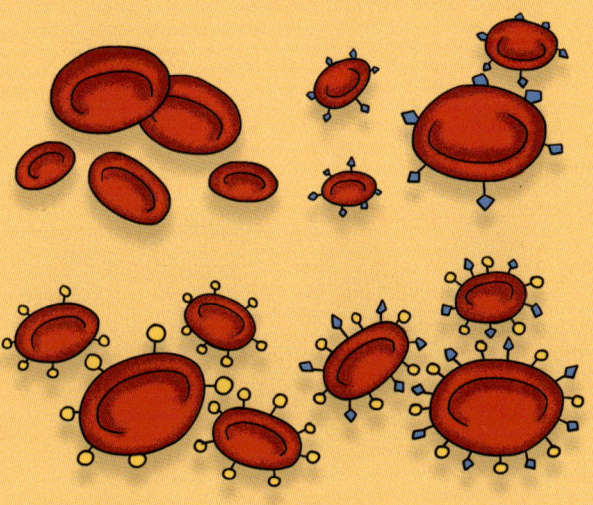

water • salts • proteins • urea (waste) • sugars

Your Own Blood

If you have a major operation or a bad accident, you can lose a lot of blood and may need a transfusion, or input, of someone else's blood. But people have blood belonging to one of four different groups: A, B, AB and O (the most common)—and they don't mix, because your body's immune system will fight against blood from the wrong group. So you must be given the right type.

How Much Blood Do You Have?

A newborn baby has about the same amount of blood as liquid in a soft drinks can. By the time you're about eight years old, you have enough blood to fill a 0.5-gallon (2 L) bottle. By the time you're an adult, you can fill two or more of these bottles!

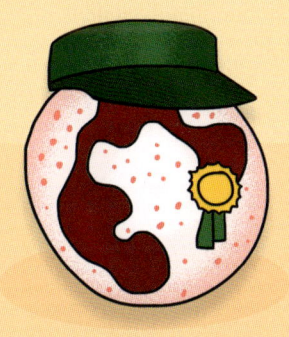

Neutrophils
are an army of pink-grained cells that fight bacteria and fungi. When they've done their job, they end up as white pus.

Eosinophils
are a select bunch of peach-grained cells that handle parasites and things you might be allergic to.

Basophils
are the look-outs, with large blue grains. They react to irritants by sending out a chemical alert called histamine.

63

Blood in Action

When your body comes under attack from disease-causing bacteria, viruses, and other germs, it's time for your body to mount a defence. It does this with an array of biological weapons known as the immune system. The most important part of the immune system is your white blood cells.

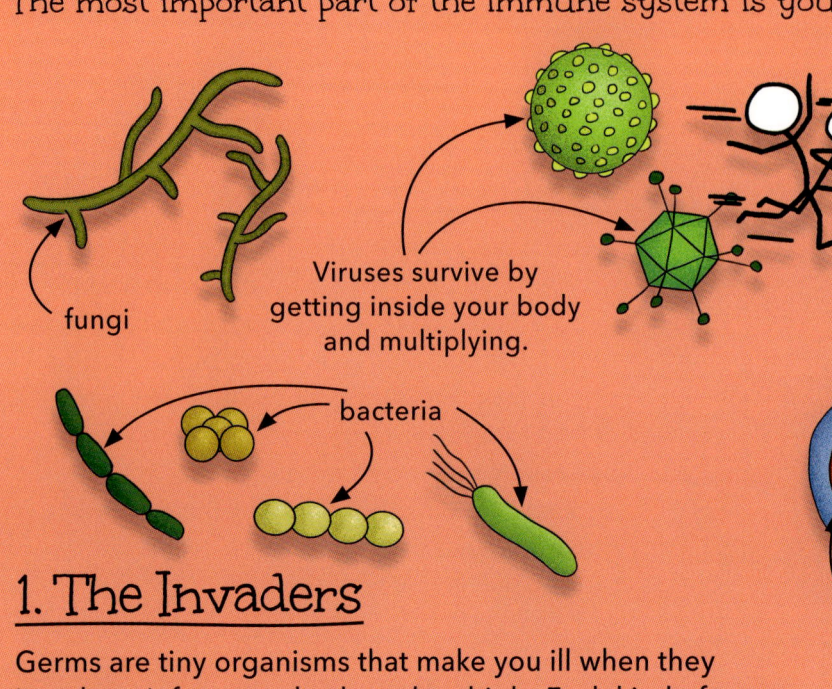

fungi

Viruses survive by getting inside your body and multiplying.

bacteria

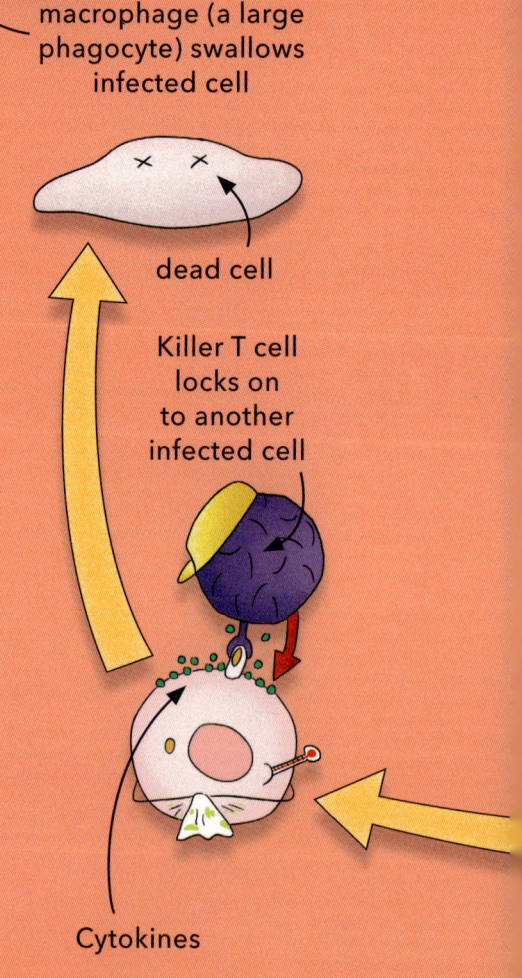

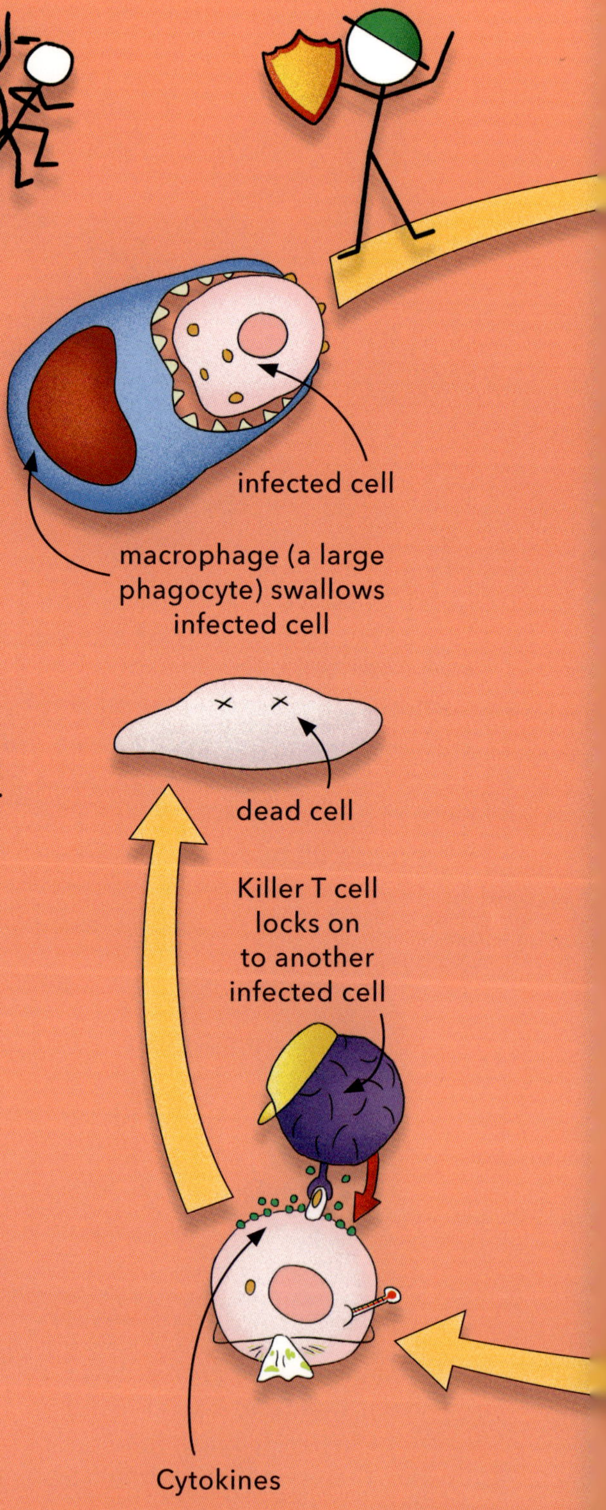

infected cell

macrophage (a large phagocyte) swallows infected cell

1. The Invaders

Germs are tiny organisms that make you ill when they invade or infect your body and multiply. Each kind of germ causes a particular disease. For example, different bacteria cause typhoid, tetanus, or whooping cough. Viruses cause colds, flu, mumps, rabies, and AIDS. Fungi cause conditions such as candida and aspergillosis (often affecting the lungs).

dead cell

Killer T cell locks on to another infected cell

2. Germ Swallowers

When germs invade your body, two main kinds of white blood cell go into action to fight them off: phagocytes and lymphocytes. Phagocytes form the first line of defence. Phagocytes swallow invading germs and dissolve them. Once they've swallowed a germ, they display the germ's identity tag or antigen on their outside, identifying them to other immune system cells.

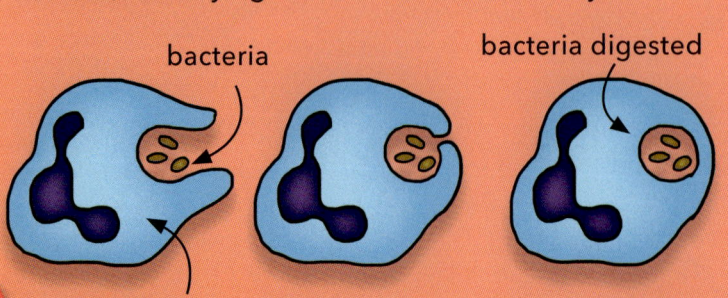

bacteria   *bacteria digested*

phagocyte

Cytokines

antibodies tag germ

B cell makes antibodies

germ

macrophage eats tagged germ

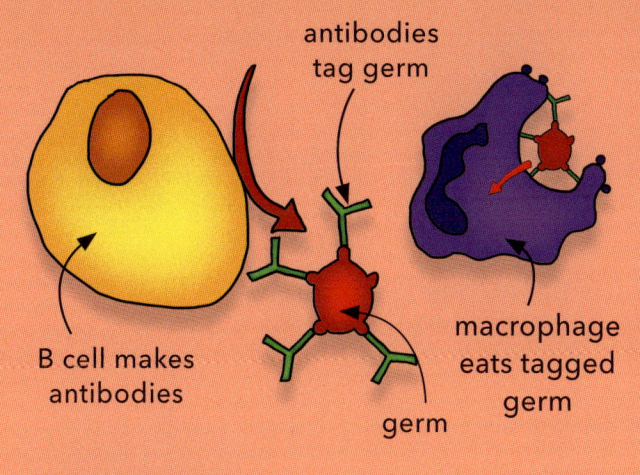

3. Targeting

Lymphocytes target particular germs. One kind, called B lymphocytes, targets free-roaming germs. Each B lymphocyte has its own antibodies: special chemicals that lock on to a particular germ's antigen. When an antibody meets its antigen, its B lymphocyte makes more antibodies. When they lock on to germs, they make them better targets, especially for extra-large phagocytes called macrophages.

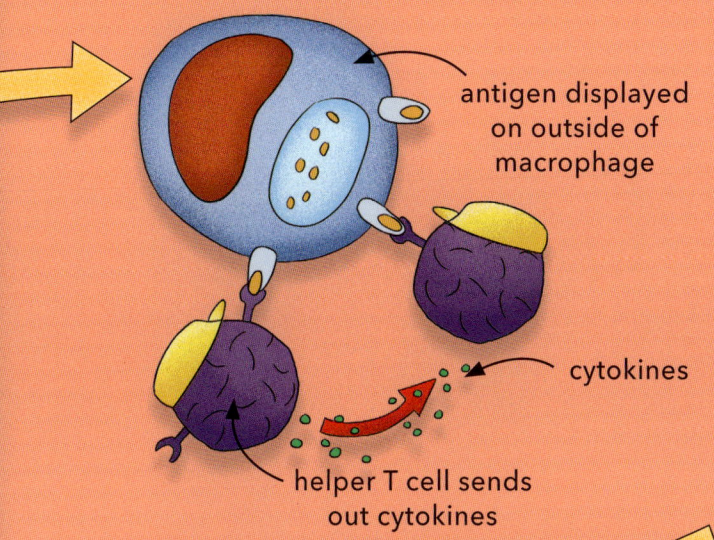

antigen displayed on outside of macrophage

cytokines

helper T cell sends out cytokines

4. Beating Viruses

Once viruses invade cells, they are hidden. That's where T lymphocytes come in. Helper T lymphocytes are alerted by telltale signs of damage and also by virus antigens on macrophages that have swallowed invaded cells. They then multiply rapidly and send out alarm chemicals called cytokines. The cytokines activate cells called Killer Ts. Killer T cells target the antigens on other cells, lock on to them, then flood them with toxic chemicals to kill cell, virus and all.

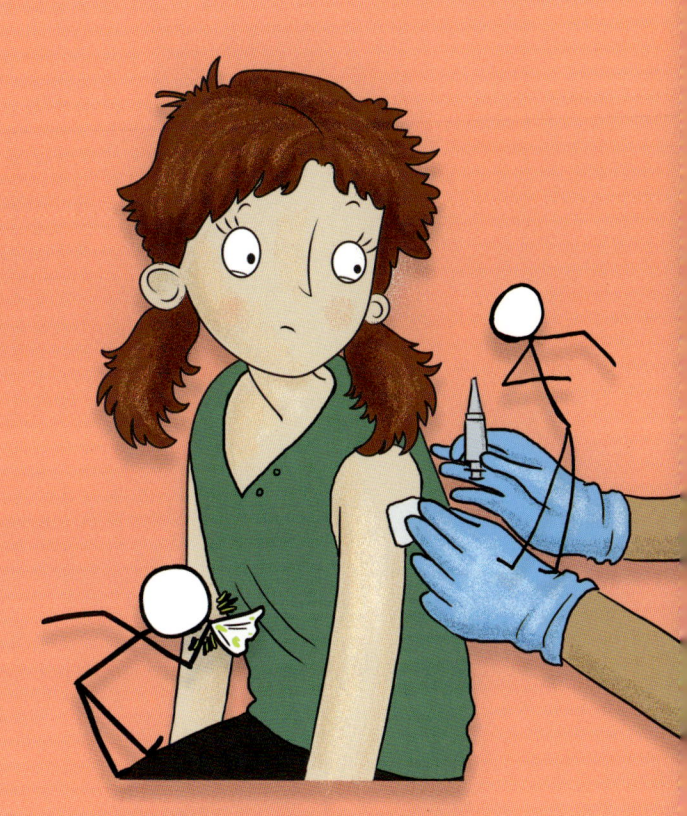

Killer T cells multiply

5. Remembering

As lymphocytes identify and attack germs, they make special memory cells. Memory cells hang around long after the battle against the infection is won. So they are on hand to mount a much more rapid and powerful response should the same germs turn up again. Vaccines work by giving you a mild infection of the germ to create memory cells armed and ready for a real attack.

Mending Hearts

The heart is an amazing organ that keeps on beating nonstop all your life. But sometimes, especially later in life, the automatic beating of the heart can go wrong or stop altogether. Fortunately, doctors are finding more and more ways of dealing with heart problems.

Heart Problems

The heart can suffer in three main ways: from a heart attack, cardiac arrest, and stroke.

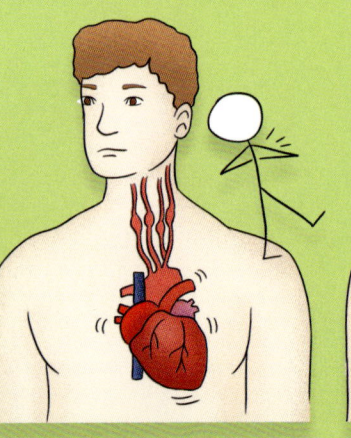

1 In a heart attack, the heart muscle fails because the arteries around the heart become blocked.

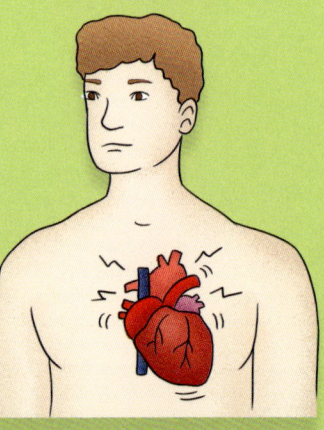

2 In cardiac arrest, the heart stops beating because the electrical signals that fire the muscle stop.

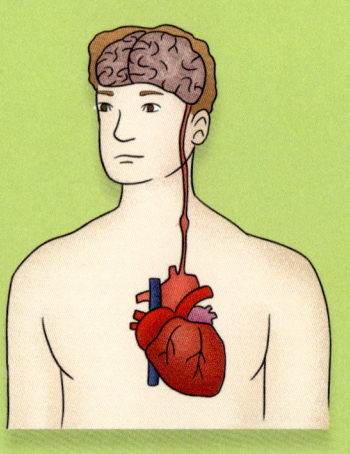

3 In a stroke, blood flow to the brain is cut off, often by a blood clot in an artery.

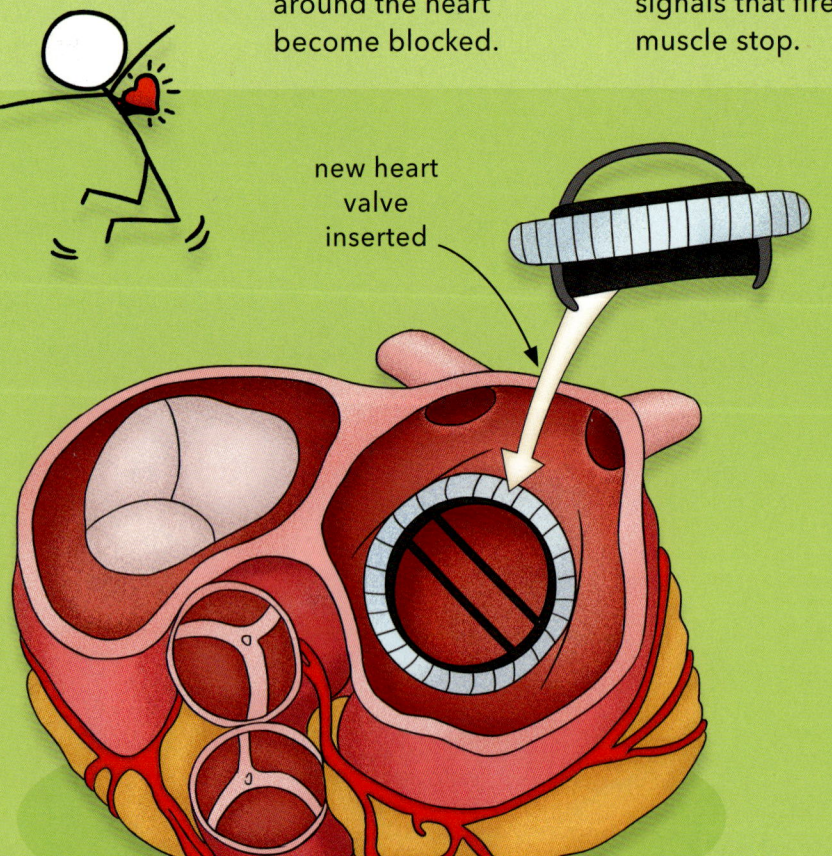

new heart valve inserted

Heart Valve

Sometimes the valves in the heart can become floppy and fail to shut properly, weakening the pumping action. If this happens, doctors may try replacing it with either a mechanical valve made of carbon fiber and Teflon or animal tissue.

66

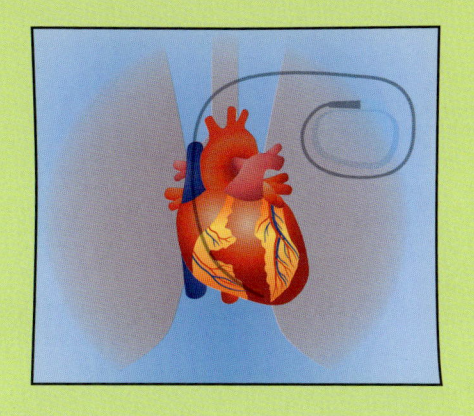

Keeping Time

Sometimes, a person's heartbeat may become dangerously irregular and they may be given an artificial pacemaker. This is a simple battery-powered device that senses any unsteadiness in the heartbeat and sends an electrical stimulus to the heart to get going properly again. The pacemaker is installed just under the skin, then wired to the heart, in a minor operation.

Heart Transplant

If heart disease is very severe. the only solution may be a heart transplant. In this, the diseased heart is removed and swapped for the healthy heart of a donor who has just died. The transplant takes about four hours. The new heart is stitched in and the patient is given drugs to make sure their immune system does not reject the new heart.

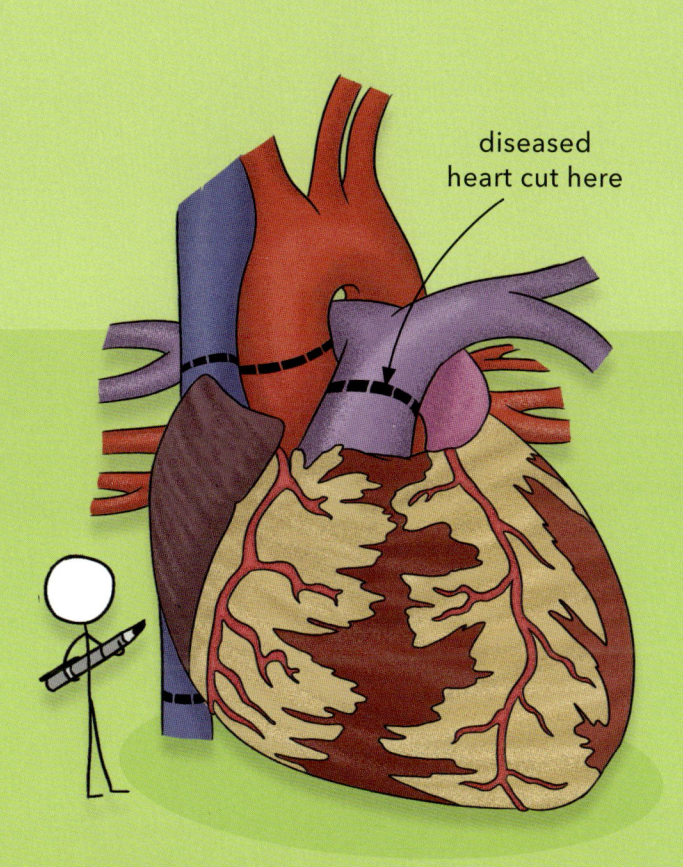

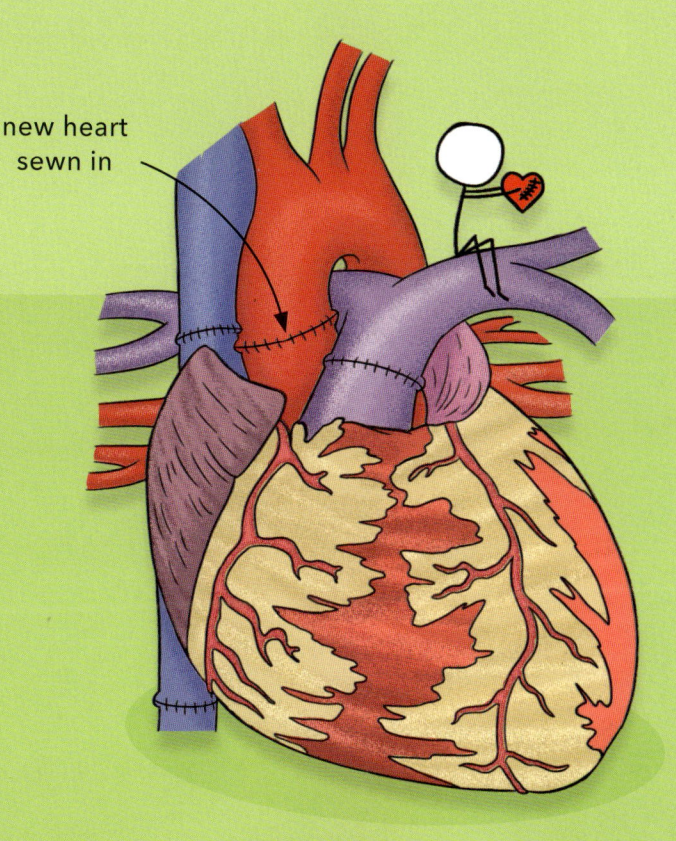

diseased heart cut here

new heart sewn in

Heart on Ice

A patient waiting for a donor heart must be on permanent standby because the transplant must be performed within a few hours of the donor dying. Once the donor's heart has been removed, it is stored in an icebox and shipped as fast as possible to the hospital where the operation will take place.

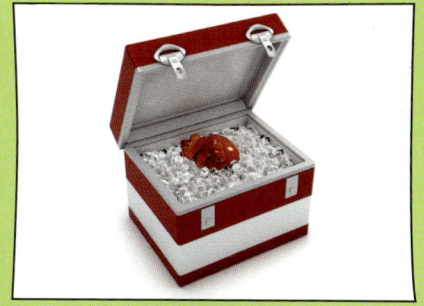

Staying Fit

One of the key signs of being fit and healthy is having a strong heart and lungs. That means your heart and lungs can supply your muscles with all the oxygen they need. If you get out of breath easily, it's a sign that your heart and lungs aren't fit enough.

Hard Work!

When you exercise, your body reacts in some of the ways shown here. If you're fit and you haven't pushed too hard, your body will return to normal in just a few minutes. If you're out of shape, or have really worked hard, it may take hours.

- body temperature rises and you sweat
- you breathe faster and deeper, taking in up to 10 times more air every minute
- heart rate soars; the heart pumps more blood with each beat
- the liver converts more of its stored sugar (glycogen) to glucose
- blood vessels widen to increase blood flow to muscles
- muscles consume up to 20 times more energy
- acid builds up in the muscles as they burn glucose without enough oxygen

Exercise: What is it Good For?

Different kinds of exercise do you good in different ways. Running is great for your heart and lungs, but it doesn't do much for flexibility. Cycling is good for muscles and for balance and coordination.

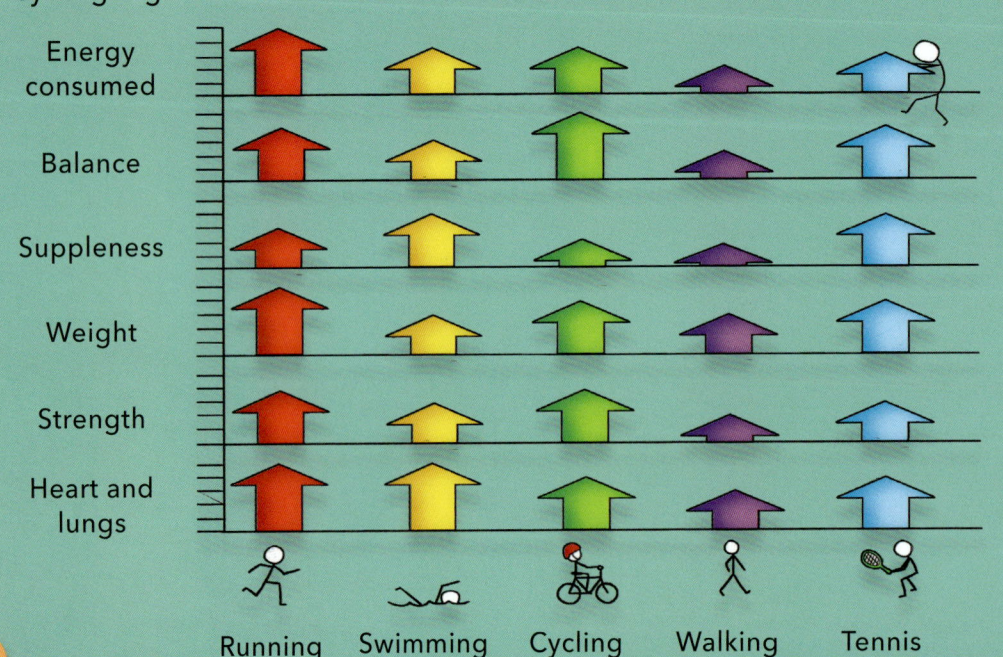

	Running	Swimming	Cycling	Walking	Tennis
Energy consumed					
Balance					
Suppleness					
Weight					
Strength					
Heart and lungs					

muscles grow

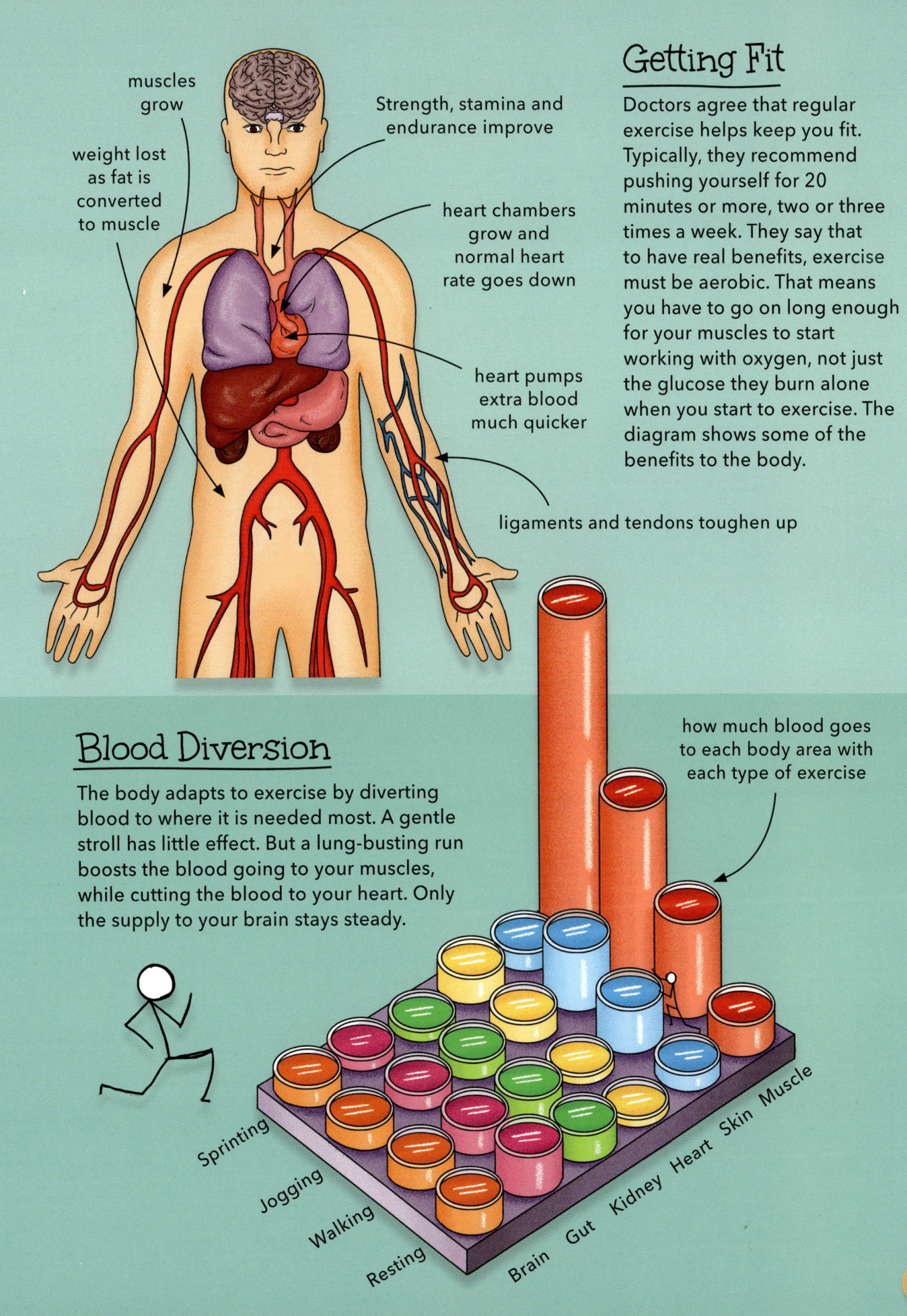

weight lost as fat is converted to muscle

Strength, stamina and endurance improve

heart chambers grow and normal heart rate goes down

heart pumps extra blood much quicker

ligaments and tendons toughen up

Getting Fit

Doctors agree that regular exercise helps keep you fit. Typically, they recommend pushing yourself for 20 minutes or more, two or three times a week. They say that to have real benefits, exercise must be aerobic. That means you have to go on long enough for your muscles to start working with oxygen, not just the glucose they burn alone when you start to exercise. The diagram shows some of the benefits to the body.

Blood Diversion

The body adapts to exercise by diverting blood to where it is needed most. A gentle stroll has little effect. But a lung-busting run boosts the blood going to your muscles, while cutting the blood to your heart. Only the supply to your brain stays steady.

how much blood goes to each body area with each type of exercise

Sprinting
Jogging
Walking
Resting

Brain Gut Kidney Heart Skin Muscle

Your Gurgling Guts

Eating gives you a constant supply of fuel and materials that keep your body going. But food comes in big lumps. That's where your digestive system plays its part. Your digestive system is an amazing chemical refinery that first breaks down food into the chemicals your body needs, then absorbs them all into your blood for distribution.

The Big Meal

Every year, the average person in the USA eats about 0.55 tons (0.5 metric tons) of food! Typically, Americans eat over 75 lbs (34 kg) of red meat (beef, veal, pork, and lamb) and 54 lbs (24 kg) of poultry (chicken and turkey). So altogether they eat nearly 20 million tons (18 million metric tons) of meat every year! That's about 160 billion quarter-pounder burgers! If all the red meat eaten by Americans each year were cows, they could form a continuous line of cattle stretching nose to tail all the way from New York City to Los Angeles, California, and back nine times!

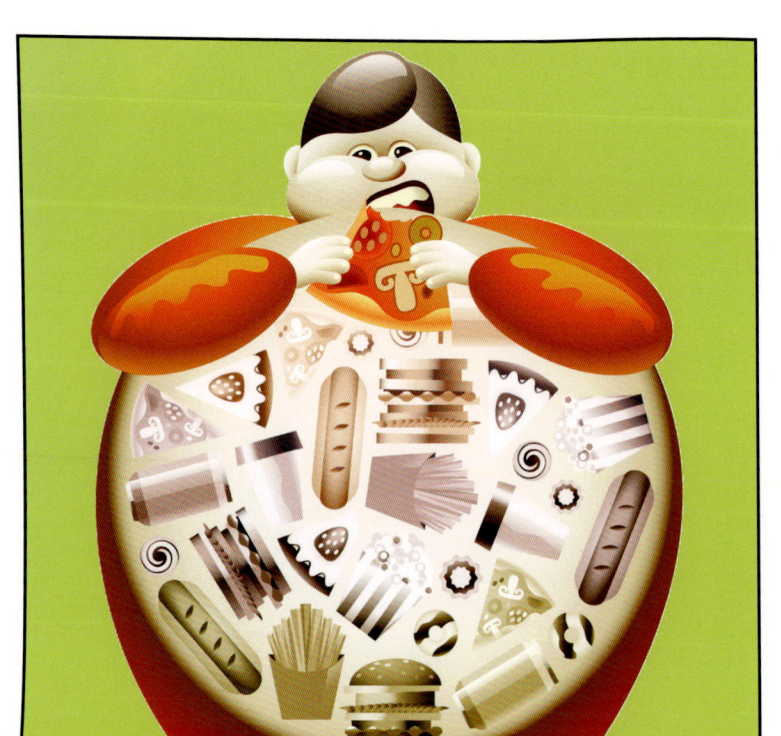

2,449 miles (3,941 km)

Fed Up

In the last 50 years, more and more people have been eating too much or doing too little exercise. So now, far more people are overweight than ever before. The World Health Organization describes those who are extremely overweight as obese and they say that 1 billion or so people around the world are now obese. Obesity can cause health problems such as heart disease and diabetes.

70

Cooking!

Humans are the only animals that cook their food. We cannot really digest much raw meat, so cooking softens it and allows us to eat and digest nearly any kind of meat. Meat contains a lot of protein, and some scientists think discovering how to make it edible by cooking is what gave humans clever brains.

Basic Foods

Although we eat a far greater range of food than most other animals, we rely on a small range of simple, basic foods known as staples. These include maize, wheat, and rice, and they are crucial for giving us vital energy. Amazingly, just 15 food plants provide 90 percent of the energy needs of the whole world.

Fast Work

While no one can live more than a few days without water, people can survive weeks, or even longer, without food. The famous Indian leader Mahatma Gandhi managed to survive 21 days without food as a protest. But going without food or living only on poor quality food, can make you ill.

Body Fuel

Food is the fuel that keeps your body going. It also provides the materials your body needs to grow and stay in good repair. Some animals eat only meat. Others eat mostly plants. But we humans eat a wide range of foods—and to stay healthy we need to get the right balance of ingredients from different foods.

Carbs

Carbohydrates are the number one energy fuel. They are different kinds of sugar and starch, made from big molecules of carbon, hydrogen, and oxygen. They are converted in your body into glucose that the cells use for fuel, or they're stored temporarily in your liver and muscles as glycogen.

Protein Power

Proteins make up pretty much everything in your body. They are built from different combinations of 20 amino acids. Your body can make 12 of these itself, but it needs to get the others from food to repair cells and make new ones.

Fat Stuff

Fats are the greasy parts of food that won't dissolve in water. They are sometime known as lipids. Some are solid, like cheese and meat fat. Others are liquid, like olive oil. Like carbs, fats are used for energy, but your body stores them for future use rather than using them at once.

Quantity vs Quality

People around the world eat 2,870 calories of food a day, on average. In the US, people eat 3,640, including a high proportion of sugar, fat, and dairy products.

Average World Diet
- dairy and eggs
- meat
- other
- produce
- grain
- sugar and fat

Average US Diet
- dairy and eggs
- meat
- other
- produce
- grain
- sugar and fat

Vital elements

By far the bulkiest item in your diet is carbs. But you also need tiny, tiny traces of chemicals called vitamins that your body cannot make for itself. Vitamins are known by letters A to K, and each has its own role. For example, Vitamin D is vital for healthy bones, and Vitamin A helps cell growth. Each is found in particular foods.

Mineral essentials

Your body needs certain other minerals, too. Salts maintain the right levels of water and help the nerves to work. You need calcium for building bones and iron to make red blood cells. You also need iodine and potassium and a range of other chemicals in small amounts.

Rough Stuff

Cellulose is the tough fiber in plants that your gut can't break down. But even though you can't digest them, your body still needs this fiber, called roughage. It exercises the muscles of your gut wall and keeps them fit.

Energy-rich

Scientists measure the energy that things use in kilojoules or calories. An average person would use about 7,000 kilojoules or 1,700 calories of energy just sitting still for 24 hours. When you exercise hard, though, your energy consumption may double.

Calorie Consumption

1,000 calories — 14-mile (22 km) walk

370 calories — climbing stairs (30 mins)

100 calories — swimming (15 mins)

Throwaway

Your body carefully extracts every last useful substance from food. But a lot of food is wasted before it even gets to your mouth. About a third of all food produced around the world is thrown away each year. If just a quarter of the food wasted were saved, it would feed 870 million hungry people!

Eating

Food provides most of what your body needs, from energy sources to building materials. But it's rarely in just the right form. So every time you eat, an amazing chemical processing factory gets to work inside you. This is what your digestive system does, and it's much more elaborate than you might think.

Mouth Power

The processing of food begins as soon as food pops into your mouth. Your teeth crush the food and break it up. Your saliva has powerful chemicals called enzymes, including one called amylase, which soften the food. Together, chewing and saliva together reduce your food to a soft pulp.

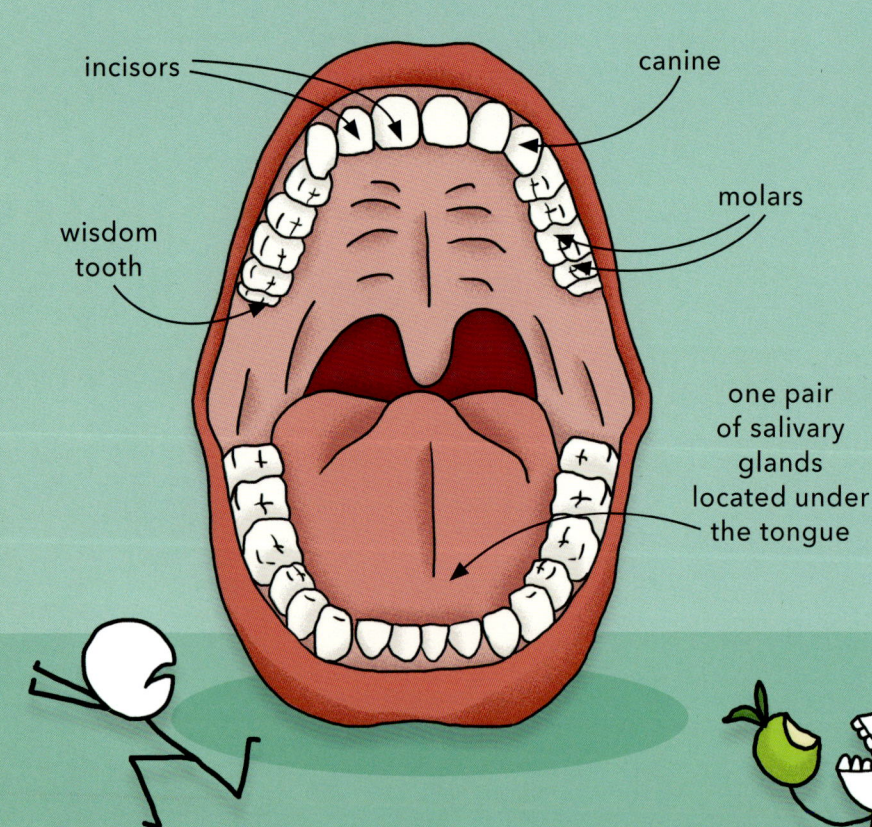

incisors

canine

molars

wisdom tooth

one pair of salivary glands located under the tongue

larynx

to lungs

1 The esophagus, the pipe to your stomach, is normally blocked off by a ring of muscle, called the sphincter muscle, to let air through the larynx into your lungs.

Gnashers

For their size, the jaw muscles are the most powerful in the body. They can bring your teeth together with enormous force. Although you don't have the biting power of a shark, you can still give a nasty nip.

Down it Goes

Your teeth and saliva reduce food to a pulpy ball called a bolus, ready for you to swallow. But of course your throat is also the passage to your lungs. So the food in your mouth must go straight to your stomach so that it doesn't choke you!

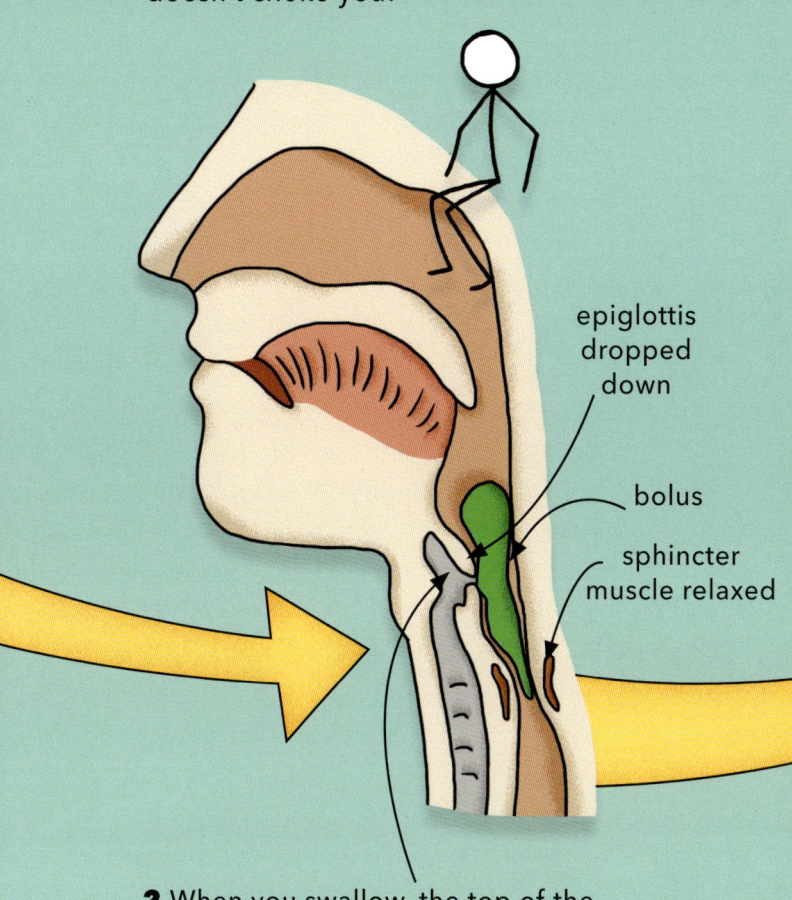

epiglottis dropped down

bolus

sphincter muscle relaxed

2 When you swallow, the top of the larynx rises out of the way, and a flap called the epiglottis shuts it off.

epiglottis up

sphincter muscle contracted again

3 Once the bolus is in the esophagus, the larynx drops and the epiglottis opens to let you breathe again.

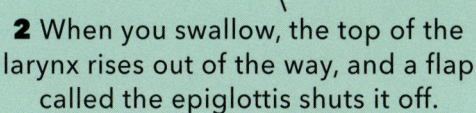

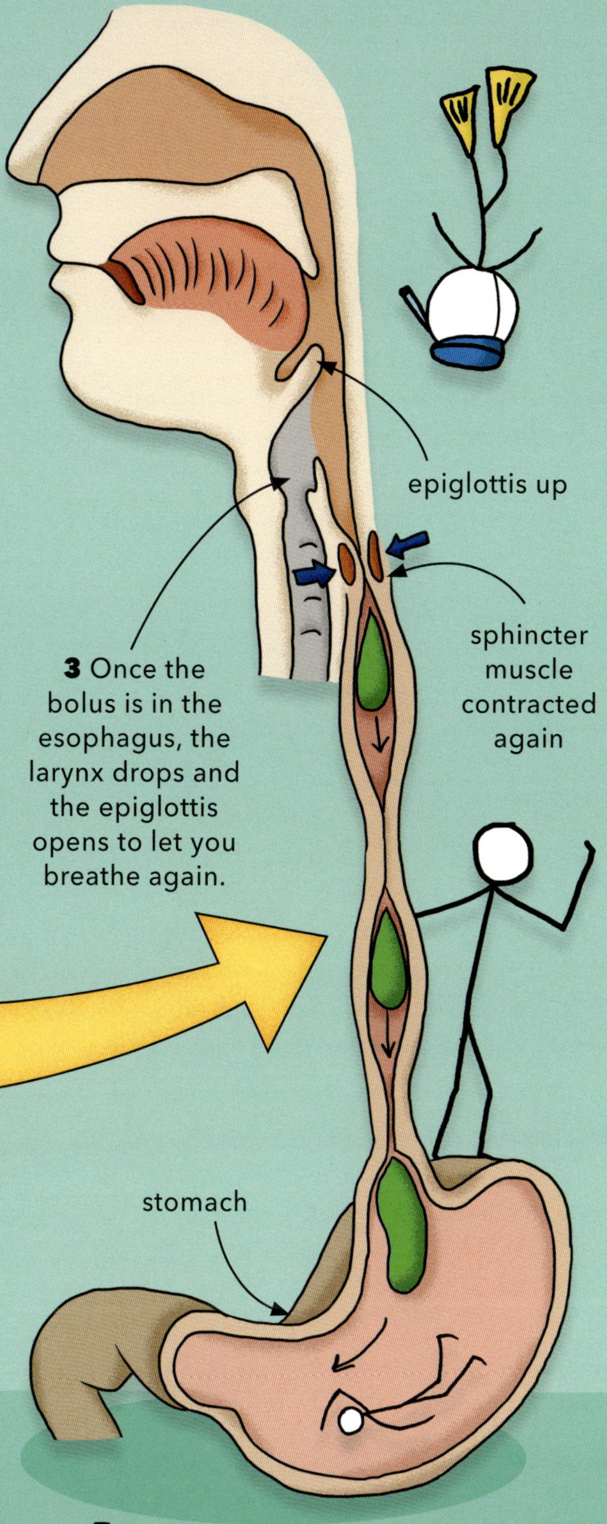

stomach

Sucking Up

The secret to sucking up liquid through a straw is air pressure. Your lips seal the air in the straw. To drink, you inflate your lungs. This creates a bigger space for the air in the straw and in your lungs, and it lowers its pressure. The pressure of air inside the straw is now less than the pressure of air on the drink. This pushes the drink up the straw and into your mouth.

The Food Masher

After being swallowed, food slides quickly down into your stomach. Then processing begins. Food really comes in for a rough time in your stomach! It is attacked by acids and enzymes and beaten to a pulp by squeezing muscles.

Inside the Masher

The stomach stores food and lets it through gradually to the next stage of the system. But it's not just a bag. It has strong muscular walls. As soon as food enters the stomach, the muscles begin to squeeze and relax to pound and crunch the food into a soft pulp called chyme. At the same time, the food is attacked chemically by acids and the gastric juice pepsin.

The pyloric sphincter muscle opens and closes, like a rubber ring around the neck of a bag. This lets food through, bit by bit, into the small intestine.

A sphincter muscle opens to let food from the esophagus into the stomach, then quickly closes behind it.

Muscles are in three layers to squeeze in different directions. At the top, they run lengthwise.

ring muscles

The fundus, or upper part of the stomach holds gas that comes off the food.

The pylorus or lower part of the stomach links it to the small intestine.

diagonal muscles

duodenum, first part of the small intestine

Inflatable bag

When your stomach is empty, it's like a flat balloon and holds very little. But as soon as food enters, it starts swelling. The size it can inflate to depends on how old you are. When you're born, it's no bigger than a strawberry. But by the time you're grown up, it can expand to the size of a melon!

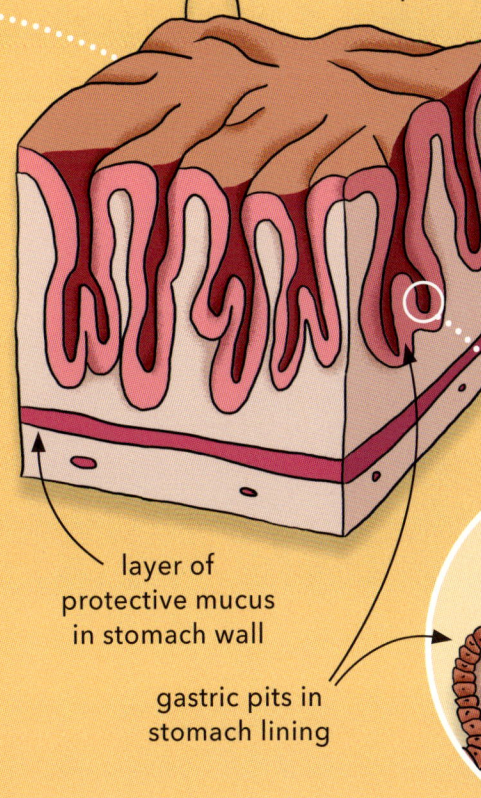

layer of protective mucus in stomach wall

gastric pits in stomach lining

mucus cell

Your stomach is lined with tiny pits called gastric pits. The gastric pits ooze gastric juices made of three things: acid, a substance called pepsinogen that helps the acid break up large food protein molecules, and a natural slime called mucus.

Acid Attack

Believe it or not, stomach acid is strong enough to dissolve metal. It is a mix of potassium, sodium chloride, and hydrochloric acid so powerful that it would need a safety warning if stored in a bottle. That's why the walls of your stomach must be protected by a lining of extra thick cells and a layer of slimy mucus.

It Makes You Sick

What goes down doesn't always stay down. If the vomiting center in your brain gets the message from your gut that something is wrong, it will send signals to your stomach to throw up. The muscle rings that block off your gut and the stomach suddenly open wide, and your abdomen muscles squeeze. And up come the contents of your gut and stomach! Ugh!

Guts

After food has been turned into chyme, it moves on from your stomach into your intestines.

pancreas

duodenum: the breakdown of energy foods begins, aided by chemicals oozed from the pancreas

small intestine, a tunnel about 23 ft (7 m) long!

Small and Large Intestine

Your intestine, or gut, is divided into two sections: the narrower small intestine where food is digested and absorbed, and the wider large intestine where undigested food is dried out and prepared to exit your body. To perform all its tasks, the gut has to be incredibly long, so it is folded over and over inside your abdomen.

large intestine, or colon, where water is sucked out of waste food

ileum: more food is absorbed into the blood and swept to the liver for further processing

jejunum: food molecules seep through the gut walls into the blood

rectum, where slimy mucus helps waste to slide out through the anus

Big Gut!

The gut needs a huge area to absorb food, bit by tiny bit. So its surface area is enormous. Estimates vary, but most scientists agree that if laid out flat, it would cover an entire badminton court!

Villi

Blood vessels in gut wall

Foodie Fingers

Many billions of tiny food molecules have to be absorbed by the gut. So its lining is covered in millions of fingerlike projections. These are known as villi. They hugely increase the surface area of the gut, so food absorption is spread out over a vast area.

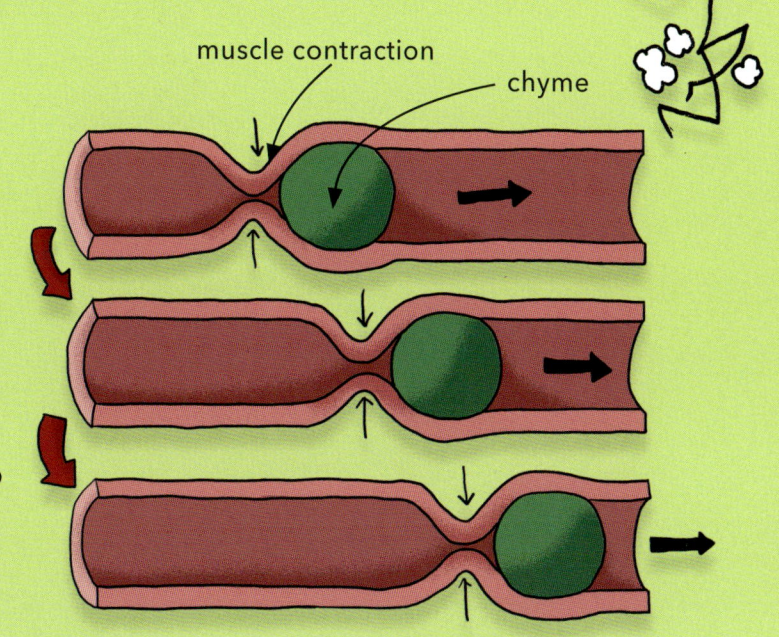

muscle contraction

chyme

Move along!

Food is moved through the gut by muscles in the gut wall. This process is called peristalsis. Rings of muscles just behind each chyme of food contract sharply, while muscles in front relax. So the chyme is eased gradually forward as muscle waves pulse along the gut.

good bacteria

Gut Bugs

You might think of bacteria as germs. In fact, there is a vast community of bacteria inside your gut that helps you digest your food. These friendly bacteria break down any food that your normal digestion cannot deal with. Waste smells as it does because of the chemicals made by these bacteria snacking on food.

lactobacilli are good bacteria found in the colon

bad bacteria

79

The Chemical Refinery

Digestion is a complicated business. It's not just a matter of breaking food into little bits. It has to be sliced into tiny particles, or molecules. So the gut is an amazing chemical refinery as clever as any pharmaceutical factory. It involves acids and those chemicals called enzymes.

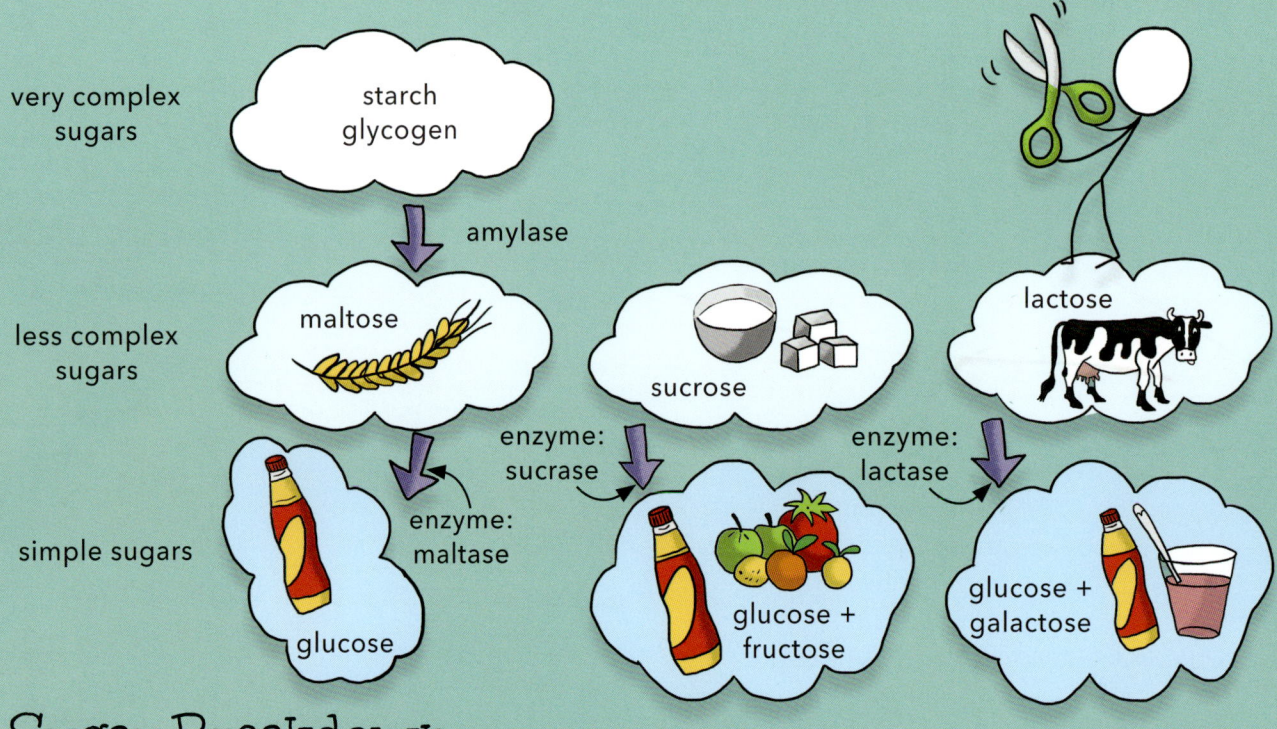

very complex sugars — starch glycogen

amylase

less complex sugars — maltose, sucrose, lactose

enzyme: maltase / enzyme: sucrase / enzyme: lactase

simple sugars — glucose / glucose + fructose / glucose + galactose

Sugar Breakdown

The living world gets energy from chemicals called carbohydrates, including starches and sugars. They come in many forms in food, but your body can only use the simple sugar glucose. So it assigns a different enzyme to change each kind of starch into three simple sugars: glucose, fructose, and galactose. Then your liver converts the last two to glucose.

Biological Scissors

Enzymes in your digestion do not break up food themselves; they just get things going. They work like biological scissors, snipping away at big food molecules just as kitchen scissors snip at a string of sausages. For example, the enzyme amylase chops up the big starch molecules in bread and potatoes into simple sugars.

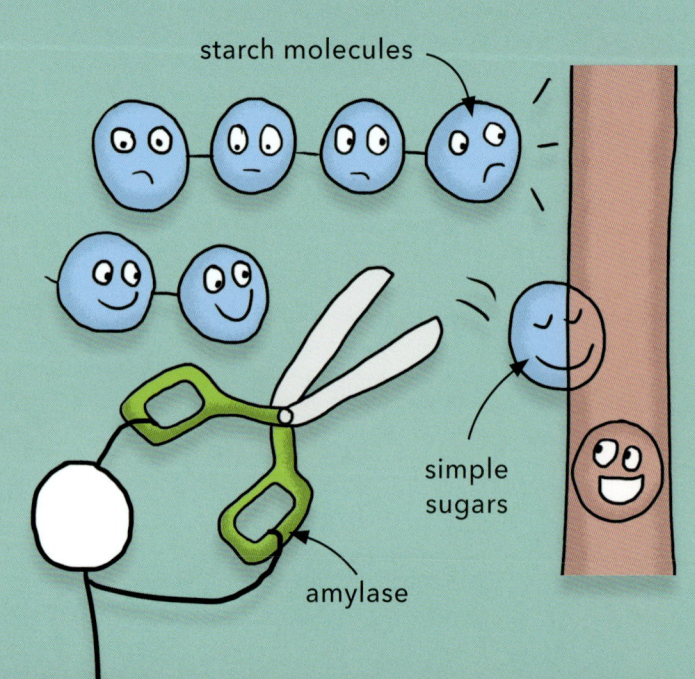

starch molecules

simple sugars

amylase

Chemical Breakdown

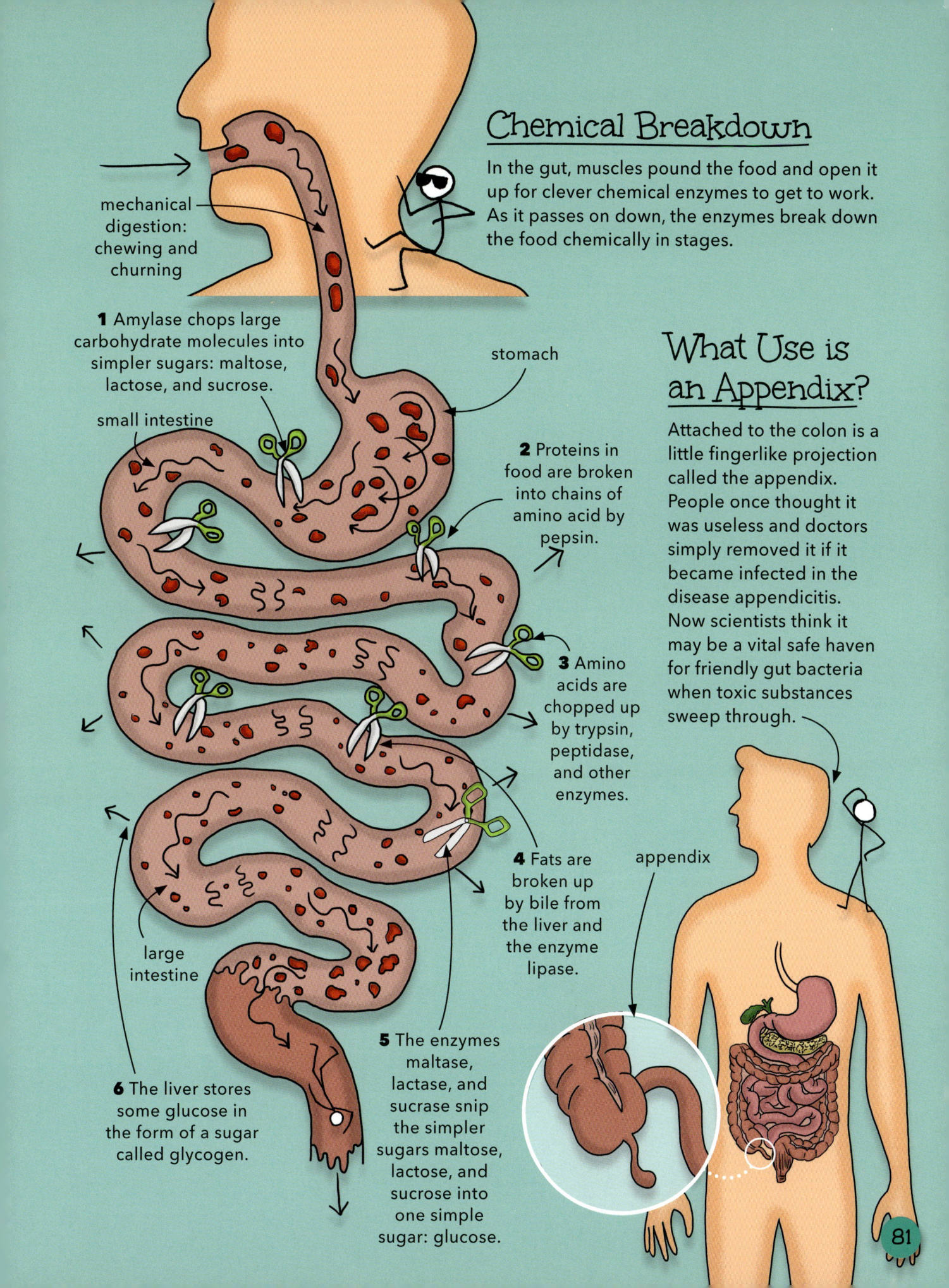

In the gut, muscles pound the food and open it up for clever chemical enzymes to get to work. As it passes on down, the enzymes break down the food chemically in stages.

mechanical digestion: chewing and churning

1 Amylase chops large carbohydrate molecules into simpler sugars: maltose, lactose, and sucrose.

small intestine

stomach

2 Proteins in food are broken into chains of amino acid by pepsin.

3 Amino acids are chopped up by trypsin, peptidase, and other enzymes.

4 Fats are broken up by bile from the liver and the enzyme lipase.

large intestine

5 The enzymes maltase, lactase, and sucrase snip the simpler sugars maltose, lactose, and sucrose into one simple sugar: glucose.

6 The liver stores some glucose in the form of a sugar called glycogen.

What Use is an Appendix?

Attached to the colon is a little fingerlike projection called the appendix. People once thought it was useless and doctors simply removed it if it became infected in the disease appendicitis. Now scientists think it may be a vital safe haven for friendly gut bacteria when toxic substances sweep through.

appendix

Chemical Powerhouse

Your liver is your body's biggest internal organ and one of its cleverest. It's a super hot powerhouse of chemical activity, generating a lot of your body's warmth and working on 500 different chemical processes at once, from purifying blood to making bile to break down fats.

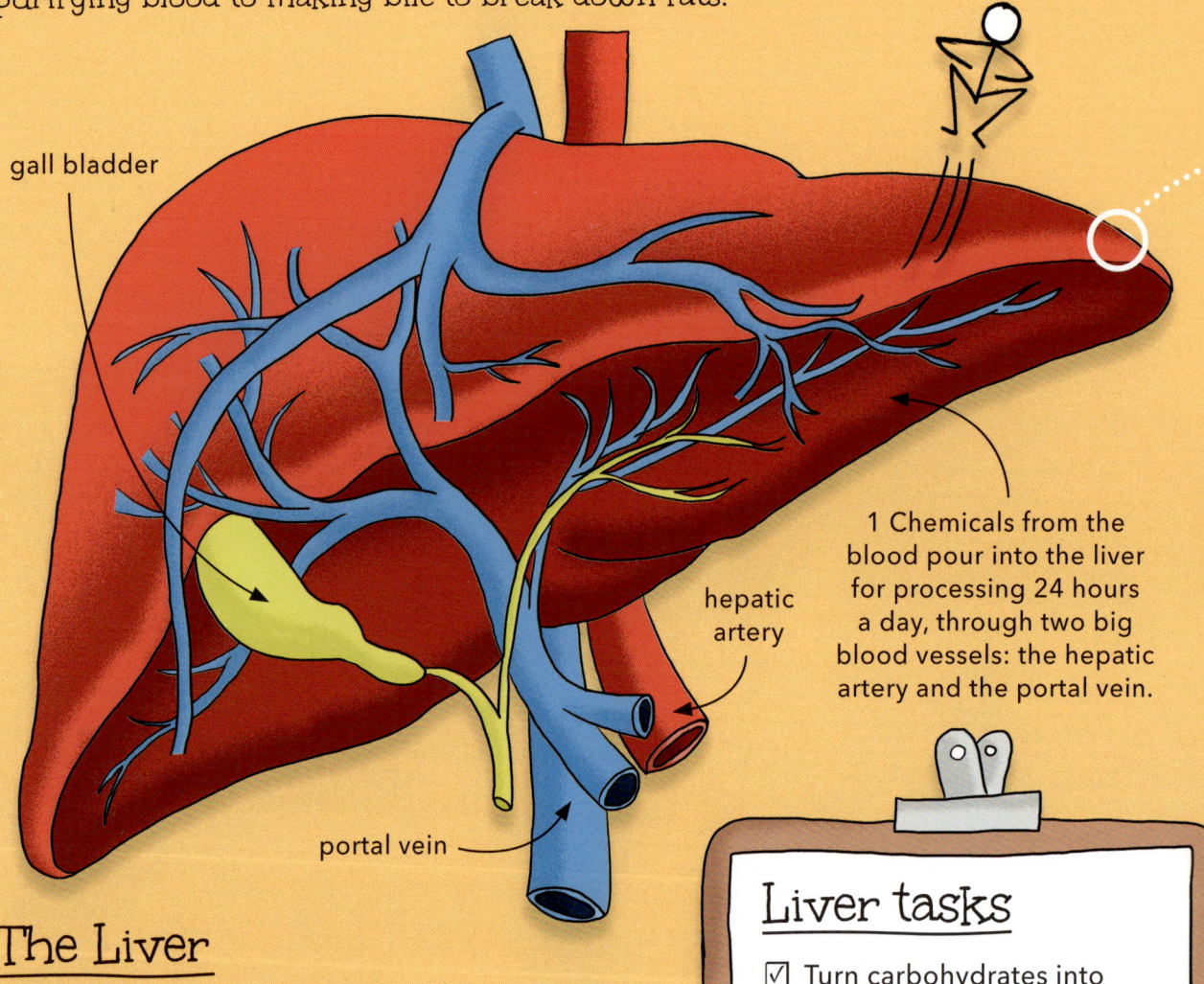

gall bladder

hepatic artery

portal vein

1 Chemicals from the blood pour into the liver for processing 24 hours a day, through two big blood vessels: the hepatic artery and the portal vein.

The Liver

The liver's most important task is to repackage the chemicals from food into just the right form for them to be used around your body. Most important of all, it keeps your blood supplied with glucose, the cells' key energy food. Guided by two chemical signals, glucagon and insulin, it helps ensure your blood Is always supplied with the right amount of glucose.

Liver tasks

- ☑ Turn carbohydrates into glucose
- ☑ Store energy in the form of glycogen
- ☑ Pack away excess energy for long-term storage as fat
- ☑ Clean out old blood cells
- ☑ Make new blood plasma
- ☑ Break down waste proteins
- ☑ Turn fat into cholesterol
- ☑ Store vitamins

2 Blood vessels carry chemicals into thousands of processing units called lobules.

3 Blood flows into the lobules through pipes called sinusoids.

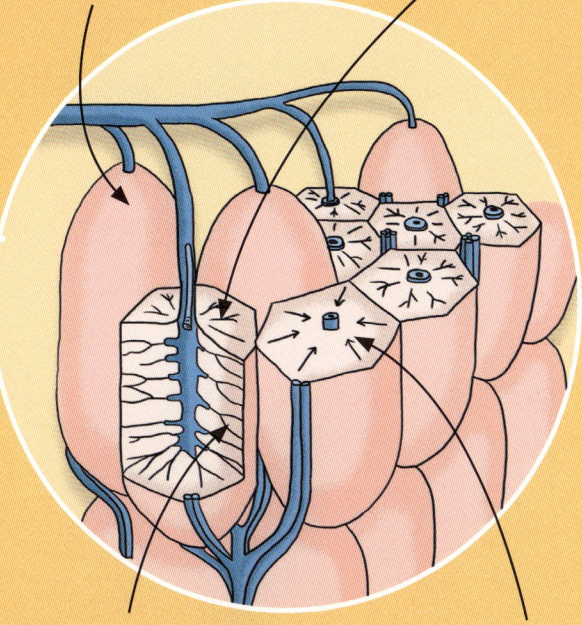

4 Cells called hepatocytes line the sinusoids. They extract the right chemicals and process them.

5 Hepatocytes return the processed chemicals to the blood.

Diabetics have the insulin levels in their blood monitored to ensure the amount of sugar released by the liver stays under control.

Blood Sugar

Your blood sugar (glucose) levels are kept steady by two chemical controls—insulin and glucagon. These are made in the pancreas, an organ just beneath your liver. When you eat, your liver makes lots of glucose and releases it into the blood. Sugar levels soar and the pancreas oozes insulin. Insulin tells your body cells to get busy using glucose and your liver to store more as glycogen. Soon blood sugar levels drop again, and the pancreas releases glucagon, telling your liver to turn glycogen into glucose. In people who have diabetes, the control goes wrong. The diagram shows what happens.

How Diabetes Occurs

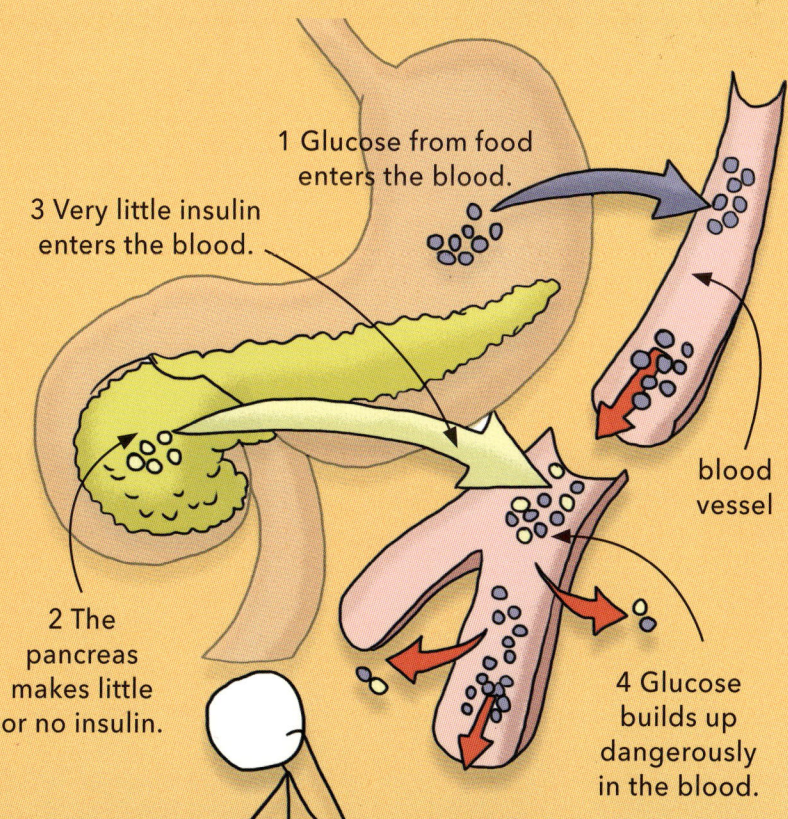

1 Glucose from food enters the blood.

2 The pancreas makes little or no insulin.

3 Very little insulin enters the blood.

4 Glucose builds up dangerously in the blood.

blood vessel

83

Warm Body

For your body processes to work, your body has to stay at exactly the same temperature all the time, whether it's hot or cold. And it has an amazing mechanism for making sure it does just that. Unless you are sick, your body will stay at precisely 98.6°F (37°C) all the time. Even when you're sick, your temperature only goes up by a few degrees.

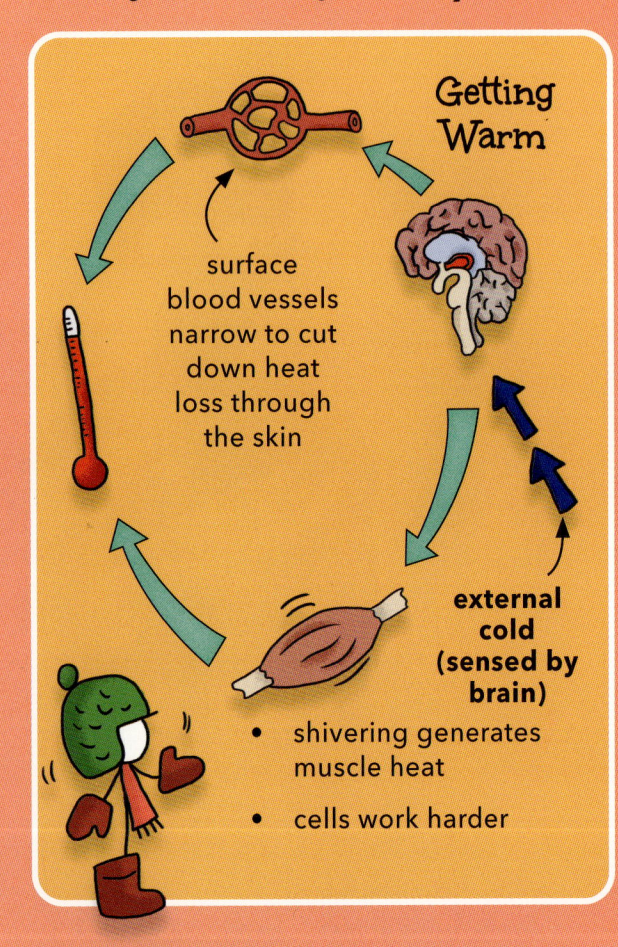

Getting Warm

- surface blood vessels narrow to cut down heat loss through the skin
- external cold (sensed by brain)
- shivering generates muscle heat
- cells work harder

How Do You Keep Warm?

You keep warm mainly by eating. Most of the food you eat is turned into heat by the workings of your cells—especially those in your liver and muscles. Inside every cell are little units called mitochondria which are like furnaces, releasing the energy from glucose and creating heat. All your countless mitochondria working together can make as much heat as a small electric fire!

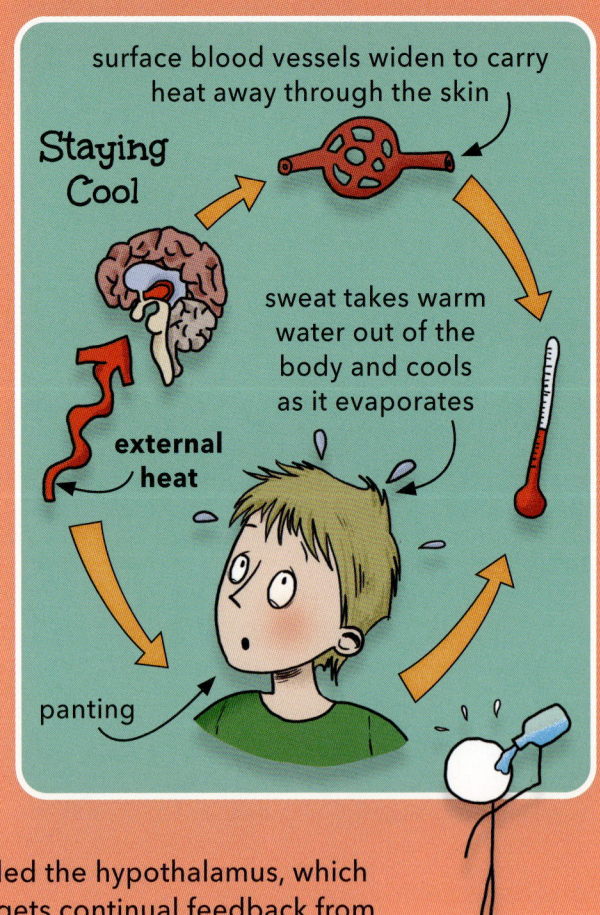

Staying Cool

- surface blood vessels widen to carry heat away through the skin
- sweat takes warm water out of the body and cools as it evaporates
- external heat
- panting

How Do You Keep Cool?

You keep cool mainly by breathing—as long as the air outside is cooler than your body. You also lose heat through your skin and by sweating.

Your Body Thermostat

You have a special heat control in your brain called the hypothalamus, which makes sure you don't get too hot or too cold. It gets continual feedback from heat sensors in your body's core and in your skin. It also senses the temperature of the blood flowing past it. Then, if it is too hot, the front of the hypothalamus sends out signals to the body. If it is too cold, the back sends out signals.

Goose Bumps

When you're cold, you may find little bumps appearing all over your arms. These are called goose bumps because they look a little like the skin of a plucked goose. If you look closely, you may see that in each, the skin hair stands erect. This may all be a holdover from the days of our hairier ancestors, since raising the hairs trapped warm air next to the skin.

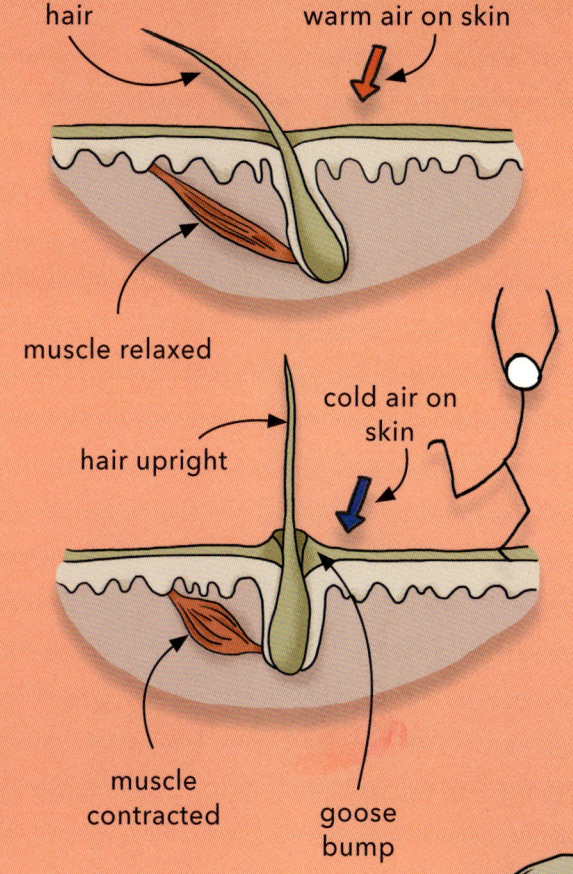

hair warm air on skin

muscle relaxed

hair upright cold air on skin

muscle contracted goose bump

Love Happiness Anger Depression

Warm Heart, Cold Fish

It's sometimes said that people who are friendly are warm, and those who are unfriendly are cold. Well, that might be literally true. Scientists used special heat sensitive cameras to reveal changing body heat patterns in different moods—and the results are marked. See how love makes the body hot and depression makes it cold.

Cold Extremities

Thermal image cameras confirm what you might have guessed. The coldest parts of the body are the extremities, such as the fingertips and toes. These are far away from the core of your body, which is much the hottest place at all times.

If your temperature goes up a few degrees above normal, it's a clear sign that you are unwell. When you have an infection or are sick in some other way, your body may boost its temperature to help its defences fight the germs better. This is called a fever, and it can make people who are sick sweat heavily and go red. Once the fever is past and your temperature drops, it's a sign you are getting better.

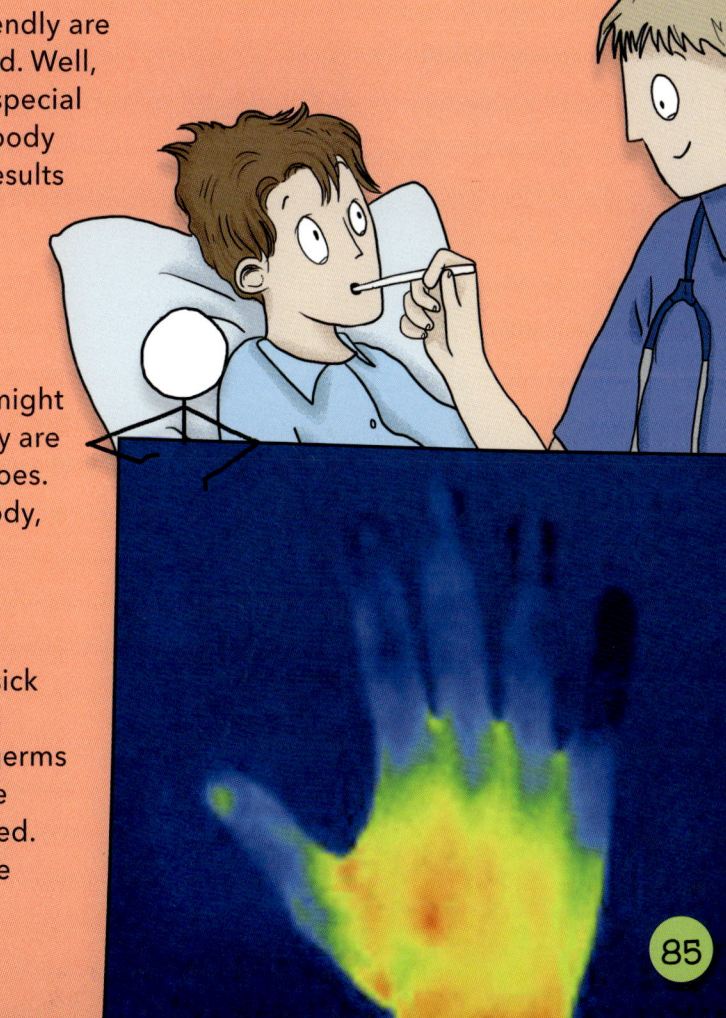

85

Staying Pure

Your body absolutely depends on water to work—and the key to controlling water is your kidneys. Your kidneys hold water back when needed and let it run out as urine if there is too much. They are also filters that draw any poisonous waste out of the blood.

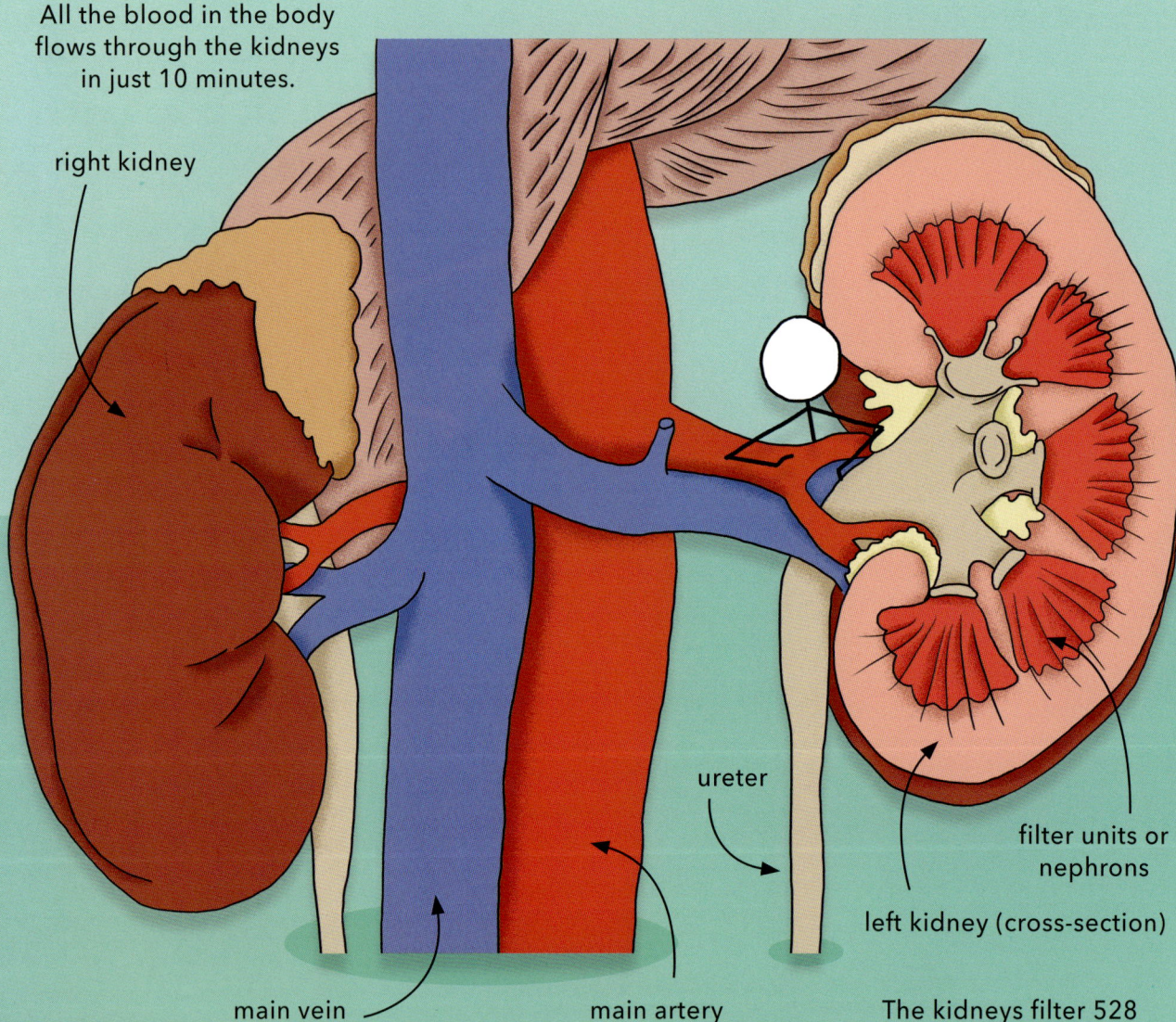

All the blood in the body flows through the kidneys in just 10 minutes.

right kidney

ureter

filter units or nephrons

left kidney (cross-section)

main vein

main artery

The kidneys filter 528 gallons (2,000 L) of blood a day. From that amount, they release only 0.4 gallons (1.5 L) of water.

Human Beans

The kidneys are a pair of bean-shaped organs in the middle of your back. They are located on the main arteries and veins, so they have easy access to the blood. Basically, their task is to clean blood as it washes through, catching larger materials and letting smaller ingredients pass on to the next stage. They then release the necessary ingredients back into the blood and let the waste and unwanted water flow away via the ureters as urine.

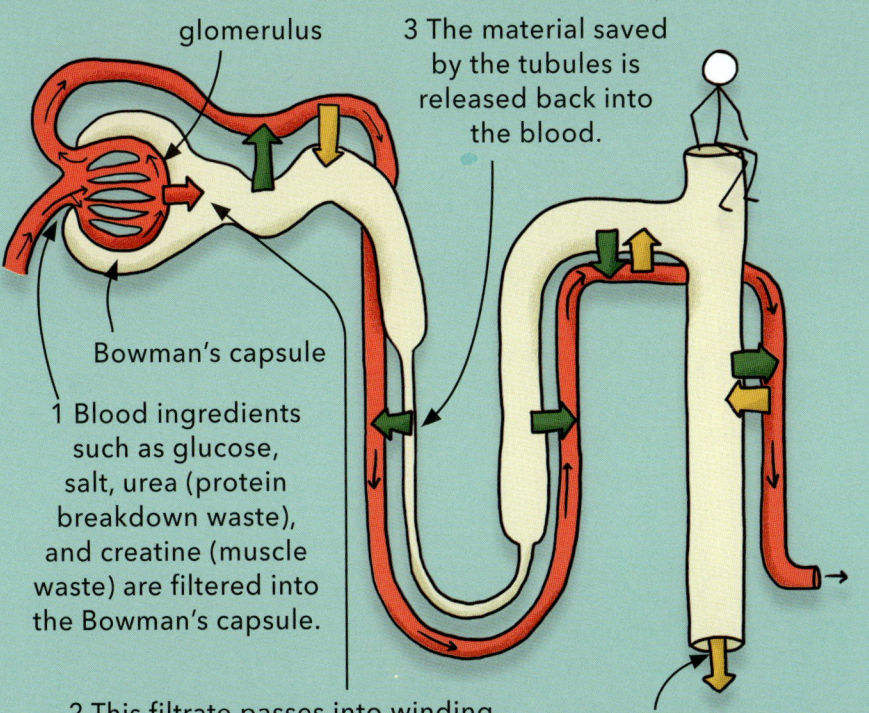

Kidneys at Work

All the kidney's work is done in filter units called nephrons. Blood is fed into each nephron through a bundle of tiny blood vessels called the glomerulus. This is held in a cup called the Bowman's capsule.

glomerulus

3 The material saved by the tubules is released back into the blood.

Bowman's capsule

1 Blood ingredients such as glucose, salt, urea (protein breakdown waste), and creatine (muscle waste) are filtered into the Bowman's capsule.

2 This filtrate passes into winding tubes called tubules, which absorb vital amino acids, glucose, and salts.

4 Unwanted ingredients flow out in the urine.

Kidney Swap

It seems we can manage pretty well with just one kidney. This means someone with two healthy kidneys can donate one to someone whose kidneys have failed. When this happens, the old ones that are not working are left in place. Surgeons insert the new kidney through a narrow slit in the abdomen and attach it to an easily accessible major artery lower down in the body. It seems to work perfectly well here.

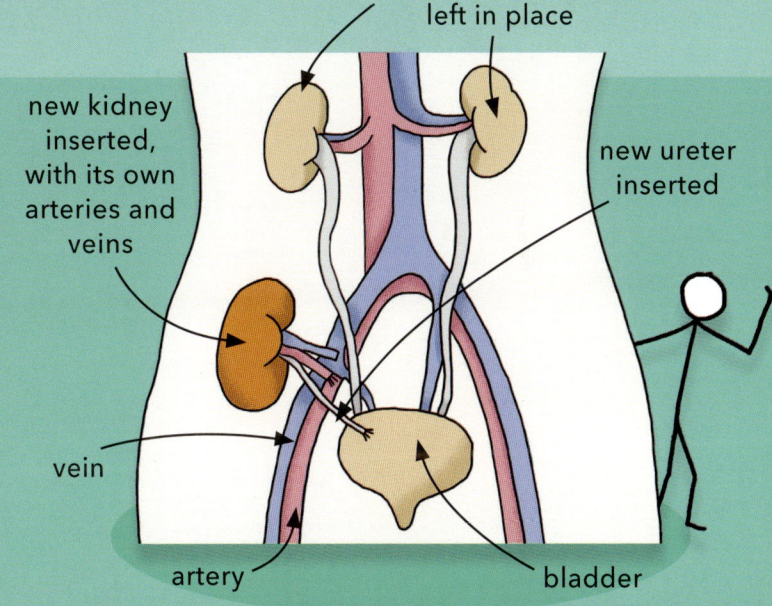

nonfunctioning kidneys left in place

new kidney inserted, with its own arteries and veins

new ureter inserted

vein

artery

bladder

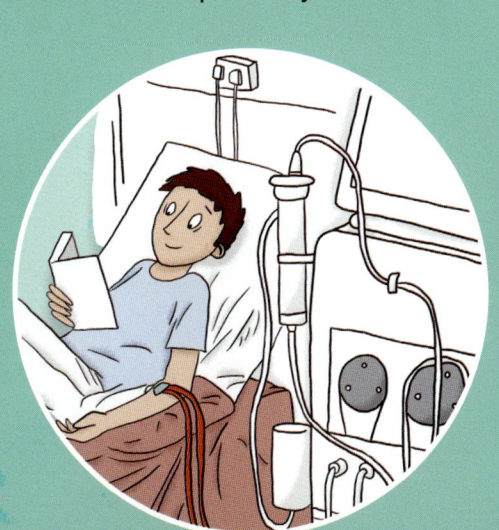

Artificial Kidney

Many people suffer from kidney disease. A kidney transplant may solve the problem, but until a suitable donor is found, many kidney patients have to be regularly hooked up to a dialysis machine. All the patient's blood is diverted through this machine, which filters blood just as the kidneys do. It works, but it is not a comfortable experience for the patients, and is very time-consuming.

Body of Water

You are remarkably wet. Every cell contains water, and body fluids, such as blood and another one called lymph, are almost entirely water. Your body needs water to dissolve the chemicals that make every process happen. Indeed, you can't survive for more than a day or two without water.

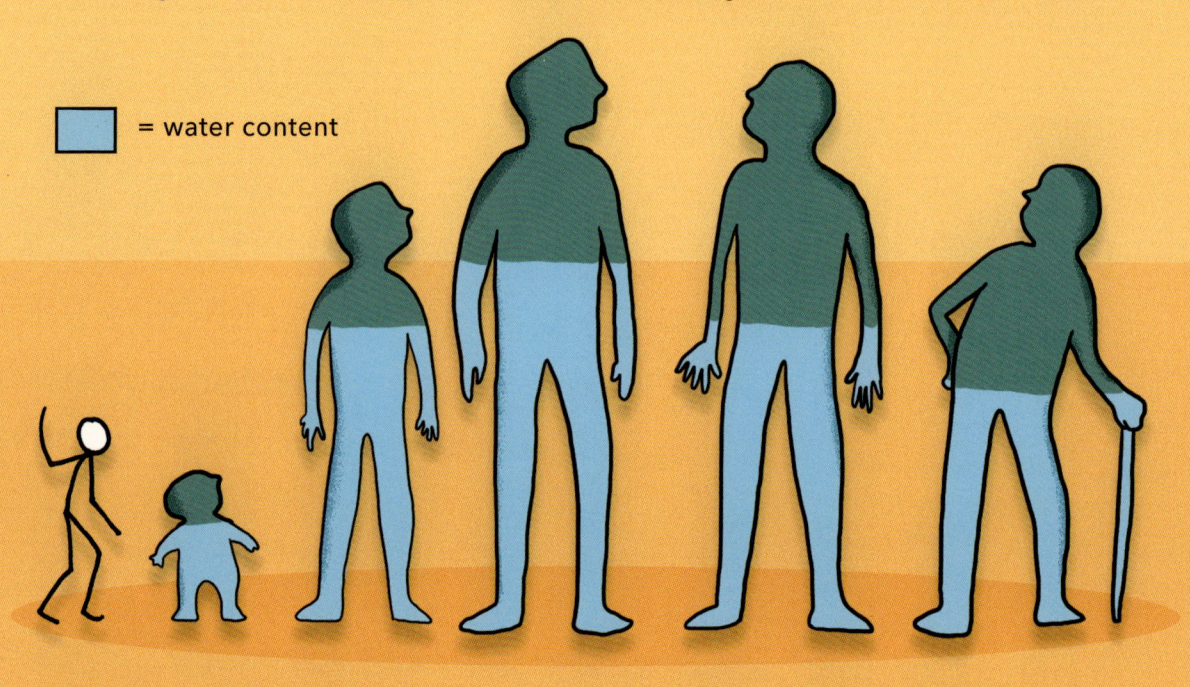

☐ = water content

Made of Water

Amazingly, babies are 86 per cent water – it's almost surprising you can't hear them slop as they move. You gradually dry out as you grow older, though. When you're a teenager, you are still about 75 per cent water. Not until you're really old do you really dry out and become barely half water. It's all that water that helps people keep young-looking.

Sweating it Out

On average, you lose about 0.5 litres (1 pint) of water a day by sweating. That's so much you'd think you might be permanently wet. But mostly it evaporates almost at once, so you keep dry. Only when you're hot and sweat a lot do you stay wet for long. You sweat more when it's hot because the evaporation helps keep you cool.

Waterworks

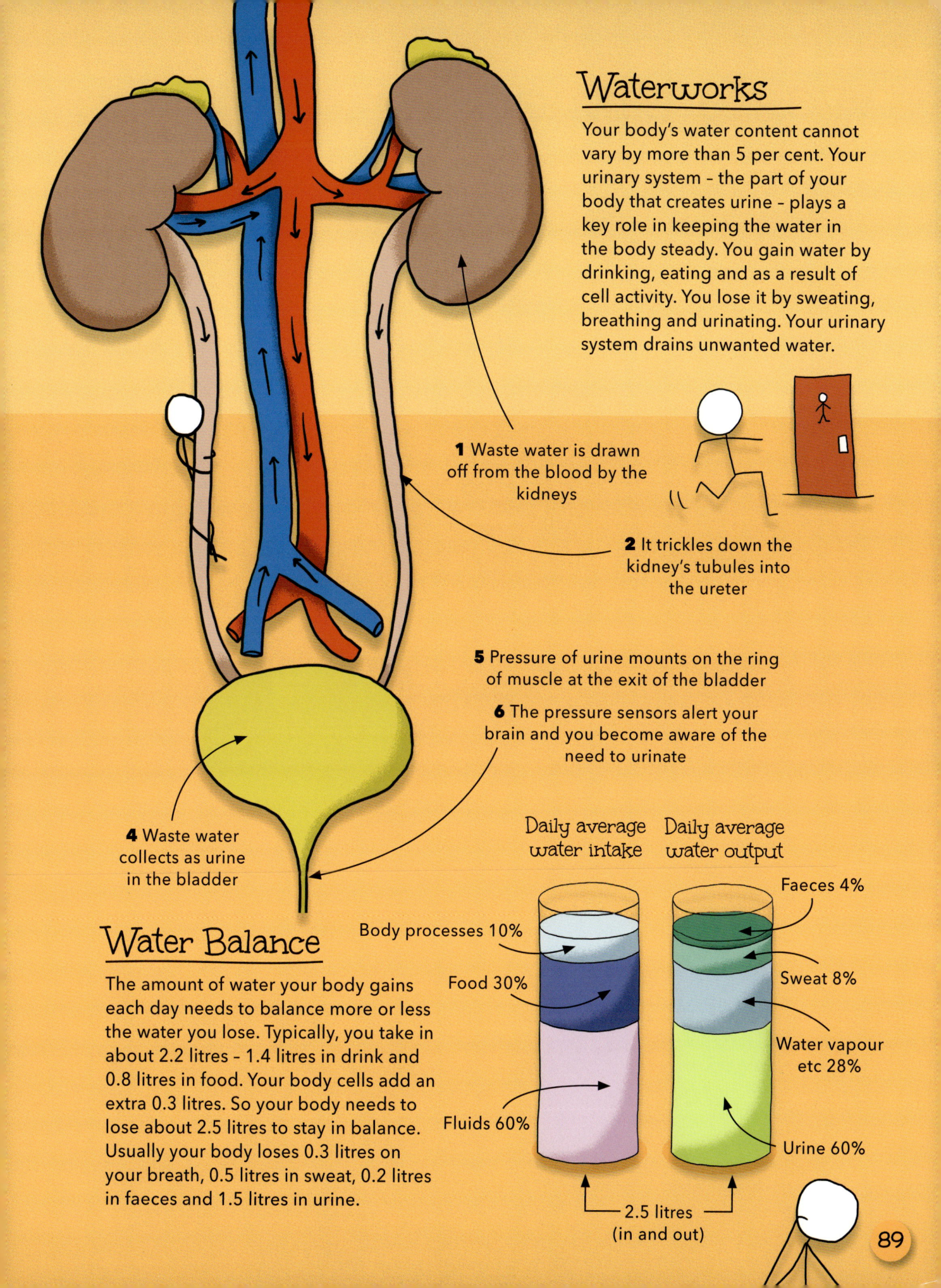

Your body's water content cannot vary by more than 5 per cent. Your urinary system - the part of your body that creates urine - plays a key role in keeping the water in the body steady. You gain water by drinking, eating and as a result of cell activity. You lose it by sweating, breathing and urinating. Your urinary system drains unwanted water.

1 Waste water is drawn off from the blood by the kidneys

2 It trickles down the kidney's tubules into the ureter

4 Waste water collects as urine in the bladder

5 Pressure of urine mounts on the ring of muscle at the exit of the bladder

6 The pressure sensors alert your brain and you become aware of the need to urinate

Water Balance

The amount of water your body gains each day needs to balance more or less the water you lose. Typically, you take in about 2.2 litres - 1.4 litres in drink and 0.8 litres in food. Your body cells add an extra 0.3 litres. So your body needs to lose about 2.5 litres to stay in balance. Usually your body loses 0.3 litres on your breath, 0.5 litres in sweat, 0.2 litres in faeces and 1.5 litres in urine.

Daily average water intake
- Body processes 10%
- Food 30%
- Fluids 60%

Daily average water output
- Faeces 4%
- Sweat 8%
- Water vapour etc 28%
- Urine 60%

2.5 litres (in and out)

Waste Disposal

Your body is remarkably good at breaking down food into the bits it needs. But there are some parts of food it has no use for at all. It's the task of the last section of the digestive system, the large intestine, to deal with this unwanted waste and bundle it up for disposal

Getting it all Out

To stay functioning well, your body needs to regularly get rid of all kinds of waste materials besides food waste. This process is called excretion, and it happens in five main ways.

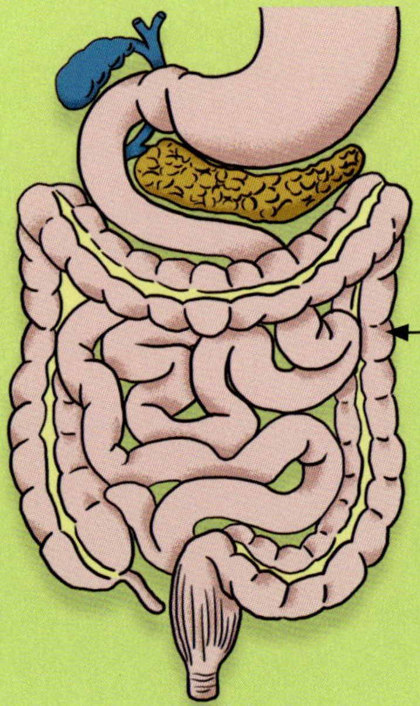

Food waste from your gut is expelled as feces via the rectum.

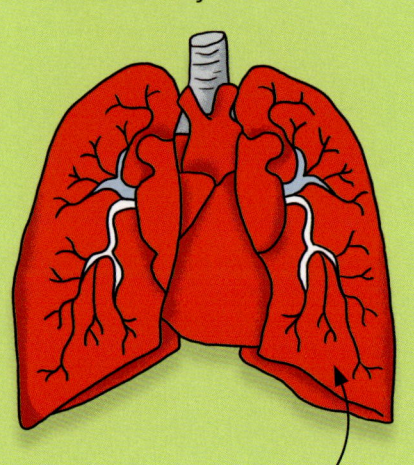

Your lungs get rid of unwanted carbon dioxide gas expelled by every cell after it uses oxygen.

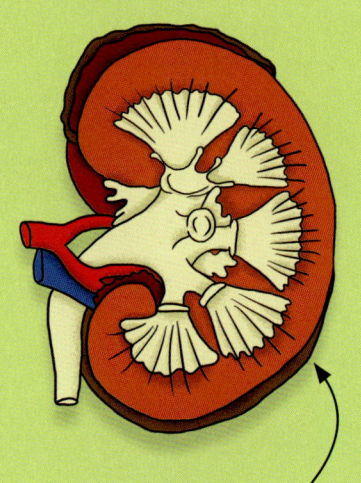

Your kidneys despatch unwanted water and dissolved chemicals in urine.

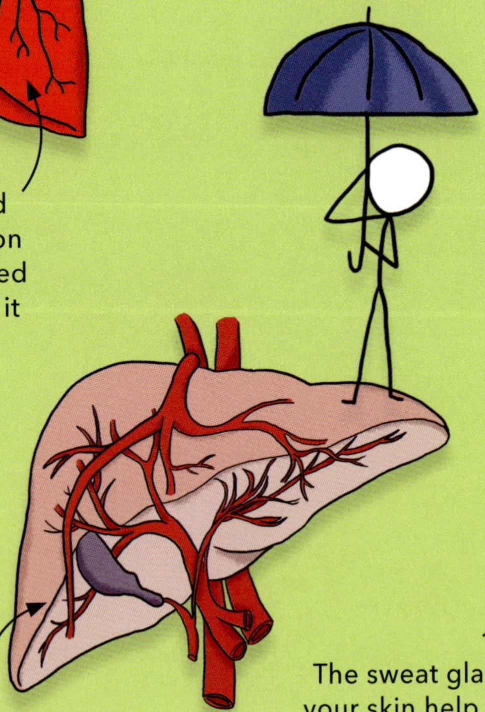

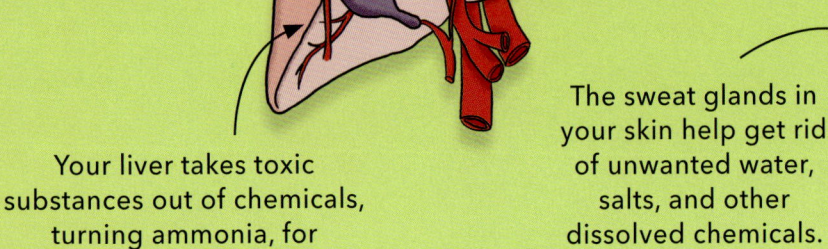

Your liver takes toxic substances out of chemicals, turning ammonia, for example, into urea.

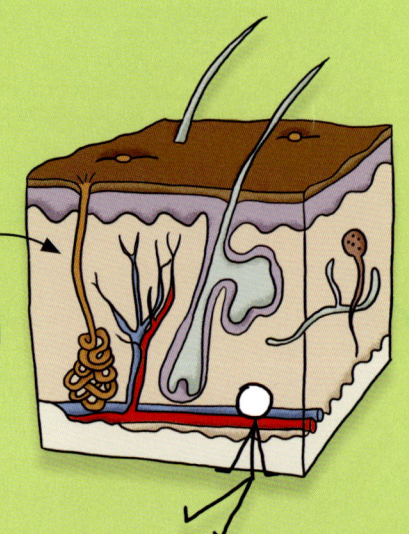

The sweat glands in your skin help get rid of unwanted water, salts, and other dissolved chemicals.

90

Sewer System

The main winding part of the large intestine is the body's sewer system. It is called the colon, and its task is to convert gloopy food leftovers into feces. The colon absorbs a lot of water and salt from the food waste to dry it out, helped by the bacteria that live there. In fact, a third of all feces is solid bacteria.

The colon breaks food waste into short packages.

The first part of the colon, called the ascending colon, is on your right and carries food upwards.

In the process called peristalsis, the muscular walls of the colon move on the packaged up feces.

Peristalsis movements in the descending colon squeeze feces towards the rectum.

Besides water, the colon walls absorb sodium and chlorine and replace them with bicarbonates and potassium.

Losing Skin

Your skin is an amazing organ—protective, waterproof and acting as a major sensor—and it's also constantly changing and regenerating itself. So you lose 30,000 to 40,000 cells from your skin, just flaking off the surface, every hour. Over a day, you lose almost a million skin cells. Over a year you shed 8 pounds (3.6 kg). The dust that collects on your tables, TV and other surfaces is mostly dead human skin cells! A man's skin flakes have more germs than a woman's—but a woman's have a greater variety.

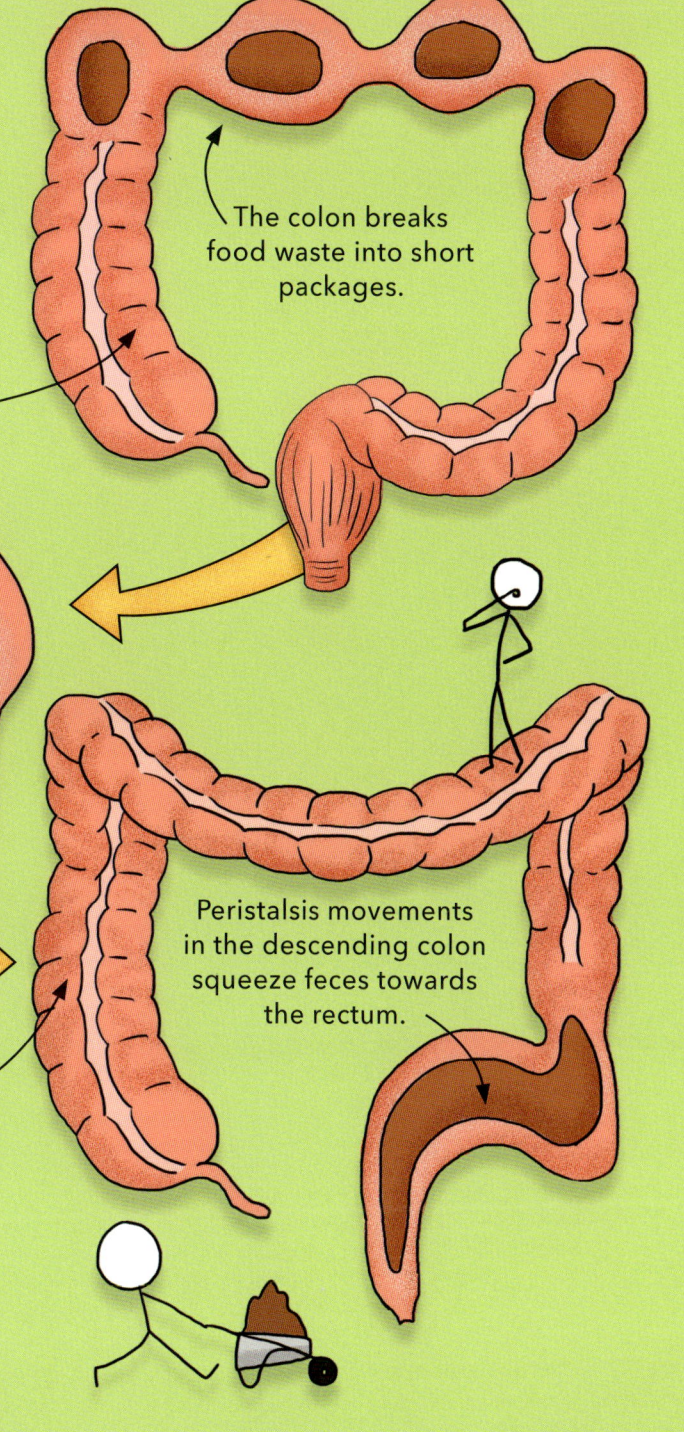

INDEX

A
acids 76, 77
Achilles heel 25
amino acids 81
appendix 81
arms 12, 24
arteries 58, 59
Autonomic Nervous System (ANS) 31

B
backbone 19
bacteria 79
blood 62, 63
   cells 62, 63
   circulation 54, 55, 58, 59
   groups 61
   pressure 59
   transfusions 61
   vessels 58, 59
blood sugar levels 83
bodybuilders 16
bone cells 20
bone marrow 20, 21
bones 6, 18, 19, 30
   inside 20, 21
   joints 22, 23
   strength 20, 21
brain 28, 29, 34, 35, 52
   inside 36, 37
   map 38, 39
   memory storage 48, 49
brainstem 36, 37
breathing 50, 52, 53
Broca's area 38, 39

C
calories 72, 73
carbohydrates 72, 80, 81
cardiac arrest 68
cardiac cycle 57
cardiovascular disease 61, 66, 67
cardiac muscle 9
cartilage 25
cells 60, 71, 72, 73, 74, 75
Central Nervous System (CNS) 28
cerebellum 36, 37, 49
cerebral cortex 37, 38
cerebrum 36, 37
circulation 54, 55, 58, 59
colon 78, 81
connective tissue 8
cooking 71
cramps 17

D
diabetes 83
dialysis 87
diet 70, 71
digestion 80, 81
duodenum 76, 78

E
ear muscles 31
eating 74, 75
ears 44, 43
enzymes 74 80, 81
eyes 42, 43
exercise 68, 69

F
feces 80, 81
fasting 71
fats 72
feet 19, 25
feeling 40, 41
fiber 73
fitness 68, 69
food 71, 72, 73
funny bone 31

G
gastric pits 77
germs 64, 65
goose pimples 85
glucose 70, 80, 81, 82, 83

H
hands 18, 24
heart 56, 57
   attack 66
   disease 66, 67
   symbol 51
   transplants 51, 67
   valves 56, 66
heat control 61
hippocampus 36, 36, 49
history of muscle and bone 28, 29
hypothalamus 61

I
immune system 64, 65
Intelligence Quotient (IQ) 28
intestines 80, 81, 83

J
jaw 11, 27
joints 22, 23

K
knees 23
kidneys 86, 87, 90
   transplant 87

L
legs 10, 11
ligaments 24, 25
liver 82, 83, 90
Lucy 6
lungs 52, 53

M
memory 48, 49
minerals 73
mitochondrial DNA 61
motor neurons 40, 41
movement 37, 40, 41
mouth 74
muscle fibers 14, 18
muscle pairs 12
muscles 7, 30, 31
   growth 16, 17, 31
   inside 7, 14, 15
   moving 12, 13, 14, 15
   skeletal 9, 10, 11, 12, 13
   strength 16, 17
   types 8, 9

N
Neanderthals 28
neck muscles 30
nerves 29, 30, 31, 32, 33, 35, 40, 41
neurons 32, 33, 40, 41
neurotransmitters 33

O
obesity 70
esophagus 73

P
pacemakers 67
pain 41
Peripheral Nervous System (PNS) 30
plasma 63
platelets 62
poo 79, 90, 91
Push-ups 13
protein 71, 72 81
pulse 57

R
red blood cells 62
reflexes 41
roughage 73

runners 16, 17

S
saliva 74
sciatic nerve 31
science of the brain 29
sight 42, 43
shivering 31
skeletal muscles 9, 10, 11, 12, 13
skeleton 6, 18, 19, 30
    joints 22, 23
skin 90
skull 18, 26, 27
smell 46, 47

sound 44, 45
spinal cord 30
stomach 76, 77
    acids 76, 77
stroke 66
strongest man 7
sugar breakdown 80
swallowing 74, 75
sweat 84, 88, 89

T
taste 46, 47
temperature 84, 85
tendons 24, 25
thoughts 29, 35, 36
tissue 8
trepanning 27

U
urinary system 89
urine 86, 87, 89

V
vaccines 65
vagus nerve 31
veins 58, 59
vitamins 71
vocal cords 70, 71
vomiting 77

W
waste disposal 90, 91
water 86, 87, 88, 89
weightlifters 7, 15, 16
Wernicke's area 38, 39
white blood cells 62, 63, 64, 65

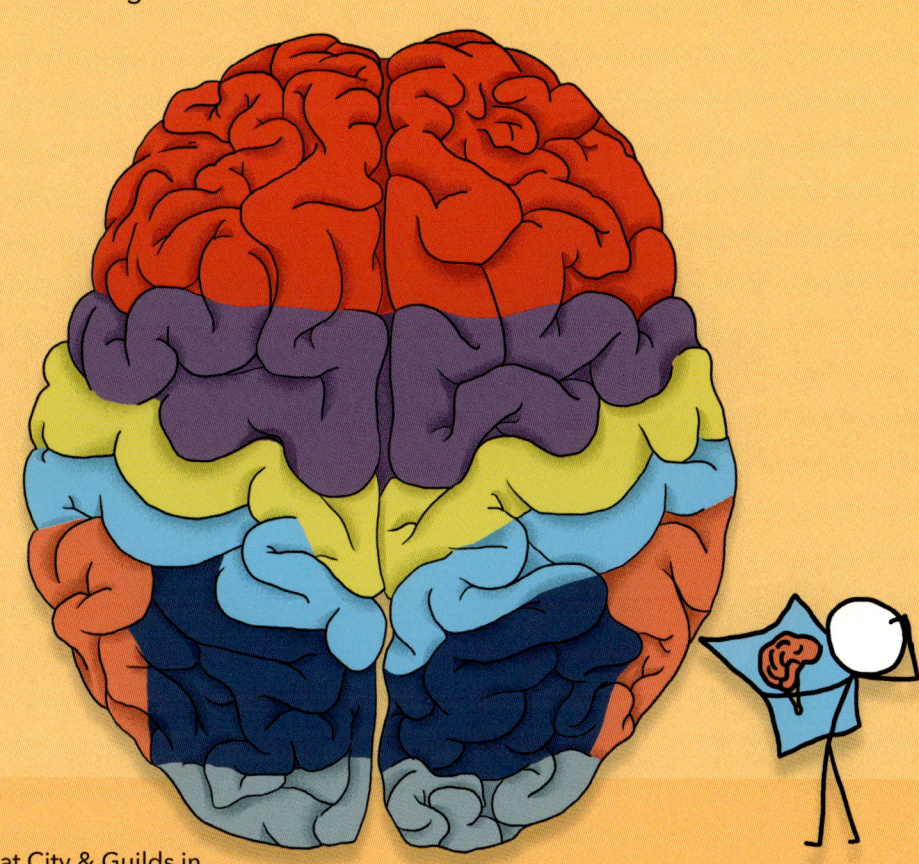

The Author
John Farndon is Royal Literary Fellow at City & Guilds in London, UK, and the author of a huge number of books for adults and children on science, technology, and nature, including such international best-sellers as *Do Not Open* and *Do You Think You're Clever?* He has been shortlisted six times for the Royal Society's Young People's Book Prize for a science book, with titles such as *How the Earth Works, What Happens When?,* and *Project Body* (2016).

The Illustrator
Venitia Dean is a freelance illustrator who grew up in Brighton, UK. She has always loved drawing ever since she could hold a pencil! As a teenager she discovered a passion for figurative illustration and when she turned 19 she was given a digital drawing tablet for her birthday and started transferring her work to the computer. She hasn't looked back since! As well as illustration, Venitia loves reading graphic novels, and walking her dog Peanut.

Picture Credits
(abbreviations: t = top; b = bottom; c = center; l = left; r = right)

© www.shutterstock.com:
6 cl, 6 br, 7 tl, 7 cr, 7 bl, 8 bl, 9 tl, 9 cl, 9 bl, 17 cr, 21 bl, 23 br, 25 br, 26 bl, 28 bl, 29 bl., 28 tl, 28 br, 29 tl, 29 cr, 29 bl, 37 tl, 43 tr, 48 bl, 50 bc, 50 br, 50 tc, 50 bl, 51 tl, 51 cr, 51 bl, 64 bc, 65 cr, 58 br, 60 cl, 60 bc, 18 cl, 65 tl, 65 br, 70 tr, 70 bl, 71 tl, 71 cr, 71 bl, 75 br, 81 br.
6 br = Juan Aunion / Shutterstock.com, 7 cr = meunierd / Shutterstock.com, 29bl = Tony Baggett / Shutterstock.com, 76 bl = Bangkokhappiness / Shutterstock.com

Every effort has been made to trace the copyright holders. And, we acknowledge in advance any unintentional omissions. We would be pleased to insert the appropriate acknowledgment in any subsequent edition of this publication.

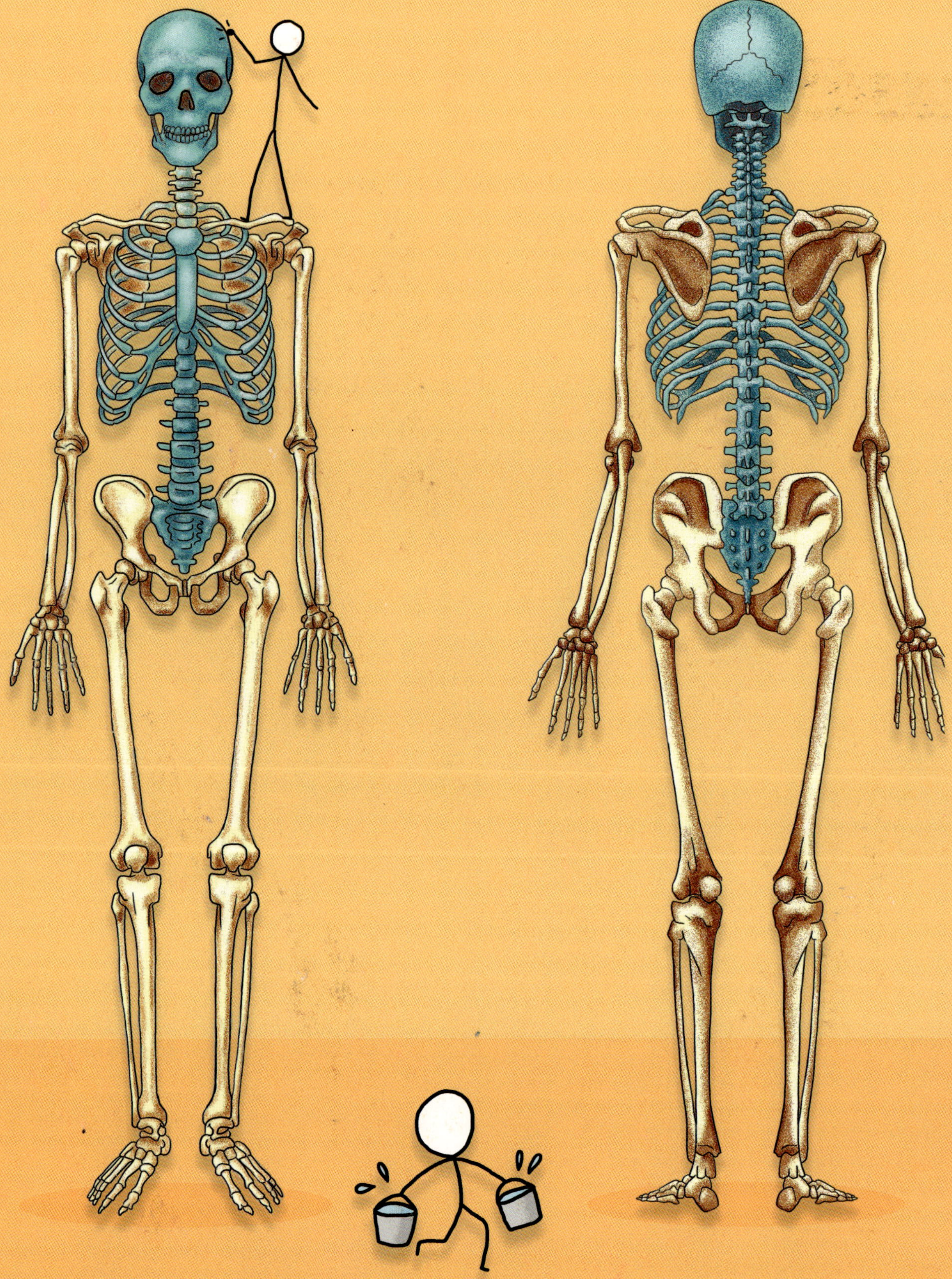